TREASURE
YOUR
LOVE

...

J.C. REED

Cover art by Larissa Klein

Editing by Shannon Wolfman, Edee Fallon, and Indie Author Services

ISBN: 1492886181
ISBN-13: 978-1492886181

TO ALL WHO FIND LOVE:

Love is a wild ride. Without the passion, we wouldn't
surrender and conquer what we never thought could be
ours.
True love stories don't have happy endings, because for
those who treasure it, true love never ends.

PART 1

1

MAYFIELD REALTIES WAS situated on the sixtieth floor of Trump Tower in one of the most popular business districts of New York City. I was standing in front of the large windows in my new office, watching the busy street below. Hundreds of people passing by, barely acknowledging each other. Soon forgotten. Twenty-four hours a day, seven days a week, something was always happening. I could feel their rush of excitement, the dread, the stress, the anticipation, and their uncertainty whether a particular day would turn into an episode of a comedy, a tragedy, or anything in between. I liked the idea of them chasing their dreams and their futures. Just the way I had once been. Ever since I was hired by Jett Mayfield, I had entered a whirlwind of chaos. I had met the man of my dreams in the city of my dreams. New York, the city that never sleeps, was my home; Jett was the man I wanted to be with, and while everything seemed perfect, I felt something was missing: the answers to my questions about the Lucazzone estate I was about to inherit. Even though I had promised Jett I'd stay in NY with him, because it was the only way he could protect me from *them*, I felt no peace knowing that people were after me.

A soft knock on the door made me flinch. A second later, Emma's head appeared in the doorway. Her cagey glance told me she hadn't yet fully digested the fact that I had been promoted from mere assistant to a higher position than hers. We had been close to becoming friends when I started working at Mayfield Realties. Now she was distancing herself, which I attributed to my change in position. The past two weeks she had been eyeing me with suspicion, her previous friendliness replaced by badly disguised arrogance.

"I hope I'm not interrupting anything important, Brooke?" Her voice was cold and sarcastic as her glance swept over me standing at the window. She was holding a huge bouquet of red roses decorated with pearls in between their velvet petals. I gaped at the rich burgundy color and the exquisite perfection of the petals.

She placed the rose bouquet on my desk. "Mr. Mayfield asked me to *personally* take these to you."

2

Emphasis on "personally," as if the word on its own conveyed a secret meaning.

I felt myself blushing at hearing Jett's name.

I wondered if she knew I was dating the CEO of Mayfield Realties. As if sensing my thoughts, she turned, her light blue eyes piercing through me with disdain and something else.

Envy.

Pure, undiluted envy.

The kind that could turn melting lava into ice. If looks could kill.

I groaned inwardly. Of course Emma knew. She wasn't stupid, just like the rest of the company's NY headquarters. In the last two weeks, Jett and I had tried to keep our contact at work limited to a strictly professional level, but of course there were subtle signs: the way he touched the small of my back when he led me out of the room or the way his fingertips grazed my arm too long whenever he tried to get my attention during a meeting. Or maybe it was the way we had been sitting together—too close, too intimate—my frantic heart threatening to burst out of my chest with each beat. Surely, if I could hear it, then others might as well.

"Thanks," I said, and watched her leave. The door closed behind her, and I was alone again. I retrieved the card tucked in between the roses, and opened it, my glance sweeping over Jett's harried handwriting.

For my beautiful, pregnant girlfriend,
Jett
P.s. Thanks for the wild ride yesterday.

I smiled and turned the card around.

I'm in my office. We have a deal to go over.
Join me if you're not too busy.

Ever since starting this position, Jett had involved me in various company deals, telling me he trusted my judgment. I had learned the ins and outs of his company, the projects they had been working on, dealing with the top clients and seeking out the most desirable properties. So, naturally, when Jett inquired if I wanted to go over a new deal, I was ready to jump at the opportunity. Not only did I enjoy working with him, to me this was another excuse to see him.

It had been hours since I last saw him, and already I missed him like crazy. Big needy girlfriend alert, but I couldn't help it. I fished my mirror and lipstick out of my handbag to fix my makeup, and tucked a few stray strands of hair out of my face. Happy with the result, I grabbed my smartphone and acquisitions folder, and left my office. The folder contained all my research, notes on past and current deals, my schedule, and daily to-do list—in case Jett needed anything. I carried it with me at all times, not least because Jett wasn't known for his patience. My stomach twisted into knots, and my knees began to shake with apprehension as I knocked on his door.

"Yeah," his deep voice called out, betraying his irritation the way it always did at work. I had yet to get used to his briskness and one-syllable commands.

I opened his door and stepped in, catching my breath. He was sitting in his leather chair, his dark hair framing his face, the newspaper in his hands hiding his green eyes. His jacket was thrown carelessly on a visitor chair, and the sleeves of his white shirt were rolled up, exposing his strong forearms. His shirt clung to his broad chest, leaving little to the imagination.

Sexy.

He looked like the kind of man you could be obsessed about. I never knew the meaning of the word "sexy" until I met Jett Mayfield.

Just looking at him, I had to force myself not to smile.

"Close the door."

I followed his command. "Thank you for the flowers. They're beautiful." Regarding him, I inched closer and placed the folder on his desk. He remained silent so I continued, filling the silence. "I'm done with the Colton estate deal. It's all in the folder, ready for you to sign." I pointed at the folder needlessly, waiting for him to look inside. Jett folded the newspaper and placed it on his desk, and stood, his intense gaze finally fixing on me. His expression was unreadable as usual, but there was something in his eyes. He was watching me, taking in my every movement, which made me nervous.

How could he remain so cool when my heart was fluttering in my chest, and I wasn't unsure whether to jump into his arms or leap out the door?

"Anything specific you wanted to talk about?" I prompted.

Jett's gaze remained glued to me.

Unreadable.

Unfazed.

Ever so slowly, he walked around his desk, his height both intimidating and arousing me. His lips curled into a dazzling smile. His green eyes sparkled, reminding me of a dark wild forest. I could stare into them forever and lose myself in their depths.

"What else do you have for me?" His deep voice was barely more than a whisper, caressing my senses like silk. His fingers clasped my chin, forcing my head up. I drew in a shaky breath and held it, both mesmerized and terrified by his proximity. His thumb brushed my chin while his other hand traced my hips. His body moved against me, pinning me against the closed door, knocking the air out of my lungs. "I hope it's more interesting than the deals I had to take care of when all I wanted to think about was all the different ways I'd like to fuck you."

He was doing his sexy thing again without even trying.

"The file's all I have for you," I whispered, mortified by my sudden arousal. My body was like a button for him— easy to press, and the heat was on. Every cell of my body wanted him and protested whenever my brain tried to keep at bay the cascade of lust wreaking havoc within me.

"You sure? Because I think you're missing something." His hand traveled south, past my abdomen.

"I recall a deal," Jett whispered in my ear, sensing my confusion. And then his lips were on my neck, biting, nibbling, turning millions of my sense buds into sparks. His hands cupped my ass. "Or should I say a bet? Someone's about to lose and I want to claim my prize."

My cheeks flamed.

Oh, God!

I'd completely forgotten that.

Ever since challenging me to a game of Spades in Italy, Jett had been delaying the inevitable. The most likely explanation I had was that he was afraid I'd win, because I was the best Spades player I knew, and I made no secret of it.

"Are you talking about our arrangement?" I pushed him away, but he didn't budge. His touch became more focused.

His hot breath continued to caress my skin as one hand traced the contours of my breasts over the thin fabric of my shirt. His mouth was so close to my lips, I could smell the faint aroma of coffee, mint, and his intoxicating scent.

"I'm talking about our bet, Brooke. Whoever wins the game gets to have whatever they want, and right now I'd love to tame you."

A rush of excitement washed over me.

"You can't tame me, because taming would imply I've surrendered, and as far as I know you haven't won yet," I whispered. "If you're ready to lose, I'm challenging you today after work. Even though we're dating and women are supposed to let their boyfriends have the upper hand, I'm not going to let you win."

"Not after work...I want it now." He laughed quietly into my ear. "Which is why I've set up a table outside. In the open, where I can be sure there's no cheating."

I slapped his arm in mock annoyance, ignoring the sudden urge to run my fingertips over his stubble. "I'd never cheat."

"I know." He winked. "But I'm not sure *I* wouldn't."

I raised my eyebrows, and his grin widened. He knew how I felt about cheating.

"I was talking about gaming, Brooke." He laughed at my scowl, revealing perfect white teeth. "I'd cheat...to let you win, baby."

8

I scowled again. "No cheating, Jett."

He ignored my statement. His teeth grazed the sensitive spot behind my ear, then moved down my neck. Stifling a low moan, I waited a few seconds, and when no reply came, I added, "I'm serious, Jett. If you cheat—in any way—I'll be pissed. I want you to give your best because it won't be enough. I'll still win."

"Sure." He laughed, and his hand tucked my shirt out of my skirt.

"Seriously?" I stopped his impudent movement before he reached my bra and shot him my most menacing glare, hoping my heavy breathing wasn't giving away my excitement at the prospect of his hands roaming over my body. "You haven't won yet."

"I was just giving you a taste of foreplay." Jett removed his hand and grimaced, almost disappointed. "A game of Spades, then. Are you really up for it?"

"More than you think." I shot him my most self-assured grin. Soon the guy wouldn't know what hit him. "You say when and where, and I'll be there."

"Then grab your stuff, Miss Stewart. Because we're doing this now." He picked up his jacket from his chair and a black leather bag from the couch, and ushered me out of his office.

Within minutes, we stepped into the cold afternoon air. Visitors and co-workers were gathered in groups, turning as we walked past. I smiled but paid them no attention because I couldn't peel my eyes off the only person who mattered.

"Where are we going?" I asked Jett as he ushered me into a waiting taxi and communicated to the driver an unfamiliar address.

"It's a surprise. It always is."

I smirked at his mysterious smile.

Oh, God. I hated surprises.

Jett knew this little fact, and yet he was still trying to get his way. I could only hope he wasn't aiming for crazy.

2

"I'M NOT GETTING on that thing. Sorry," I said. Jett and I were standing on a narrow landing strip in front of the tiniest helicopter I had ever seen. Okay, I had never seen one in real life so I couldn't really judge it based on its size, but it looked horribly fragile, with barely an inch of metal standing between me and a deep plunge into sure death. Jett knew how much I liked solid ground beneath my feet. "I don't want to crash and die."

"No one's dying, Brooke." His brows shot up, amused. In fact, he was having a hard time not to laugh, which I could tell from the way his lips kept jerking at the corners. My temper boiled just a little bit. I had issues with height. No big deal. A lot of people did. And I was ready to tell him just that when he interrupted me.

"Do I have to remind you that you also went on board

with me? What's the difference?"

"It was a boat, Jett. There was water all around us, and I can swim. I cannot fly. I don't want to get on a helicopter, thousands of miles up in the air with no ground under my feet."

"You'll like it, I promise." He wrapped his arms around my waist and pulled me close. Glaring, I inhaled his scent, fighting with the voice inside my head that kept telling me to give it a shot.

Try everything once.

No frickin' way in hell.

"I've done this a thousand times, and as you can see, I'm still alive. Just close your eyes and hold on to my arm while I get us to our destination—safe. I'll help you overcome your fear of heights," Jett said, soothing me with that deep voice of his that could probably persuade a grizzly to give up his half-eaten prey.

"Tell that to my subconscious. Even if I closed my eyes, I'd still know you were flying. I'd feel it in my bones that I'm high up in the sky with no way but down." The thought made me shiver with dread, and a trickle of sweat ran down my spine.

Jett took a half-step back, regarding me. "What's wrong with me flying?"

Oh, God. Was that the only thing he was worried about? That I might be questioning his competence and abilities? I groaned inwardly.

"I'm sure you're an awesome pilot." How could I explain to a man who loved taking risks and who had once been addicted to adrenaline, that I was scared of a lot of things, including flying, and that I harbored absolutely no wish to overcome this particular fear—and especially not in a helicopter, which was more prone to crashing than an airplane.

"But?" Jett drew out the word, prodding. Why couldn't he just drop it?

Okay, I admit, maybe I couldn't pay him the same level of confidence I might give a professional pilot. The way I saw it, would I rather have surgery performed on me in a hospital ER by the person I had hot sex with, or by a person who was unbiased, with plenty of experience and a resume to demonstrate his skills? As much as I loved Jett, the decision was a no-brainer.

"Look. I know I'm being unreasonable." I heaved an exaggerated sigh. "But I'm not like you." It was true. The guy had no fears. He'd jump headfirst into any situation just so he could demonstrate he wasn't scared.

"It's not that different from a plane. It just feels more real." His eyes glimmered with pride. I could hear it in his voice. I could see it in his confident stance, and I was once again reminded he did all kinds of crazy stuff, thanks to his father's competitive upbringing and bank account. And what did he mean by "real?"

My fear was instantly magnified at the thought of sensations up in the air being more intense. I didn't want intense. I wanted earth—or at least a working parachute.

Taking one step back, I shook my head and crossed my arms over my chest. I *was not* getting on a helicopter where I could feel every jolt, jerk, and shaking. Not when the tiniest possibility existed that a bird might collide with us, or something dropped from the sky, making us crash. And particularly not when Jett might be tempted to show off with some impressive aerobatic maneuver in midair such as loops and spins. I had seen those on TV, and while the crowd usually cheered, I preferred to stare, horrified, thankful for choosing my profession wisely.

"My point is, I'm not keen on being strapped to a seat with no option to exit. I want to be able to jump."

The corner of his lips twitched again at my choice of words. Jumping off a plane—why was it so easy to imagine him suggesting just that?

Because it's probably one of his favorite hobbies? Do not even go there, Stewart!

I felt sick already. Holding onto Jett's arm for support, I took a deep breath and let it out slowly. Jett began to rub my back, but the movement didn't manage to soothe me.

"Baby, there's nothing to be afraid of. We're not flying far," he insisted. "Everyone's doing it in NY. It will be fun."

Yeah, right!

Fun for him to fly. Nightmare for me. But fun for him, nevertheless, to see me sweating a river.

"Why can't we just take a taxi?"

"Because it'd spoil your surprise."

I covered my eyes and groaned, hating the fact that I had to disappoint him, hating the fact that he kept persisting. "As much as I want to, I can't."

He cupped my face and placed a soft kiss on my lips. "I want you to see your hometown the way you've never seen it before. And don't say you can watch it all on TV, because that's not the same and you know it." He forced my gaze up to meet his, and his voice softened. "I know you're scared, but do you know why I want to show you everything? The boat, the sea, Italy?" I shook my head, not knowing where he was heading. "I want to be on your side when you experience things for the first time. I want to be the first one in everything you do."

My breath hitched in my throat. "Why?"

"Because you taught me that first moments matter. We don't forget them. Like our first kiss or our first date. Or the way I'm going to kiss you, right here, right now."

In one swift movement, he pulled me to him. His lips found mine with a hunger I had never seen from him before. It was delicate yet possessive, soft yet determined. A delicious shiver tore through me with warmth that radiated from inside out, filling me, calming me a little, persuading me that I was ready. My head was spinning when he pulled back, and for a fraction of a moment I forgot he was still waiting for my decision.

There was so much hope and warmth in his gesture and expression that I knew I had lost the battle with myself. For him I was going to face my fears.

As if sensing my crumbling resolution, Jett said, "You were right when you said that no matter how many years may pass or how many good or bad experiences you have in life, first memories are priceless. From now on, I want to be in all of yours, so no one can take them from you. From us."

"I'm still afraid."

The wind blew a strand of hair in my face. Gently, he pushed it back, his eyes focused on me.

"All beginnings are scary, like all endings are sad, but that's the journey and everything in between is worth experiencing. He gestured at the helicopter. "I was joking about me flying. I want to sit next to you and enjoy the tour. I want to hold your hand, help you get over your acrophobia, so I've hired a professional who'll show us the view. If you see it through, you take the fear out of flying. You know, fear is nothing but a trick of your mind, because we both know you've never been in a helicopter. You've never crashed. The odds are one in a billion."

I took a deep breath and nodded slowly before I could change my mind. I figured in the event we crashed, at least I'd die with a sexy guy on my side and plenty of happy memories. And nobody could say I hadn't tried to talk him out of this madness.

"Okay." I whispered. "But if—"

"No ifs," Jett said, determined. "Everything will turn out fine. It always does. You'll see this entire experience is good for our baby, too."

It's not even born yet, I wanted to point out like I had several times during our heated conversation when he mentioned his rigid beliefs on prenatal education. Jett supported the belief that the majority of neurons in an adult's brain were formed during the first five months inside the mother's womb. Soon after our arrival from Italy, he had started to implement his belief by giving me more responsibilities and tasks at work so our unborn could *learn*. Not that I complained, but claiming conquering my fears would benefit my baby was ridiculous.

Shortly after, our pilot arrived. His reassuring smile calmed me a little, and after we went through the usual precautionary safety and emergency instructions, I decided he seemed competent enough. I didn't know if my fear was written across my forehead or whether Jett had mentioned something to him, but he assured me he had thirty years of flying experience. And then my decision was made.

Jett helped me to get into the helicopter and the pilot handed us both aviation headsets. As he switched on a few buttons, my head started to hurt and my heart began to beat so hard I feared it might be about to burst. Being afraid was an understatement. I was paralyzed to the spot, barely able to suck in one shaky breath after another. Sitting next to Jett, with him smiling at me in that confident way of his, I realized that agreeing to give this a try was pure madness. I opened my mouth to tell him I had changed my mind when the machine whirred to life and we began to take off. My nails dug into the seat because it was the only thing that felt real—until Jett grabbed my hand. The warmth of his fingers seeped into my skin, soothing me, reminding me that he was here for me. Whether I wanted it or not, I had to trust his word that everything would be okay.

***

Jett had promised that the trip would be over in twenty minutes. And it was, down to the exact minute, even though it felt like an eternity. During our flight, the pilot showed us the breathtaking scenery New York City's skyline had to offer. As we soared above the Hudson River and flew right by the magnificent Statue of Liberty, my awe, eventually, grew bigger than my fear. Looking down at the high buildings, the lines of vehicles, and the small dots that I assumed were people, I couldn't shake off the feeling that we had been transferred to a different dimension where reality had become fantasy, and the ordinary had turned into the extraordinary.

Jett's eyes connected with mine. "Are you okay, baby?" he whispered, the deep baritone of his voice barely audible over the engine's whirring. Only then did I notice that I had tightened my grip on his arm. I let go quickly and placed my hands on the armrests, my knuckles turning white as I clutched at them for support.

"I'm fine." I nodded just in case my thin voice betrayed my lie.

The helicopter dipped low over the beach. Gazing out the window, I realized that, being rich, Jett had probably seen it all before, and that everything he did—he was doing it for me. To our left stretched out the city. To our right was nothing but sparkling water. The sun was shining, heating my frozen insides and melting my core. Or maybe it wasn't the heat, but the way Jett kept regarding me, his thumb stroking my skin, his fingers interlacing with mine.

Jett's arm wrapped around my shoulders, and he pulled me to his chest. Too late did I realize why. My pulse pounded hard and my stomach turned as the helicopter hit a downdraft, and then the pilot descended. I closed my eyes, sending a short prayer to any higher power out there.

Jett laughed, but the sound barely registered with me. My back was slick with sweat and my legs felt so weak I thought I might faint on the spot. And then the helicopter hit the ground with a soft thud, and the pilot switched off the engine.

I opened my eyes warily, not quite trusting the sudden silence. Jett was staring at me with an irritating grin on his lips. I glared at him and grabbed his outstretched hand as he helped me up.

"Don't say a word," I whispered.

"I wasn't going to." He laughed, which was worse than words.

My limbs continued to shake, and I felt oddly lightheaded as he helped me out of the helicopter. With a sigh of relief, I stepped foot onto solid ground, thankful that it was over. We were still alive, and for that I was tempted to kiss the ground beneath my feet. The pilot said his goodbye and took off, leaving Jett and me alone.

"You did great." Jett grabbed his bag from the floor and hung it around his shoulder. "How are you feeling?"

"I'll live so I guess—" I shrugged. Maybe it was the happiness at the prospect of having made it out alive that urged me to tell the truth, or maybe it was the adrenaline coursing through my veins, but for some reason I felt on top of the world. "To be honest, it wasn't as bad as I thought it would be."

Jett cocked a brow. "You'd do it again?"

I snorted.

Hell, no.

Reading my mortified expression, he let out a deep rumble that resembled a laugh. "I know you, and you're changed, baby. Do it again, and you'll never want to step foot *out* of this thing."

I bit my lip, fighting hard to come up with a kickass comeback. But Jett was right. Something in me had changed. I was proud of myself. And while I'd be scared to get into a helicopter again, deep down I knew I'd do it.

Who would have thought that I, the most responsible person I knew, had a danger-seeking bone in my body? I had to take a picture, because Sylvie would never believe it otherwise.

"It's not that different from a plane, right?" Jett said, grilling me, winding me up, waiting to drop the "I told you so" bomb. I ignored the amused look on his face and shrugged again.

"I'd say you can't compare them. When we hit the turbulence, I felt like I was the one holding up the chopper by the armrest." I scanned the area of the heliport. "By the way, where are we?"

"In the Hamptons."

"Ah." What the heck where we doing there? I opened my mouth to ask when Jett held up his hand to silence me.

"Come on, Miss Stewart. I have big plans for us." Touching the small of my back, Jett guided me across the platform to a door and down the stairs until we reached the lower level and a reception area, where a man in his thirties was waiting.

"Sir. Ma'am." He held out his hand as he saw us approaching.

Jett shook it and whispered to me, "He's our driver."

"Where's he taking us?"

Jett winked. "You'll see."

I grumbled but didn't comment as I followed him to our waiting limousine.

3

TEN MINUTES LATER, the driver let us out in front of a huge Renaissance property with Greek-style columns and a stone pavement leading to an arched front door. The kind of mansion that screamed high society and celebrities, luxury and buying stuff no one needs. The kind of mansion that can only be found portrayed in magazines alongside a multi-million dollar price tag. While I had seen it all before during my visit to the Lucazzone estate, this was different. Even though I loved the estate in Italy, with its magnificent backyard and the vastness of its rooms, it paled in comparison to the cream-colored building in front of us.

"Wow," I whispered. "Magnificent."

"It belongs to one of our clients." Jett held out his hand and I placed my palm in his, our fingers connecting. "May I invite you in?"

"Sure." I stifled the giggle forming at the back of my throat at hearing his Southern accent so pronounced. It was strange, because usually he tried his best to hide it.

He pulled a set of keys out of his pocket and dangled it in front of my face. "It's ours for the night."

Ah, the *night*. I swallowed hard at the sudden blast of heat running through my body.

"Does he know?" I didn't know what made me ask such a question.

"You mean 'she'? No, she doesn't know. It's been empty for months because the price she's asking is ridiculously high and no one wants to buy it. I told her, but she won't listen." He trailed off for a moment, as though annoyed that someone would not listen to his expert opinion. He *was* an expert when it came to prime real estate, so the owner was probably an idiot. "Anyway," Jett continued, "why don't we take a tour around this place?"

I squeezed his hand to stop him before he unlocked the door. "Jett, we can't stay in a property that we're supposed to sell. It's not right."

His intent gaze fixed on me, and for a moment I thought I caught a hint of amusement in his eyes. "Why not? We're here to get a feel for it so we can come up with the right sales pitch. How else are we supposed to flock it off if we don't know what we're talking about?"

I couldn't argue with that.

Jett unlocked the door and entered to switch off the silent alarm. I didn't move from the spot until he peered out again with a quizzical look. "Are you coming?"

I shook my head. "I don't feel comfortable with this. What if she finds out?"

"She lives in Florida and asked me to personally take care of it." He winked. "Which I'm doing—literally."

"What if the neighbors see us?"

He pulled me inside and closed the door behind me. It closed with a loud bang. I regarded him, shocked by his boldness. Jett dropped the bag and turned to face me.

"Who says we can't?" His eyes had that dangerous look I had first glimpsed the day we had sex on the beach. The one that always promised a sizzling time. The one that didn't take "no" for an answer. "First of all, we're her realtors, Brooke, and it's in her contract that we enter the house in her absence at our convenience. And second, what are you afraid of?" He raised my chin, and his lips came so close I could feel his sexy breath as his voice dropped to a whisper. "After I win, I get to choose where and how I take you. What if I want it here? Will you deny me?"

His finger curled around the buttons of my business jacket as he opened them one by one. One button and then another until my thin blouse was exposed. "What if I told you that the only reason I brought you here is to have sex in the pool, on the beach, in the backyard, or on the pool table?"

"Thanks for your honesty. But it doesn't matter, Jett, because you haven't won yet." It took all my willpower to push his hand from under my blouse.

"Having you twenty-four hours just for myself sounds too tempting to let you win. You know that, right?"

"People who reach too far are the ones who fall from the greatest height." My smile matched his cocky grin, when all I wanted was to get this over and done with so we could have sex, anywhere, everywhere.

"Brilliant people like me never fall."

Seriously, his ego was so inflated it was beyond me how he could possibly squeeze it through the door. I rolled my eyes at his arrogance and walked past him, taking the place in. We were standing in an opulent foyer with candelabras and a marble floor. In the middle was a staircase leading to the upper story. Behind it was an open door, through which I glimpsed the living room. Or what I assumed was the living room, because it was huge—probably as large as an entire apartment floor in Brooklyn, with arched bay windows and a fireplace dominating the entire right wall. Jett showed me the upper floor with its five oversized bedrooms and bathrooms, and yet another lounge. Then we returned downstairs to inspect the landscaped backyard, the outdoor BBQ area, the in-house cinema, the 850-foot fitness area, the open-plan kitchen, and another leisure room. I had never seen so much opulence.

"This place is amazing. Why does she want to sell it?" I said, back in the living room. We were sitting on the cream-colored leather couch facing the fireplace, drinking a glass of non-alcoholic red wine. The glass doors covered the entire wall, through which we could see the landscaped yard with its perfectly sculpted shrubs and blooming magnolias. It was so serene, the world outside forgotten. A tiny paradise just for us. Only it wasn't our paradise, and the poor owner didn't know we were intruding. I put the glass on the table and sat up straight, my back not touching the soft leather.

Jett shrugged. "People change their opinion all the time. What they want isn't always what they need. And the moment they get what they want, it loses its spark." Jett shrugged again. "She bought the place when she was dating some musician, instantly assuming they would live here forever. When things didn't work out and she met someone else, she moved to Florida and forgot about the charm of this place."

"Are you saying she never lived here?"

He nodded. "She complained about the lack of space."

I almost choked on my breath. Lack of space?

Holy cow. Our entire neighborhood could live in here and barely see each other. I didn't want to be inquisitive, but my curiosity got the upper hand. I honestly needed to put a face to this place.

"Who is she? Is it someone I know?"

"Maybe. It depends. Do you know Kim Dessen?"

"Kim Dessen?" My jaw dropped. "Wow. You have her as a client?"

She wasn't just one of the biggest singer-songwriters in the world; she was a celebrity famous for going through guys like some people go through their underwear. Scratch that. She had more guys than people had underwear. A pang of jealousy hit me as I realized that someone as successful, well-known and beautiful as Kim knew Jett. Kim was stunning, and so was Jett. Two beautiful people born into wealth—there had to be some sort of attraction because they both weren't blind.

"So, you know her personally? Like, met her?" I tried to hide the tremor in my voice by forcing cheeriness into it, but I only ended up making it worse.

"A couple of times. It's her fourth property I'm selling." He shrugged as if it didn't matter. My heart dropped at the way he seemed to find the hardwood floor more interesting than me. He met with her at least four times. A lot could happen during four meetings. Like having drinks and ending up in a hotel room, their perfect bodies entangled in sweat-soaked sheets.

Uncomfortable silence ensued between us, during which I picked up a sparkling Swarovski crystal centerpiece from the coffee table and turned it to watch the sunlight catching in the delicate red roses. My gaze kept skidding back to Jett as my hands glided over the smooth glass. So fragile. So easily shattered. Just like my heart. One tumble was all it'd take. Such as finding out he had slept with her. Even if it happened before we met, I had no idea how to deal with it. Women like Kim Dessen with *Playboy* model looks got what they wanted. I never knew how much I loved Jett until I realized the thought of him with someone else was enough to break my heart.

I swallowed past the lump in my throat and put the centerpiece back in place.

"Did you two—" My words trailed off, filling the void between us with unspoken indictment. It hadn't been my intention to make it sound like an accusation, but somehow it came off as such because, if Jett confirmed my suspicions, I couldn't stay in a house where he once had sex with someone else.

Jett's eyes narrowed on me and his jaw set. "Fuck, Brooke. She's just a client. I don't sleep with my clients."

I averted my gaze to hide my disbelief. He signed deals—and a lot of them; he whisked off his clients to expensive restaurants and stunning vacation destinations. Did he really expect me to believe he and Kim never got intimate on such an occasion?

He walked over to me. I could feel his hands on my

shoulders as he turned me around so that I faced him, but I didn't look up.

"Brooke, just because I'm a guy doesn't mean I sleep with anything walking on two legs. Kim's not even my type. No one is, except you."

"It was just a question, Jett."

A question I would probably ask myself every time he met someone.

A question I would always be afraid to ask because I knew in my heart I didn't have the strength to handle the kind of answer I feared. As much as I wanted to believe every word he said, and as much as I loved him, I didn't trust life wouldn't send another woman his way—someone more beautiful, better suited to his social status and lifestyle. Someone able to change his feelings for me.

"It's not a big deal," I lied. My eyes met his gaze, imploring him to drop the topic because I didn't want to sound insecure. Insecurity wasn't an attractive trait.

"I just wondered. That's all," I mumbled when he kept staring at me.

"Do you trust me?" His question was unexpected. I narrowed my eyes in surprise.

"I do," I said.

"Do you, Brooke?"

He moved closer, towering over me. Peering into my heart, his gaze lingered on me too long, making me nervous. He was so tall I had to lean all the way back to look into his green gaze. Green like a haunted forest reflecting the morning sun. So deep and dark I would have dipped my fingers in it to stain my soul. Because haunted he was—we both were by our pasts—only he knew better how to deal with it.

As Jett regarded me, I could see the color of his eyes shifting—the way it often did, depending on his mood. Lighter when he was tired. Darker when he was agitated or infuriated. I realized I was getting to know him. The real Jett. And right now he was downright angry.

"Do you really trust me?" His fingertips lingered on my cheek, cold as ice.

"In some way," I whispered. But did I? His expression challenged me to tell to truth. "I don't know. I know you're interested in me, and not in the estate. I also know you wouldn't betray my trust, but I feel there's a lot more to you. Hidden layers that I still have to get to know."

His face betrayed no emotions as he moistened his lips, carefully preparing his words. "Brooke, I'm not just into you…I'm in this for the long haul. I dated others, but I always *knew* they weren't the real deal. That whatever attracted me to them would pass. With you, it's different."

"How do you know?" I asked breathlessly.

He smiled. "You make me want to be a better person, and I cannot imagine a future without you." His voice lowered to a whisper. "We haven't known each other for long, but deep inside I feel like we understand each other. I feel like I've been waiting for someone like you all my life. Besides, you make me think of sex nonstop and that's always a good sign."

I could feel myself blushing, my insides turning all warm and fuzzy. He wasn't the only one who couldn't stop thinking about sex.

"That's your libido talking," I pointed out.

He shook his head. "No, it isn't. You turn me on like I know I'm turning you on. Your wet panties are proof enough."

His fingers brushed my neck, and then his lips gently touched the sensitive skin. His hot breath sent a delicious shiver through me. "If we're both honest with each another, if we trust one another and we mention whatever is on our mind rather than keep things buried, then nothing can go wrong in this relationship. We won't lose this." He pointed to the air between us. "I won't let it happen. It doesn't matter what we once did and who we slept with, because they didn't matter and the knowledge is all that counts. That's all you, or I, ever need to know."

He was right. Of course. The mere mentioning of my ex was enough to make him jealous. If it upset him seeing me with others and he was ready to never ask, then it was time for me to let go of my dark thoughts. I couldn't expect from him something that I couldn't give in return.

"I brought us here to spend time alone." His tone dropped to a sexy whisper again. "Are you ready for our game?"

I put on my poker face. "You bet. If I win, I want to go back to our apartment, and I want to torture you in your own walls. I'll tease you all night and drive you crazy until you beg for mercy."

He grinned. "Now, that sounds tempting, Miss Stewart. I like the idea of you punishing me. But to be honest, right now I like the idea of fucking you, in every possible position, even more. We're not going home today."

Holy cow. He looked like he meant it.

I laughed as he walked over to his black bag to retrieve a set of cards. And for the first time I wondered why he had brought such a huge bag. What was he hiding in there?

4

DAMN!

I was losing big time.

"This game sucks," I said. As much as I wanted to cross my arms over my chest to express my frustration, I first needed them to hide as much skin as possible. It wasn't because I was ashamed of my body. It was Jett's hungry stare that made me want to hide behind a curtain. I didn't need to ask him about his thoughts. I could see them written all over his face as he pondered all the things he wanted to do—with me, to me.

Sitting inside the open pavilion in the backyard with barely any clothes on, I felt more exposed than ever.

Jett hadn't been kidding when he demanded we play our little game *outside*. I just didn't expect him to want it outside on private property—he didn't own. In the yard, where anyone could see us lounging, laughing, and being competitive half-naked.

"You're so sexy when you're pissed, Brooke." He grinned, and my heart melted a few inches. "I promise when I win the last round, I'll consider going inside. If you ask nicely."

So far, he had won five rounds straight in a row, each time giving me a chance to "redeem myself and get a chance to win the twenty-four hours of pure sex" by winning the next round, which he ended up winning…again.

If I could have wiped the smug smile off his face, I would have. With every loss, Jett requested that I remove one piece of clothing, and with every protective layer removed, his smug grin widened. He had already removed my shoes, socks, business suit, and bra…oh, God. Was he sniffing my blouse?

"What the hell are you doing?" I asked, mortified, fighting the urge to snag my blouse from his hands.

"Smelling the scent of success. I'm giving you one more chance, baby. You know six is my favorite number. It's my lucky number." He winked, just in case I didn't get his drift. "If I win one more time, I have to remove your panties and get to do what *I* want to do with you."

"Stop bragging, Mayfield." I pulled up my legs to my chest so I could rest my head on my knees and hide my smile. To call my pink sheer thong "panties" was ridiculous when it was so tiny and see-through you could see all the way to Alaska.

He sniffed my blouse again.

"Give me that." I leaped up to snag my top out of his hands, covering my exposed breasts in the process. Jett evaded my assault, laughing, as his gaze focused on the sides of my breasts where they seemed to spill out of my hands.

"You smell amazing, baby. Like a summer dream."

"It's called perfume."

He took another sniff, then pointed to my tiny thong. "Whatever it is, I'm sure what I'm going to smell next is even better."

I scowled. "I can still win."

He laughed out loud as he shuffled the cards. "You keep saying that after each lost round."

"Let's get this nonsense over and done with," I said through gritted teeth.

"Didn't you say it used to be your favorite game?" He could barely hide his wicked grin as he pulled playfully at one of my curls. "Sounds like someone is a sore loser."

"I am not," I protested.

I was. Big time.

But I was nowhere near ready to admit that to him, and particularly not when I didn't expect him to win. My father used to say I was the best Spades player. I hadn't lost in years. I knew I was being childish, but I couldn't help myself. That annoying grin of his was driving me nuts, which in turn managed to make me bold and careless, taking risks I wouldn't usually have taken. What drove me even more crazy was the fact that he always seemed to know my next move. The idea of having sex with him in a stranger's house filled me with shame because it was immoral. I had to win, just for the sake of stopping him from turning me into a mirror image of his wanton, sex-starved self. I wasn't going to lose my morals.

"You have one more chance." He kissed my shoulders, his hot breath both arousing and irritating me. "I'll let you win if it makes you feel better."

"I told you, no cheating. I'll beat you fair and square. And then we'll go back to your apartment. Because there's no way I'd ever sleep with you in a stranger's house. But let me guess, you'd only let me win if I agreed to do it here?"

"You're damn right about that."

"Well, in that case, I'm not changing my plans." I drew in a long breath and let it out slowly, imploring my mind to focus on the game rather than Jett's presence and his lips on my skin.

"Me, neither." He winked. "Luckily, I won't have to, which makes this round even hotter."

I shook my head at his inflated ego.

Maybe this time *I* was lucky. Nobody could win six times in a row. It was impossible. Right?

One win was all it'd take to have my say and take control of the situation.

Just one out of seven. The odds weren't so bad.

"How's it going?" Jett asked. He was sitting in a wicker chair, relaxed, as he surveyed me the way someone would look at potential prey. His gaze brushed over my neck, my exposed breasts, then moved up to my lips. He was clearly relishing his pre-coital fantasies, unleashing roaring chaos inside me with just a glance. So sure of himself, which made me nervous and unable to think.

Damn, I needed my brain to work—and fast—before it was too late.

"It'd be great if you were naked, too," I admitted. "I can't focus."

"You think you'll be able to focus once I'm naked?" He laughed. "Sure, baby. Whatever rocks your boat."

"It wasn't a compliment," I said, irritated. "I can't focus because you're staring at me."

"Fair enough. Then let me help you feel more at ease." He grinned and undid the top button of his shirt. My eyes followed his fingers, drinking in each movement, as he unbuttoned his shirt all the way down—slowly as if he had all the time in the world, revealing rows of toned muscle. My gaze lingered on the tribal tattoo on his upper arm before moving to his chiseled chest and the narrow trail of hair on his abdomen.

He was pure perfection.

Forget perfection—he was a god, sent into the world to mentally torture women with his impossibly sexy body.

I swallowed hard and clenched my legs together to hide the betraying signs of my arousal. It took every ounce of my willpower to fight the need to close my eyes for a second, just to escape the film playing inside my mind. His lips on mine. Our bodies entwined, moving in accord, pleasuring the other as we sought our own release. I groaned inwardly. Why did I have to tell him to take off his clothes? I should have known better.

He dropped the shirt on the floor.

Not your brightest idea, Stewart.

Knowing too well the effect he had on me, Jett sat back in his chair, his gaze lingering on me, and I could've sworn I could see the sex movie playing before his eyes, too. A sharp electric shock ran down my spine and gathered in my abdomen, sending delicious jolts through my private parts.

Focus, Stewart. He wants you to lose. That's why he's piling on the sex appeal. Why the hell did you give him the idea?

"You know there are many ways we could play this?" he asked.

Pure awesomeness came to my mind.

"How?" I asked casually. It was my turn to draw a card.

39

Two of spades. I decided to keep it.

"You could give up, and I'd take it easy on you. I'd even agree to spending half a day here and the other half back in NY. Deal?"

He was about to lose. For some reason I could feel it. This was my chance. I peered at my cards, confident.

"Thanks, but no." I looked up, grinning.

"You sure, baby? It's your last chance," Jett said, grinning back.

I could see right through his bluff.

"No." I shook my head. "Because there's no way you could possibly win this one."

He did win. A couple of minutes later, I tossed my cards on the table.

Crap!

I didn't know what went wrong. It might be the way Jett was sitting, so confident and sexy with half his body exposed. Or maybe it was the way he looked at me, his eyes already making plans what he'd do to me. Or maybe—and I'd never admit that to him—he was the better player. Luckier, too. Whatever it was, I was screwed.

Jett stretched out his long legs, obviously enjoying every second of his glory. I figured I'd never get men and their competitive alpha behavior.

I shook my head in disbelief. "How did you do it?"

"It's called motivation"—his eyes sparkled—"to get laid.

Seems I want it more than you do."

"I doubt it."

His brows shot up. "You doubt I want to sleep with you more than you want with me?"

Heat shot up my neck and face. "No, that's not what I meant. I—"

He began to laugh, and I clamped my mouth shut.

"I know you were talking about my strategy," Jett said. "I could teach you my technique. In fact, I can teach *you* a lot of things, Miss Stewart. Things you never experienced before."

Holy mother of double meanings.

My heart jumped in my chest as I watched Jett get up and reach me in one step.

"You know you're mine for the night and I get to do whatever I want with you?" he continued in that unfazed voice of his.

Too cool. Too confident. Too much of everything.

Why the heck did I think I could ever deal with a man like him? If it wasn't for our unborn child, I might have run.

Maybe.

Probably not.

Because he was like a drug, and I was addicted to him.

I nodded, barely able to peel my gaze off his sculpted and very naked chest.

"Do you have any idea what's in store tonight?" He

kneeled before me, hands resting on both sides of me, and our eyes connected. I pressed a hand against my pounding heart. Did I have an idea? No, but it sounded sexy and forbidden. Whatever it was, I'd take it.

"May I have the *pleasure*?" Without waiting for my approval, his fingers moved up my legs, putting just the right amount of pressure. A whiplash of electric pulses rushed through me. Gently he pushed my legs apart. My breath came heavy as he started to kiss my knees, then his way up the inside of my legs.

His lips caressed my sensitive skin, working upward closer and closer to the growing wetness between my legs. I could feel the need inside me growing as he kissed my thong, his tongue running over the damp spot.

In spite of the layer of fabric separating his hot lips from my pulsating clit, the sensation was stronger than I ever imagined it to be. I closed my eyes and a soft moan escaped my throat...when he stopped. Opening my eyes, I glanced down, confused. Jett opened his bag but held it away from me so I couldn't glimpse what was inside. He caught my interested glance but didn't comment.

Excitement rushed through me at the though of him taking charge. He had done it before. Only, the bag made me nervous because, for some reason, it kick-started my imagination, pushing it to run wild with images of sex toys and kinky lingerie.

"You're not a masochist, are you?" I tried to read his cryptic expression and failed. "Because if you are, we need a safe word. And you should know in advance that I'm not into spanking, choking, in fact anything that involves unbearable pain."

He looked up, his green eyes full of mischief. "Pain wasn't *quite* part of my *plans*."

Holy shit!

What did he mean with "quite" and "plans?"

I would have given anything to know his plans, yet his reply was as cryptic as his expression. I grimaced but didn't pursue the issue. Eventually, he retrieved a timer from his bag and placed it on the coffee table.

"Ready?" Jett pressed a red button, and the timer started to count backward.

Twenty-three hours. Fifty-nine minutes. Fifty-nine seconds.

The seconds began to tick by as my nerves began to fray. I clasped my hands in my lap, unsure what to do.

"Back inside you said you trusted me." Jett's statement took me by surprise.

"I did. Why are you asking?" I frowned as I watched him pull out a sheet of paper from his bag and pass it on to me.

"Those are the rules."

I almost choked on my breath. "Seriously? You have sex

rules?" Why was I even surprised? This was the same guy who demanded a nondisclosure contract before sleeping with me.

"I do because I've won you for the night, which is why I'm setting the rules. So consider yourself obligatorily at my mercy." His smile was gone now, replaced by a dead-seriousness. I had never been at a man's mercy, and I didn't know how to feel about it.

I swallowed past the lump in my throat as my eyes began to scan the computer printout.

RULES

1. The losing party agrees to keep the phone switched off at all times.
2. The losing party agrees to shower and dress in the winner's preferred outfit to look most enticing in accordance with the winning party's wishes.
3. The losing party agrees to be willing to experiment with new things in accordance with the winning party's wishes.
4. The losing party agrees to pay maximum effort to both reaching and causing physical pleasure.
5. The losing party agrees not to discuss the events happening on this day with any third

party.

6. A change in Terms is to be suggested in written form through a recognized lawyer. The winning party reserves the right to decline any and all suggestions made by the losing party.

7. The winning party can't be held responsible for any strong reactions experienced as a result of this game and its rules and implications.

My eyes widened at the words losing … enticing … commands … not to be discussed … strong reactions.

"Seriously?" I repeated for the second time. "You know, this looks kind of formal, not to mention creepy."

On the bright side it wasn't an agreement to having some kind of depraved sex that might've scared the hell out of me. It was short and to the point—and absolutely non-descriptive. I was as clueless as I had been before.

I pointed to paragraph six. "It's impossible for me to suggest anything in written form because there's no lawyer around and I'm bound to the house. By the time we get back to New York, your twenty-four hours might be over."

"Exactly." He grinned. "I thought I should make it sound like you had some say in the matter."

I grimaced again. "How kind of you to think of me. Why don't you also throw in some feedback form? You know, the kind I could submit after you're done with me."

My voice dripped with sarcasm, and he laughed out loud.

As I handed the rule sheet back to him, his finger touched mine and a spark ignited between us, traveling all the way down my spine and into my abdomen. I flinched and my eyes connected with his, searching for a clue that he had felt it as well. His expression remained as composed as always.

"You sure you don't want me to sign over my soul?" I asked, joking.

"That's a tempting offer, Brooke. I might indeed take you up on it later to make sure you'll always be mine. But for now all I want is the chase."

He pointed to the shirt next to me, and I threw it to him. He caught it in midair and I watched him pull it on again, almost regretful.

"Go take a shower and get dressed." Jett opened his bag again, and this time I caught a glimpse of a white gift box, which he handed to me. "I want you to wear that."

The box was surprisingly light for its size. Curious, I opened it and retrieved a sexy red and black set of lingerie, a pair of matching high heels, a satin robe that'd barely cover my ass, and...were those stockings?

"Oh, God." I held up the narrow strip of fabric I assumed was a thong but I couldn't be sure because it was the skimpiest I had ever seen. It was sexy, made of mesh and chiffon, and left nothing to the imagination. "You expect me to wear this?" Somehow the thought made me excited.

Jett nodded slowly. "As I said, yes. My game, my rules." The corners of his lips curled into a lazy smile. "Ever since I set my eyes on you in that bar, I've been wanting to see you in something like this. Can you blame a man for living out his fantasy?"

I couldn't. I just wished it didn't involve prancing around a stranger's home half naked.

5

AS PER JETT'S request, I first took a shower. Under the hot water running down my body, the tension in my muscles slowly subsided, but my thoughts of being an uninvited guest in this mansion weren't so easy to switch off.

The bathroom was as large as a bedroom, and pure luxury, with a huge Jacuzzi to fit several people and a TV set mounted on the wall. The tiny lights in the ceiling reflected in the black marble tiles, making them sparkle like huge diamonds. I stepped out of the shower and wrapped a towel around my naked body, then went about cleaning up after myself to restore the bathroom's previous pristine condition. Sylvie used to call it OCD, but whenever something bothered me, I cleaned. And right now what bothered me was the prospect of having sex in a stranger's house.

By the time I changed into Jett's idea of lingerie, the thought of having sex with him in this mansion both scared and excited me. Even though I didn't want to admit it, my body was wet and ready for him. It wasn't just the prospect of doing something illegal. It was the idea of doing another first with him. Letting him be in control the way I had never surrendered to him before. Having to trust Jett knew what he was doing, when I had a strong feeling the house had at least one or two hidden cameras installed.

I slipped into the bra and barely there thong, rolled up the stockings, and tried to get a feel for the high heels. The robe hugged my figure in all the right places and, as expected, barely covered my modesty. The black high heels with straps made my legs look a mile high. I ran my hands through my hair to give my curls some definition and applied a tiny bit of lipstick. Pleased with the result, I regarded myself in the huge mirror. I looked sexy and felt just the same. This was the kind of outfit that would make any woman look hot. Whoever advised Jett on what to buy sure knew their way around lingerie. Only, walking in those heels required some skill. Right in front of the window was a narrow strip of white sand—prime private beach. I wondered if Jett would insist on taking a walk? If so, I hoped I didn't have to wear the heels, because they were so high I doubted I could take more than a few strides in them, let alone enjoy an evening stroll. With a last glance, I left the bathroom and joined Jett in the master bedroom, where he'd said he'd be waiting.

As I stepped inside, partly nervous, partly excited, my breath caught in my throat. He had spread a black satin cover on the sheets and red candles were arranged on the nightstand, their soft glow giving the room a romantic flair. The delicate scent of roses hung heavy in the air.

"You look stunning." Jett's voice was hoarse. I turned sharply and found him standing to my right, obscured by a massive dresser. His hands were buried in his pockets, his sleeves rolled up to reveal his strong forearms. His eyes scanned my high heels, my stockings, my half-exposed breasts, wandering farther up until his gaze met mine, and a smile lit up his face. There was something in his eyes—a glimmer I had seen before, only I couldn't remember where.

"Thank you," I whispered, unsure what to do with myself. "You have good taste, albeit a bit kinky." I pointed down my front.

"No." He shook his head and walked over to me. "You're beautiful, Brooke. Everything would look amazing on you."

My glance swept back over the candles, to their soft flickering glow, the king sized bed, then back to Jett, all the while ignoring the one thing that scared the hell out of me.

I had never done tying up and we barely knew each other. While I trusted him, I didn't know whether I trusted him that much. His previous questioning of my level of trust made so much more sense now.

"What?" he asked.

"You didn't strike me as this kind of guy." I shrugged and pointed around me, as though it didn't matter. "I thought you would go for outdoor, daring. I don't know. I just thought you would be more—" I trailed off, looking for the right words. He regarded me intently, but didn't help me out.

Romantic? Daring? He had been all of those things so far, including the exhibitionistic outdoorsy type. I just didn't expect—

Bondage.

Being tied and at someone else's mercy. Holy cow. When I had made that joke on the need of establishing a "safe word" I couldn't have been closer to the truth.

Jett's eyes narrowed on me. "Nothing wrong with variety. At least I'm experiencing it with one and the same woman. I can't claim the same thing for many men." His tone was half accusing, half amused. "But I guess you're right to some extent."

"How so?"

"You don't know half of the things you should know about me. This—" he pointed to the candles "—is meant to set the mood and relax you. Nothing more and nothing less."

What the heck did that even mean? That it wasn't his style? That he wouldn't have done it, if he didn't feel a need to make me feel comfortable?

My stomach fluttered and my mouth went dry as I watched him walk across the room with slow measured steps. His feet were naked, barely making a sound on the hardwood floor. His eyes remained focused on me, and for the umpteenth time I felt like his prey, scared but hypnotized, waiting for him to capture or release me. Tonight I harbored no false hope that it would be the latter.

"We can't stay here for the night. We could get in big trouble," I protested weakly.

He stopped in front of me, and his arm wrapped around my waist. At first I thought it was to caress my back. Only when his fingers trailed up my spine and gathered in my hair did I feel the gentle pull, urging me to raise my head and meet his burning lips.

It was a gentle kiss, his lips barely grazing mine.

"My rules." He spun me around slowly. "That's why we're here. I'm teaching you to break a few rules." His gaze brushed my lips with such hunger it sent a tingle through them. "I'll love you in any way I want. I'll love you in any way you need. As long as we stay here, baby, you're mine." He grinned as he pulled me down on the bed. "You had your chance to win. Not my fault you didn't want to."

I had wanted to, but I had been too weak to make it happen. Or maybe, on an unconscious level, I had wanted to surrender to him. Either way, I was at his mercy, and he knew it.

"Stop rubbing it in, Mayfield."

"Why don't you admit you like when I'm in charge?"

I swallowed.

"I'm not into all that submission crap," I muttered. Giving up control was kind of nice every now and then, but he didn't need to know that, or I'd live to regret it. Jett had the unnerving tendency to get a little too intense, like with this game. He couldn't just establish that he was the better player by winning and shutting up about it; he had to translate his dominance into our lovemaking and risk criminal charges by breaking a few laws in the process.

"I didn't expect you'd do it without putting up a good fight." He raised my leg and started to trail soft kisses on the inside, the movement sending a delicious shiver through me.

I suppressed a moan as his lips kissed my inner thigh. His tongue started to draw small swirls on my skin, inch by inch moving down toward my knee.

"I'll always be your best, Brooke," he whispered.

I had no doubt about that.

Slowly, he peeled off my high heel and dropped it near

the bed.

"No one will ever love you more than I do," Jett continued. The second high heel hit the floor with a thud.

Intense? Yes, but I loved it.

My heart raced as his attention shifted to my other thigh and he proceeded to torture my body. His teeth grated my skin gently and turned into soft bites.

"Close your eyes."

I followed his command, anticipating his next move. Something silky tickled my skin. I opened my eyes and looked down at the ties in Jett's hand and the naughty glint in his eyes.

"Are those yours from the apartment?" I asked, sitting up. He pressed me back down.

"Yeah. They're just right for this particular purpose." He stretched the material, conjuring images of punishment, whipping, and bondage inside my head.

"I'm not—"

His hot mouth stifled my protest and his hands pulled my arms over my head. I could feel the silky fabric first on my left wrist, then around the right. I pulled gently, and then with a little more fervor as I realized I was being bound to the bedpost.

"Relax," Jett whispered. "I'd never hurt you."

I nodded, even though my heart was beating a million miles an hour, and not from the sexual tension in the air.

The smooth material felt cool against my skin. Sexy. Erotic. Menacing.

"This was actually my idea. You realize that, right?" I laughed nervously. "I told you what I'd do to you if I won, and now you're claiming it as your own."

His brows shot up in mock offence. "Are you implying I'm stealing your ideas, Miss Stewart?" He shifted his weight off of me and moved to my ankles. My breath caught in my throat as I realized what he was about to do.

"Maybe I'm implying I have no free hand to help you." I hoped he got the hint and untied me.

"I'm doing just fine but thanks for offering."

He grinned with the kind of glint in his eyes that said he harbored no intentions to follow my unspoken request. In fact, he was going to tease me and tease me hard. I wondered where he was heading. The tie brushed my skin, the cold satin against my ankles sending shivers of delight up my body.

"Are you going to keep on talking?" he asked. "Because right now I'm thinking of shutting your sexy little mouth so I can follow through with my plans."

"What plans?" At his displeased expression, I halted the hundreds of questions inside my head. I had been talking again. I always was when I was nervous. "Sorry," I muttered.

He shifted back on top of me and propped up on his

elbows, his mouth so close to mine I wanted to reach up and suck his lower lip between my teeth.

"Dirty plans. I'm going to ravish you until you can't get me out of your system. There are a million ways to make you come and I'm planning on testing each and every one of them. But first you'll need to be—" He lifted the last tie to show me.

"Of course," I muttered.

I lifted my head so he could blindfold me.

The sudden darkness, his hot breath on my neck, and the weight of his body on me made my heart pound harder. It was so dark I couldn't see a damn thing and the idea both scared and aroused me. My legs were spread wide open, inviting him to do whatever he wanted to me. What was he doing? Why didn't he move? I bit my lip hard to stop the need to ask.

I could feel his gaze on me, caressing my body, making my skin tingle all over. I could sense the smile on his lips but couldn't read his intentions.

"I want to fuck you," Jett whispered. "Slowly. Recklessly. Teasingly. However I feel like doing it. In all possible ways. Scream as loud as you want because no one will hear you. And I want you to scream, baby."

His fingers began to trail my abdomen, gathering between my legs. I felt him prodding me, spreading my gathering juices. Tied and in a stranger's house, I was open for him. My senses heightened, my primal instincts asking to be filled. His finger slipped inside me slowly. I moaned and lifted my hips, welcoming the sensation, drawing him deeper.

"Not yet," he whispered. His finger pulled out of me, leaving me empty and frustrated. I frowned as I listened to his footsteps walking across the room, Jett picking something up, then laying back down on the bed.

Something rustled.

"Open your mouth." His sharp tone left no room for discussion. My heart pounded frantically against my ribcage. I swallowed hard but didn't follow his command.

"Do it, Brooke." His deep voice dripped with impatience.

This was his chance to prove he loved me and would never hurt me—his chance to earn my trust. I had to take the plunge to see it for myself. So I opened my mouth and in that instant I knew I did far more than trust him. My passion for him was big, but my love for him was bigger. I wanted to please him because when I lost my heart to him, I also gave away my vulnerability. I surrendered to him and he conquered me—body and soul. Trust was the only thing left to give freely. The only thing we could earn, the only thing we are still learning.

Something sticky hit my tongue. Sweet, soft and creamy like chocolate.

"Bite," Jett instructed.

I bit and sucked, then swallowed and opened my mouth again, realizing it was chocolate transitioning from a rich cocoa flavor to an intense, sweet hazelnut cream. His mouth descended upon mine again, the chocolate melting between our tongues.

I moaned because it was delicious.

His kiss was heavenly chocolate melting delicious.

Heat gathered between my legs and my clit began to pulse gently, silently demanding attention. As though reading my thoughts, Jett's mouth left me and began to move down my chest and abdomen as something cold and sticky poured between my legs, trickling down my entry.

"What is that?" I asked breathlessly.

"Chocolate." I could hear his amusement and it drove me nuts that I couldn't see his expression. His hot breath traveled down my abdomen, and then his tongue touched the right spot, the sensation of licking and sucking sending my pulse into a frenzy. My nipples peaked for him, urging him to touch them, but his attention was focused elsewhere.

More chocolate dripped down my skin—so much I was sure he was using the whole tube, smearing it all over the bed, when I remembered the spread. He had thought of everything. I made a mental note to give him credit for that, but the thought was short-lived because his tongue began to swirl in a circular motion, and his finger found my entry, filling and stretching.

Oh, God.

I was dying.

Scratch that.

I was dying and going straight to heaven.

Or maybe he was my downfall and I was going to hell.

I moaned and switched off my brain as heat began to pool into my abdomen. His finger thrust inside me, twisting and circling as his lips sucked my clit so hard my whole body reacted. Moisture gathered between my legs, spread by his fingers thrusting rhythmically until I reached the brink of lust. From there it was a mere step into total surrender.

"You're so good," I moaned. "I want more."

"I love when you demand," he whispered. "Chocolate and your juices. It's my favorite combination."

My cheeks caught fire, but I had no time to feel mortified because his teeth began to graze my clit, sucking gently.

And then his mouth was back on my lips. One hand squeezed beneath the nape of my neck, the other lifted my leg. In one swift movement he slammed inside me, his thick erection burning its way deep into my core. The bed shook, or maybe it was my body as he began to crash into me. I didn't care that we were spreading chocolate all over the sheets. I wanted him. I wanted every bit of what he had to offer. I moved my hips to meet his thrusts, listened to the sexy noises coming out of his hot mouth as his thrusts became deeper and faster. Hot waves of heat rocked my abdomen, promising to erupt in a raging fire.

I lifted my hips to give him deeper access, and more he took. Feeling every hard inch impaling my flesh, I lost reason, consumed by his passion for me. The hot flames of a nearing orgasm began to build inside my womb, and my body rocked with the first tremors.

"You're so damn addicting. Like a narcotic." His hips pushed his erection deep into me in fast short thrusts. He was close. I could feel his shudders, and my clit ached in response, desperate for relief.

In darkness, I moaned and lifted off the bed as far as my restraints would allow, my mouth searching his. Our tongues connected in a fast erotic dance mirroring the movement of his hips, sending electrical shards of pleasure through my heart and soul. Jett's fingers pressed against my clit hard, the sudden sensation unbearable. I gasped against his mouth. My soft flesh tightened around his hard shaft, and I came undone around him, faintly aware of Jett's groan of fulfillment tearing from his chest.

My skin sizzled with electricity as our bodies merged into one, over and over again, until there was nothing more to give. Exhausted, I slumped against the sheets and closed my eyes. Fingers removed my restraints and blindfold. Jett pulled me against his hot body and wrapped his arms around me. The intoxicating scent of chocolate and our lovemaking was my last conscious thought.

6

AN HOUR LATER, my fingers traced the contours of his tribal tattoo. It was a gang thing, he once explained, and part of his former life. He had done so many things, seen the world from different perspectives, and in some way touching it was my chance to connect with some aspect of it.

I watched the light of the candles reflected on his bronze skin and wondered for the umpteenth time whether I might ever know him—the *real* him, the parts he so carefully kept hidden.

"What's wrong, sleeping beauty?" Jett asked, sensing my emotional undercurrents.

I shook my head and took a deep breath to clear my thoughts. "Nothing." I knew he wouldn't drop it, so I said the first thing that came to my mind. "I just realized I never had sex in a puddle of chocolate before. It's kind of strange to wake up surrounded by the scent of chocolate."

"I feel the same way, and I'm glad you were the one to experience it with." He kissed the top of my head.

"Hope I'll get to return the favor one day. That's if I ever win one of your games."

"We'll see about that."

I hated to be away from him, but some needs couldn't be ignored. "I need to visit a certain room," I said with an apologetic smile.

"Ah." He moved aside, but his grip didn't let go of me immediately. "Be back soon."

"I will," I whispered, and left for the bathroom. After a quick shower, I wrapped myself in an oversized towel and decided to borrow Kim's hairdryer. It usually took me a while to get my hair dry, courtesy of my unruly curls, so I left it half damp before Jett got bored and kicked in the door. Not that he had ever done that, but he was on a schedule, so I figured he might have a few more plans lined up before his twenty-four hours were up.

I shrugged into the robe again, ignoring just how short it was in the bathroom light. Knowing Jett's appetite, I reckoned we probably wouldn't venture far from the bedroom, so no one beside Jett would ever see my ass. With a last glance in the mirror, I stepped out of the bathroom and stopped dead.

The first thing I noticed was the light streaming in through the windows. Jett must have pulled back the curtains, bathing the room in glaring brightness. The next thing I noticed was that, in my absence, he had removed the candles, and the sheet covering the bed was gone, together with his bag.

"Jett?" Calling his name, I walked downstairs and stopped. His voice carried over from the living room. I strained to listen but couldn't make out any words, so I inched closer as a sense of *déjà vu* gripped me. On the last day in Italy, Jett had almost shot two intruders who got away with all evidence we had gathered on the Lucazzone estate. The fear of having someone watching us, waiting to strike when we least expected it, had caused me a few nightmares and never quite left me. And now it was coming back full force.

Ignoring the frantic drumming of my heart, I sucked in air a few times, forcing oxygen into my lungs. Unlike back in Italy, no one knew we were here, so my sudden pang of fear was unreasonable. Still, I couldn't stop the beads of sweat gathering at the nape of my neck. I took another lungful of air and stepped into the living room. Jett was standing near the windows overlooking the backyard; his back was turned to me, and his phone was glued to his ear.

"You do that." His voice sounded strangely anxious and strained, which managed to worry me even more.

I knocked softly on the doorframe to get his attention, and he turned to signal he had acknowledged my presence before turning away again.

"I'll be fine," he said. "Don't worry. I'll take care of things...Okay." He hung up, his hand clutching at his phone, his gaze fixed on a point outside the window.

Hesitating, I inched closer and stopped next to him. His eyes were distant, and his face was a mask of fury. From the way he was standing, motionless, with his shoulders slouched, I couldn't shake off the feeling that something bad had happened. Something felt horribly wrong. My fingers itched to touch him, but I didn't dare. Not before he told me what had happened.

"Jett?" I probed softly.

He didn't stir, didn't look at me.

"Jett? What's wrong?"

A few seconds passed in silence. His troubled gaze brushed our feet, as if recalling where he was, or maybe he just fought for strength.

"My father died," he said at last. His voice was so low, strained and choked, I wasn't sure I heard right.

"What?" I whispered. I shook my head, unable to comprehend the meaning of his words. It couldn't be. I clasped my hand over my mouth in shock. "Oh, my God."

Jett turned to me, his eyes meeting mine. They were filled with pain.

"My brother was called to the morgue this morning. He phoned to say my father had been on his boat when it blew up yesterday." I watched him walk over to the couch and slump down. "He didn't survive it."

I sat down next to him.

"I'm so sorry, Jett." I squeezed his hand in the hope the gesture would convey more meaning than the probably most overused phrase in the world. Even though they had not been close and Robert Mayfield used to belong to Alessandro's secret club, he was still Jett's father. I watched the way Jett sat, defeated with his head buried in his hands, and couldn't stop my tears from falling. We never got the chance to tell his father we were expecting. I had never even met him.

"It's all my fault." Jett looked up, his eyes meeting mine, searching for the confirmation I wouldn't give him. I inhaled a sharp breath and let it out slowly. It killed me to see him suffering like that.

"No, Jett. You can't blame yourself."

"But it is, and we both know it." He pulled his hand out of my grip and got up, his face turning into a mask of anger. He punched the wall and I jerked back in shock. "He called two weeks ago, right after we returned from Italy. I didn't want to talk with him because I was angry. If only I'd met with him, maybe this wouldn't have happened."

"What are you saying?" I asked, shocked. "You think it

wasn't an accident?"

"No, Brooke, it wasn't." He glanced back to me with so much anger I flinched. "A boat doesn't blow up. He would've noticed a fire and called for help. Maybe whoever did this shot him first before setting fire to get rid of any evidence. It was arson, I'm sure of that."

I didn't know what was more frightening: that I had never seen him so upset, or the fact there wasn't a single thing I could do to help him. I regarded Jett's angry face, afraid of his next move. Afraid of what this could mean for us.

Seconds passed, which turned into minutes, and Jett didn't budge from the spot.

"Fuck," Jett mumbled.

"I wish there was something I could do," I whispered.

"There isn't." His tone softened, and for a moment the anger in his voice disappeared, only to come back directed at himself. "I should have known."

I shook my head in confusion, unable to follow his changes in mood. "Known what?"

His eyes glazed over, lost in thoughts. He walked back to the couch and sat down. Another minute passed, and no reply came.

"What makes you think he was killed, Jett?" I asked cautiously. "Your brother would have said something. The police would be all over it."

"Do you remember the five people on the list?" he asked.

I nodded, thinking back to the little black book we had found in Alessandro's basement. Jett had mentioned five names, and one of them was Robert Mayfield.

"I think that was a hit list," Jett continued in a tone that made shiver.

I sat down next to him on the couch, watching him in silence, as his words slowly sank in.

"There's no way the five names were the only club members. It's impossible. My father said—" Jett's voice faltered with emotion "—he said there were seventy-eight members before he left. Maybe the other four decided to opt out as well."

"You think he was killed because he wanted out?" I asked needlessly. I hadn't seen this perspective before and it certainly didn't make a hell of a lot of sense to me, but I couldn't rule it out. A club like that probably thrived on wealthy members and their dedication for life. Maybe someone had taken the "silence to the grave" oath a little too literally. Possible. I thought back to Jett's words.

I don't think your way is the way they're working. They're not as peaceful.

Even I had known at that point that no one was let in

easily, and definitely not out with a mere handshake.

"My father said it was a mistake to join the club," Jett said. "They probably wanted to get rid of him. If I had mentioned the book and the list, I could have prevented his death. I know he would have listened to me." His voice sounded choked. "I would have been able to save his life."

"No, Jett." I shook my head, my heart hurting because Jett blamed himself.

"Don't think like that," I whispered and shook my head again, my hand clutching at his arm to force him to listen to me. His eyes bored into me and for the first time his anger wasn't directed at himself, but at me.

"But it's the truth. The fucking truth, Brooke. Why won't you accept that I made a mistake?"

7

LIFE HAS A way of throwing everything around. Sometimes I couldn't stop the feeling that we were all trapped inside a cup called life, and like dice shaken around and thrown out. Ready to be tested and played. Ready to risk and face the unthinkable. Ready to lose and get hurt. And it didn't matter how high the social status was or how much money a person had, it could affect everyone, anytime and anywhere. We were all at the mercy of the shaking cup called life.

Watching the various emotions crossing Jett's features, I realized how much I loved him and that I'd do anything for him. However, whatever I did or said, there was no recipe for taking away the pain. Nothing to ease his mind or guilt. Nothing to rid his conscience of the demons haunting him. As much as I loved him, love was not enough to release him from the guilt he'd probably carry with him for the rest of his life. It was as if guilt had become his companion and I had become his shadow—one trying to heal him and the other causing as much havoc as possible. And I knew all about guilt and the dirty tricks it played so it could haunt you forever.

The moment Jett found out about his father's death, I felt him distancing himself from me. We packed up quickly and drove back to his apartment in freezing silence. The moment he unlocked the door, I felt like an intruder in his world.

"Gotta go to work," Jett mumbled, and disappeared again, leaving me alone in the perfection of his place.

"Okay," I said weakly, but he was gone already.

Work had to be an excuse to bury himself in his grief—or why else would he leave without giving me a kiss goodbye? That night he didn't come home. And the following night, he was there with me and yet not there. Listened to me, and yet none of my words reached him through the shield he had built around himself. I knew this would happen. I almost expected it. What I didn't expect was for him to shut me out of his world. To not let me get close, refusing to talk, refusing to listen. He had become emotionally distant and at times unavailable, but the worst was that I could feel him changing.

It was as if guilt had created an invisible barrier that

began to separate us, harming our relationship, his playful nature replaced by something that scared the hell out of me. Like sickness, leaving a bitter aftertaste in its wake.

With each day, the walls grew higher, distancing him from me. And no matter how hard I pounded and shook at the gates, they seemed to be stronger than I, my love for him, or anything that used to matter to him.

Maybe I hadn't known him as well as I thought I did. The silence and determined continuation of his rituals consisting of nothing but work and sleeping was *his* way of coping. However, the way he was shutting me out— physically and emotionally—made me feel as though he was shutting me out in his heart, too.

I preferred tears. They were good. They would purify, cleanse, and help him heal. I preferred anger because it would draw out the poison of guilt. But they never came. I wanted an outburst; I wanted something to show me that he wasn't too broken to heal, the way my mother had been after my father's death: motionless, her body living and breathing, but her soul dead within the physical carcass of herself. That was a lot worse than the anger I wanted Jett to let loose so he could eventually move on.

With Robert Mayfield dead, my thoughts kept circling back to the break-in, the black book, and Alessandro Lucazzone. I could feel the connection, and it scared me. Maybe someone had panicked, and our discoveries were the reason why Jett's father was murdered in the first place. I couldn't shake off the feeling that if Jett and I had never begun to date, we would never have broken through the wall and found the black book that was so important people were ready to kill for it.

"That's why secrets should stay buried forever," I muttered to myself as I slipped into a demure black dress for Robert Mayfield's funeral.

If Jett heard me, he didn't reply.

I drew in a shaky breath and closed my eyes to get rid of the stinging sensation as a new thought entered my mind.

How terrible would it be if not Jett but I were to blame for his father's death?

8

THE SKY RESEMBLED a looming dark pit carrying the heavy promise of rain. A strong gust of wind tugged at my black dress, its cold caress keeping me strangely grounded and reminding me that amidst all the graves we were alive, continuing to swim in the river called life while the rest would be soon forgotten, whether we wanted it or not.

I glanced at Jett who was standing in front of Robert Mayfield's grave, his eyes focused on a spot on the horizon only he could see. The people around us listened to the reverend's empty words in silence. A few were crying, their souls tormented by the loss of someone they believed to have known. Most of them barely blinked, locked in a state of memories and self-reflection, their minds full of promises to re-evaluate their own life and make it better. I knew because I had been one of them after my sister and father died. I could see it in the mourners' guilty expressions and the determination in their eyes. I also knew from experience that whatever promises they made to themselves would rarely last. In the end, the stupid things we did didn't matter anyway; what mattered was appreciating the people in our life, spending enough time with them.

Material belongings always waste away, while memories never fade.

I blinked away the tears gathering at the corner of my eyes and peered around me. I'd never seen so many people at one funeral. Then again, I had never been rich or famous, while Jett's father had been both.

The drive to the funeral service was short and silent. By the time we reached the penthouse Jett's father had inhabited during his stays in New York, hundreds of people had already gathered and more were flooding in by the minute, all hurrying to offer Jett their condolences.

I listened to countless speeches, all praising Robert Mayfield as a good man who had brought many great changes to those who had entered his life. I listened to recalled fond memories while my gaze brushed the pictures on the walls and mantelpiece. Most were hidden behind countless flower bouquets and goodbye letters, but a few stood out—mostly of Robert Mayfield and women. One or two showed him with two young boys I assumed were Jett and Jonathan, and it made me wonder how many of the funeral visitors actually knew the kind of man Robert Mayfield had been hiding behind the façade of normality and perfection.

Biting my lip hard, I peered at Jett's stony expression and the hardness in his eyes, and I recalled the way he had known his father. As a hard man. As a terrible role model who neither acknowledged his mistakes nor apologized. But no one seemed to want to mention any of that.

"Will you stay here? I have to see some people," Jett said, jerking me out of my thoughts.

"Sure. I'll go check out the buffet." I pointed in the direction of the open-plan kitchen area, which I had spied upon entering. The large assortment of finger food would have done a wedding reception justice. "Want anything?"

Jett shook his head. "I'm okay." He shot me a tender smile, and then he was gone.

I walked over to the buffet and grabbed a plate, then got in line, unable to decide whether to get the oysters or the salmon rolls. Everything looked delicious, and the baby inside me knew it.

"You're Brooke, right?" A voice behind me startled me. I turned sharply to regard a tall guy with dark hair and blue eyes. The first thing I noticed about him was the tailored black designer suit; the second was the confidence in his eyes. His lips were curved into just a hint of a friendly smile—not too much and not too little, given the circumstances.

"Yes." I nodded. "And you are?"

"I'm Jonathan, Jett's brother. Call me Nate. Everyone does." He shook my hand. "Jett's told me everything about you."

"I'm sorry for your loss," I said.

"I appreciate it." Nate's smile didn't shift, but I caught the sudden glance at the floor. I remembered a time when I had to smile and pretend the world was all right when all I wanted was to crawl into a corner and bawl my eyes out. Maybe finding common ground was what made me like Nate instantly.

"It was a terrible accident," Nate murmured and for the first time I noticed the dark circles framing his eyes. I swallowed down the lump in my throat and nodded.

"Terrible and sad." Unaware of my gesture, I brushed a hand over my flat abdomen. A brief moment of awkward silence ensued between us, during which a waiter carrying glasses of champagne walked past. Nate picked up two, handing me one glass, then pointed to a couch in the corner of the huge living room. I nodded and followed him, my hands clutching the glass of alcohol. He sat down and invited me to do the same.

"How's Jett holding up?" he asked. His voice was strained. A shudder ran down my spine at the thought that he was the one who'd been called to the morgue in order to identify his father's body, scorched beyond recognition. I couldn't imagine how difficult it must have been for him. I was glad it wasn't Jett.

"As okay as the circumstances allow."

"My brother's a tough guy. If something's troubling him, he works hard to get rid of it." He took a sip from his glass and watched me for a moment before continuing. "After our mother left, he took charge. It's the way my little brother copes."

I leaned back, hiding my surprise. Of course Nate knew his brother well. They had grown up together. But talking about him so intimately jarred me. As though sensing my thoughts, Nate smiled and took another sip of his drink. "Just be there for him, and he'll be fine."

"You two used to be very close," I said matter-of-factly, remembering the few stories Jett had told me back in Italy. Two boys watching the Lucazzone estate in secret, their imagination thriving with theories of mystery and conspiracy. Back then they didn't know just how spot-on they were.

"Correction. We still are." Nate's eyes bored into me. "We're friends. We've always been. Too bad we're living in different states."

"Jett said you work in Austin?" I asked.

His eyes moved to my glass. I fought the urge to take an

obligatory sip.

"Yeah. I'm managing the southern division of Mayfield Realties. Not missing New York a bit."

"Why?" I asked, a little stunned. It was one of the best cities in the world. So many people moved to New York to follow their dreams, I almost expected everyone to love the city, the magic of the holidays, the best shopping strips, and the spirit in general. He pointed at the gray sky outside the wall-to-ceiling window. In spite of the rainy weather and the crowded skyline, it was still a stunning view.

"I'm a southern guy, and to me New York is touristy. I'm not saying Texas is better—I just prefer it due to its weather, good schools, the best steaks in the world, low crime, the high employment rate, to name just a few thing." He laughed, and I found myself laughing with him. "I'm not trying to sell anything to you, but you should come visit. You might end up wanting to persuade Jett to move down there."

"I might," I said.

"In which case I'll have to insist you do it sooner rather than later. We could use someone like Jett. Not least because I want to go on a vacation every now and then. We sure miss him."

I leaned forward, listening intently as I sensed my opportunity to find out more about my boyfriend's past. "Jett used to live in Texas?"

"We were raised in Smithville on a huge ranch. When our mother got sick—" he paused, and I knew he meant her addiction to various substances "—our father decided that the South wasn't good for us, so we moved to New York. I was sixteen and Jett was just ten when we moved from countless horses and lazy afternoons to smog and concrete buildings. It wasn't easy. When I saw my chance to go back to attend college, I took it, but Jett stayed behind with Dad."

Nate paused long enough to help himself to another glass of champagne before resuming his smalltalk.

"So, Brooke, this is probably one of those cliché questions, but how did you two meet? Were you doing your catwalk and he happened to sit in the front row?"

"No." I laughed. "It's a long story, actually. It was in a bar, and we were supposed to have a business meeting, which never took place."

"Supposed?" His blue gaze bored into me again with a strange interest.

"Supposed, yes, because I didn't know who Jett was, and his style didn't exactly scream business meeting, so I brushed him off." I smiled uncomfortably at the memories in my head. I hadn't just brushed Jett off; I had been downright rude, which was justified, given Jett's intentions at that time. I wondered whether Nate knew of those. "Didn't you say Jett told you everything?" I asked, eager to change the subject.

"Ah, you caught me. I know the story, actually. I just wanted to hear your version." He held up his hands in mock resignation. "Unfortunately, Jett forgot to mention you were this—" he gestured with his hand and laughed "—beautiful."

He moved closer to me, invading my personal space, as he whispered in my ear, "I'm not surprised my little brother fell for you. We've always shared the same taste. If I had been the one to meet you, Brooke, I would have asked you out, too." He leaned back again, watching my reaction with the kind of self-assured expression I knew well from his brother. It seemed being cocky and full of oneself ran in the family.

"Thanks, I guess."

"I'm happy my brother met you," Nate said. "It was about time."

I hesitated, unsure how to react to his statement.

"I should get going," I said, standing. "Jett might be looking for me and—"

"Sure." Nate reached into his blazer and handed me a business card. "Here's my number. Call me if my brother needs anything or, you know, if you need someone to talk to. You're part of the family now. I'm sure my father would have loved to meet you." His expression seemed pained but disappeared quickly. "Maybe you could convince Jett to visit us for a weekend. It'd be great to have you guys around. Bring back some normality."

"Sure."

I fiddled with my glass. Nate's brows shot up. I frowned and followed his line of vision to the hot dark-haired guy who seemed to be a head taller than everyone else making a beeline for us, and my heart jumped in my throat. I had yet to get used to the idea that I was actually dating him.

"I see you've met my girlfriend," Jett said to Nate, a grin lighting up his face—the first I had seen since his father's death. His arm locked around my waist, and he pulled me just a little bit closer, as though to establish his territory, which made me smile.

"Look at you. You're a changed man. How have you been doing, little brother?" Nate patted Jett's shoulder a little harder than I would've expected. I regarded them as they briefly hugged each other, their eyes locked in something I couldn't quite pinpoint—until I remembered something Jett once told me.

Competition.

His childhood and teenage years had been full of battles to be the better, the stronger, the more daring out of the two of them.

"How's the lovely Natalia?" Jett asked.

"Good. She's been bugging me to make you come visit."

"I'm planning to. In a few weeks, maybe, when everything's settled."

"Hopefully still this year." Nate chuckled and shot me a meaningful look, which I took for an invitation to persuade Jett to change his plans.

"I've brought the company records you wanted to see," Nate said. "Do you want to go over them now or later?"

"Give me two minutes with Brooke, and then we can talk." Jett glanced over at me. I said a hurried goodbye to his brother, and then Nate was gone.

"Has he always been this—?" I began.

"Confident, yet complex?" Jett cut me off. "Yeah. He's like the center of a hurricane. You'll never know what you get before it hits you." His eyes met mine, and for a moment I wanted to wrap my arms around him and kiss him like there was no tomorrow. I missed the old Jett, when he wasn't angry at the world and plagued by guilt. "You can also easily push his buttons. You don't want to see him explode when he's drunk. Natalia has seen her fair share of him in that state, which is why I'm surprised she's still with him."

"Who's Natalia?" I asked.

"His fiancée."

Nate was engaged. I didn't expect that, just as much as I didn't expect him to have a possible drinking problem.

Jett's eyes fell on my full glass and he took it from my

hand. "You're not supposed to drink that."

"I didn't intend to," I said dryly.

I wanted to know more about Nate and his life but there were more important questions that needed an immediate answer.

"Does he know?" I whispered.

"What?" Jett frowned.

"About the estate?"

Jett hesitated, pondering whether to tell the truth. I scowled in the hope he wouldn't dare lying because we had sworn each other to honesty.

"I told him, but—" he heaved a sigh "—he doesn't want to believe it. In his eyes our father could do no wrong, maybe because they were so much alike. Unlike Robert, Nate's a good guy."

"You guys talk often?"

"Not as often as I wish. The distance isn't helping."

"We should head down there for a few days," I said. *It might do you good.* But that I didn't add. "We could tell everyone about the baby."

"Yeah." He glanced at his watch impatiently, signaling that my time with him was up. "I need to go over some papers. It won't take long, Brooke. Will you be okay?" I nodded, and Jett's eyes filled with worry. "If you're tired, I could have someone drive you home."

"I'm fine, Jett." I squeezed his hand and shot him a

dazzling smile. "You guys do whatever you need to do. I'll wait here."

"It really won't take long." He kissed me and hurried out.

I watched him disappear in the crowd and then returned to the buffet. Ever since I'd found out about the pregnancy, I'd felt hungrier than usual, so I grabbed a plate when my phone rang. A look at the display showed me it was Sylvie. She had called several times in the past few days, and in all the turmoil I had failed to get back to her.

"Hey." She sounded nervous. "I've been trying to reach you."

"The funeral's today," I said to remind her in case she had missed my texts.

"I know." She paused, hesitating. I could almost hear her nervousness through the line, which turned me instantly anxious. "I was wondering if we could meet tomorrow. I haven't seen you in a while."

"Sure. Is everything okay?"

"Yeah." She hesitated again. "What about you?"

"I'm fine," I lied, then changed my mind. As best friends, it was my duty to tell her the truth. "Actually, no. Jett's been blaming himself for his father's death, and I don't know what to do about it."

"That's huge, but he has to accept all the bad things that happened, and that's something you can't do for him. It's a natural process, Brooke."

I nodded, because every now and then Sylvie opened her mouth and something amazing came out of it. It was rare but it happened, and right now was one of those times. Somewhere at the back of my mind I registered that someone had started to talk into the microphone again, and a few guests had begun to eye me up and down with disdain.

"We can't really talk right now," I whispered. "Let's meet tomorrow. Three p.m. Same place as always?"

"I'll be there."

THE BISTRO WAS situated in a tiny cul-de-sac, shielded from the busy midday traffic. I pushed the door open and headed directly for our usual spot in the far corner. Since she was hidden by a huge plant, I spotted Sylvie's stilettos long before I spied her. As usual, they were mile-high and matched the rest of her. Her blond hair was glossy, her nails were done, her makeup impeccable. Dressed in a blue fitted dress that matched her sapphire eyes, she looked stunning. I kissed her on the cheek and slid into the seat opposite hers.

"I've missed you like crazy." Sylvie smiled, scanning me up and down, which was never a good sign. Either there was something wrong with my outfit, or she thought I looked exhausted, or both. Whatever was the matter, she kept her thoughts to herself and would only start dropping hints when she thought I wouldn't notice. "The apartment feels lonely without you."

"I'm sorry." I realized we had never been separated this long. "I feel terrible I neglected you. So much has happened that I didn't realize we haven't seen each other for weeks."

"Fifteen days and nine hours." She pointed at her sleek cell phone. "I've kept track in case Jett locks you up forever and I have to sue his ass to get five minutes with you."

I opened my mouth to protest when a waitress appeared to bring us two lattes.

"I've ordered the usual," Sylvie said. "Hope you don't mind. The decaf is for you. Because of the—" She was so scared of kids, she couldn't even bring herself to say the word.

"Baby." Smiling, I rolled my eyes and took a sip of my coffee. It was delicious though I could taste the lack of caffeine. Even though I was still in my first term, I couldn't wait to get this pregnancy over and done with so I could return to my usual knockout caffeine dose.

"Have you told your mother yet?" Sylvie asked, playing with the spoon in her cup.

"Not yet."

Sylvie frowned. I held up my hand before she could start her interrogation and persuaded me into making a decision I didn't want to make.

"I'm waiting to see whether it's serious between Jett and

me. Knowing her, the moment I mention a boyfriend or baby, she'll go all traditional on me, you know—" I waved my hand, ignoring the urge to roll my eyes again "—insist that we get married and all. I don't want to scare Jett." The mere thought of mentioning marriage and scaring the hell out of him almost caused me to have a panic attack. "God, Sylvie, I feel like a shitty friend not getting in touch with you sooner. How are you?"

"It's okay. I'm good. To be honest, I have been busy, too." She shot me a dazzling smile, which usually screamed one of two things: she'd snagged up a designer handbag people usually waited months for, or she was in relationship bliss. I took a sip of my coffee again, thinking I knew her well enough to guess whatever she had to say. "I got a job offer from Delta & Warren, and I'm still deciding whether to take it."

I gaped at her. "Wow. Sylvie, that's huge. That's been your dream job forever. What are you waiting for? A few weeks ago you said you'd do anything to get it."

"I know, right?" Sylvie heaved an exaggerated sigh. I narrowed my eyes in the hope I'd make sense of her cryptic expression. The way her fingers couldn't stop playing with the hem of her dress instantly raised my suspicion.

"Why?" I prompted.

"I've been doing some thinking these past few days."

Sylvie never *thought*. She acted on impulse, doing

whatever her little heart and hot body desired.

"I don't understand. This is your dream job. You worked hard for it, and now you tell me you've been *thinking*?"

"I know how this sounds." She avoided my gaze again, and in that instant I knew my initial instinct had been right. "Kenny wants to show me Arkansas. This could be my first try at a real relationship. I don't want to mess it up. Besides, he's seen so many places, I feel like I've been missing out."

I blinked several times, unable to comprehend the meaning of her words. "You want to go on a road trip with Kenny?" I asked, shocked. "What happened to 'never put a guy first'?"

"It's just for two months, after which I'd be back to my usual boring life."

Boring? Sylvie wouldn't know what boring was if it came knocking on her door.

"But you're a city girl, Sylvie. You hate sitting in a car, or sitting *anywhere*, for longer than an hour. You say it makes you itchy."

She shrugged. "Maybe I'm converted. Life changes people. I've been studying and working my butt off my whole life. Maybe I'm sick of it all. Maybe I need something new."

I narrowed my eyes on her again, assessing her. Something else must have happened, because the Sylvie I knew did stupid things, but they weren't monumentally stupid. Had Jett's father's death affected her in any way? She hadn't known him, but maybe his passing away made her aware of just how fleeting life was. Deep in my heart, I could accept that Sylvie sought something new, because I wanted to see her happy and support her, no matter how crazy it all was. I just wanted her to be aware of any consequences.

"When are you planning to go?" I asked.

"Kenny wants to leave as soon as I'm ready. I thought maybe before the month's up."

"If that's what you want, I'll support you," I said. "You don't have to please anyone. And you love vacations." Of the five-star catered kind, which I didn't add. "But before you decide, I just want to remind you this job was your big dream. It might be a once in a lifetime opportunity."

"I know," she wailed, "which is why it's so hard to decide. And then there's you and the—"

"Baby."

She waved her hand. "Yeah. I don't want to leave you on your own."

"Well, don't worry about us. I'm sure you'll be back before it's born. We still have a few more months to go."

"You sure?" She sounded doubtful. "Maybe Jett and you need a break. If you want, you can come with us."

I frowned. I had watched Sylvie for the past minutes

and somehow from the way she behaved, I just knew she was hiding something. She was nervous, more than usual. And what was she saying anyway? That I end my relationship and leave Jett alone in his grief?

"Are you suggesting I break up with him?" I tried to keep my voice low and casual but didn't succeed.

She leaned over the table and grabbed my hand to stop the sudden wave of anger washing over me. "No, Brooke. I was thinking he might need some time alone to deal with his grief. People aren't themselves when they suffer loss. I don't want things to take their toll on you."

"I can't, Sylvie." My voice came out more agitated than necessary. I took a deep breath and let it out slowly. "He needs me more than ever. Even when he shuts me out of his life, it's like a part of me is with him, feeling what he feels. It literally pains me to see him like that."

The mere idea of not seeing Jett daily and not waking up to the rough stubble of his cheeks grating my skin made me anxious to call him just to hear his voice.

"I know, sweetie, but I honestly feel you should think about it." She took my hand again, her voice changing to a whisper. "There are other things you need to worry about."

My whole body stiffened. "What do you mean?"

She bit her lip, her eyes avoiding mine. "That's why I've been calling, but you were never available. I would've texted you, but when Jett's father died, you were busy, and it's not something you should ever put in a text message."

"Please don't tell me you had the kind of surprise I had back in Italy." I laughed nervously. An unwanted pregnancy was Sylvie's nightmare. "There has already been so much drama."

"No, that's not it." She looked down, stalling, avoiding my gaze on purpose, which wasn't a good sign. Worry set in. Was Kenny abusive? Those things happened. You heard it every day, read about them in the newspaper. I didn't want Sylvie to be a victim. "Is it Kenny? Whatever's wrong, you can tell me. Just because Jett needs me doesn't mean I'm not here for you."

"Things are fine with him. We're dating. He's great," Sylvie said. I opened my mouth to push for an answer when she held up a hand. "Please stop, Brooke. It's not about me. It's about you and Jett, and it's bad…. God, this is so hard to say."

"*Bad?*" My fingers clenched around my cup so tight, I feared it might snap as hundreds of thoughts raced through my mind.

What could Sylvie know that I didn't? Was he having an affair, and she didn't know how to break it to me?

"Promise me you won't kill me," she said, squeezing my hand. "I need you to promise, because I swear otherwise I'm not telling you anything."

My heart started to race. All of a sudden, I didn't want

to know. I felt like I should just run out of the door and not look back, pretend this conversation never happened. But my feet were glued to the floor while, inside, the chains of my heart were about to unleash a tornado of chaos.

What could be so terrible that Sylvie was too worried to tell me? I knew my best friend. She was never afraid to share her honest opinion. And then it dawned on me that an affair was the only reason why Sylvie might have been so jumpy.

Jett was having an affair. I knew it because he'd been working long hours lately, often arriving home past midnight.

What did you expect, Stewart? He's a guy with an oversized ego and the kind of looks no man should possess. What woman would ever say "no" to that?

"I know what you want to tell me," I whispered. "I should have known all along."

Sylvie grimaced. "I don't think we're talking about the same thing here."

"Are you talking about cheating?"

"What? No, the book. It's been with me all along."

She stared at me, anxiously awaiting my reaction. Her eyes shimmered with something and now I understood. Her jumpiness didn't stem from frayed nerves.

It was caused by fear. Pure raw fear.

The kind that makes you want to join the witness

protection program. The kind of fear that makes you want to buy a gun, and then barricade everyone you love inside a panic room.

"What are you talking about? What book?" I asked, but even before she confirmed my biggest nightmare, I felt physically sick. "How is that even possible? It was stolen."

"Not really." She smirked. "I found it inside my bag. Somehow I must have grabbed it with the rest of my stuff before we drove back to Bellagio to buy the pregnancy tests." She squeezed my hand apologetically. "I'm so sorry, Brooke. My bag is like a tiny Bermuda Triangle that swallows up everything. I swear whatever I put in there, it's either lost or forgotten, only to resurface when it wants to. It's all my fault."

"You mean it's been with us all along?" I said slowly.

She nodded.

"What about the disk?"

She nodded again. "The book, the disk, they're all here. The only thing they took are the financial reports and the sheets of paper you found in the basement."

My mind began to spin. "Oh, God. You realize this could be the reason why they killed Jett's father, right?" I closed my eyes, wishing I could hide forever.

Descend into darkness, but into darkness I was already descending, and it seemed worse than I ever imagined it to be.

Jett's father did not die because Jett didn't warn him. He didn't die because someone had put him on some hit list. He was killed because the people involved never got what they came for, and they were dangerous enough to commit murder.

"Robert Mayfield was a potential witness," I said slowly, the words echoing in my brain with the intensity of drumrolls. "He knew the club inside and out. He held all the information we could have wanted. Being Jett's father, they feared he might say too much to us. Add his statement to the book and the disk, and we could've had real evidence against whatever's going on in there."

My head pounded hard, reinforcing the sense of sickness inside me at the thought of what this might mean for us.

"I feel sick."

I ran for the bathroom, faintly aware of Sylvie's presence as I stormed into a cubicle. I lingered over the bowl until my stomach was empty. Sylvie's hand brushed my back, but she remained quiet as I washed my face. The cold water cooled my hot skin and helped clear my head. And then I broke down. Like a bursting dam, the tears began to spill before I could stop them.

"How am I supposed to tell Jett?" I asked. "After what happened to his father, he might think I'm not worth the risk and end things with me."

"You don't tell him, Brooke." Sylvie's eyes met mine, and for a moment I was left speechless by the calculation and determination I glimpsed in them. "You just pretend nothing's happened."

"Until shit hits the fan?" I snorted. "Are you fucking nuts?"

"Then I'll tell him. It's my fault, not yours, so I'll deal with him."

"Are you sure it's your fault?" I thought back to the day I found out I was pregnant. My memories were a blurry mess because of the huge news I thought would break my world apart. I remembered a handbag and papers and us hurrying out, but who grabbed what? "It could just as well have been me. You always forget stuff, and I always make sure to remember to retrieve whatever you leave behind. Besides, I tend to shove my stuff inside your bag because yours is always larger than mine."

"It doesn't matter who did what. I honestly don't think you should tell him." She shook her head.

A cold feeling settled in the pit of my stomach. We had promised each other honesty. Technically, not telling him wasn't lying, but keeping secrets sure felt like it.

"I can't." I grabbed her shoulders in a weak attempt to make her understand my dilemma. "What if they hurt more people? He has to know."

I looked into her eyes and saw my own fear reflected in

them. Was that the reason why she was so hell-bent on going on a road trip, far away from the drama and the danger I seemed to attract like a magnet?

"If he breaks up with me, I'll be fine," I said, my mind made up. "It'll break my heart probably even more than before and it'll take a long time to heal, but at least I'd have come clean."

"Why would he do that? It'd be stupid. Jett might be many things, but he's not an idiot." She smiled, but I knew it was fake and meant to make me feel better from the way it didn't quite reach her eyes. The slight tremor in her voice signaled she was just as unsure of what the future held in store for us as I was. "You're too good for him, and he knows it."

"I'm not so sure about that." I shook my head.

I had been kidding myself.

After the break-in, Jett had assured me that it was over. I could still remember his exact words.

They have everything they wanted, so there is no need for them to come back.

But they didn't have what they wanted. Maybe they had intended to send out a message by killing Robert Mayfield. If that was the case, no one was safe. Not I, nor Sylvie, Jett, or Nate. But that wasn't my biggest fear. Jett's guilt kept nagging at him, and I couldn't shake off the feeling that everything had happened because of me. For the umpteenth time since Sylvie's confession, I wondered how Jett would react once I disclosed the truth. What if he started to blame me for his father's demise? And, most importantly, would he be able to forgive me? Because as sure as the sun comes down after a beautiful day, promising a cold night, he would be mad and I didn't know what a full confession might mean for us. Would we stay together? Would he continue loving me?

And to think of all the times I had expected Jett would let me down; of all the times I had mistrusted him. Ever since I found out Jett had lied to me, I had been worried about him hurting me, which seemed ludicrous in light of the disaster that was about to unfold. For weeks I had watched him and tried to read every gesture and word while the thought never occurred to me that I might be the one to make a mistake so grave it would cost a life. I never realized I might be the one who failed, and I hated myself for it.

If Jett loved me truly, he'd forgive the unforgivable. But even if he did, would I be able to forgive myself for killing his father? My sister was one thing. Her death had been my fault and it still haunted me in my dreams. But what about Jett's father? Could I live with a second death on my conscience?

10

NONE OF US spoke during the taxi ride to Sylvie's apartment, which we had shared for years until two weeks ago. After our arrival from Italy, Jett and I had decided that it might be safer for the baby and me to move in with him. I had agreed reluctantly because he had a point but, standing in my former living room painted the color of lavender and decorated with way too much fluff, I couldn't help the nostalgia washing over me. Maybe my memories were what prevented me from returning the key or from taking all my belongings with me, but I realized I wasn't yet ready to close the door on this part of my past.

In silence, I watched Sylvie drop her handbag on the coffee table and shrug out of her jacket, tossing it on top of the bag, before she turned to me.

"I can't tell you how sorry I am. I just—"

"Don't." I cut her off. "Let's focus on the now and worry later. Show me the book."

"Stay here. I'll be right back."

"As if I'd go anywhere," I mumbled.

Waiting for Sylvie, I figured I might as well make myself comfortable, so I got us two cans of soda from the kitchen and slumped on the couch, then opened one and took a sip. I put it down on the couch table and seriously considered checking on Sylvie when she finally returned. The tension was so thick I could almost taste it. I peered nervously at the bundle Sylvie handed me.

The black leather-bound book seemed light in my hands, but it looked just as ominous as I remembered it. There was still a chance that Sylvie had somehow gotten her hands on someone's journal with yellowed pages carrying the joy of a new relationship or maybe the secrets of a love affair—anything but five names and a few strings of numbers. I opened the first page, and my last morsel of hope that it might all be a misunderstanding dissolved into thin air. I wished it was just a nightmare from which I couldn't wake up, but no matter how many times I pinched myself, I knew I wasn't dreaming. No dream could be so terrible and shattering. No dream could ever evoke the kind of devastation those five names caused inside me.

I stared at them as they circled before my eyes like a record on replay:

David McMuldrow

Eric Statham

Clarence Holton

Robert Mayfield

Troy Bradley Wilson

"Have you told Kenny?" I finally said.

"No." Sylvie shook her head, her blue eyes meeting mine. "I wanted to show you first. What's the big deal with the names?"

"Jett thinks it's a hit list. He believes they tried to get out."

"That's fucked up." Sylvie let out a deep breath. "Actually, I Googled them."

"You did?" I sat up, interested. "Did you find anything?"

"I know Clarence Holton. Not personally, but he's friends with my father. They used to go golfing together. Owns half the gossip magazines in Europe."

"Right." I tapped my fingers on the book. I didn't like the fact that Clarence Holton was acquainted with Sylvie's family. "What about the others?"

She leaned forward conspiratorially and began to whisper, "There's a semi-famous Troy Bradley Wilson in Canada. He's teaching physics in Montreal, has won a few awards, and is a household name in various journals. But he didn't strike me as the guy we're looking for, so I dug further and I found another Troy guy. He's a successful public speaker and the co-founder of a company in San Diego called—wait!"

She disappeared down the hall and returned with a notebook, then began to read out loud. "Latrix. They specialize in, now listen, importing sex products."

"Sex products and a club. Much of a coincidence?" I said.

"Yeah." She raised her eyebrows meaningfully. "Moving on to the next. Googling Eric Statham brought too many hits but, assuming he's rich, which seems to be a prerequisite, he's either a successful entrepreneur or a famous football player from Illinois. I don't think he's a football player because the guy's hot. Like, seriously hot. He probably doesn't need that sort of club to get laid."

"So the entrepreneur it is." I glanced at the last two names on the list. "No need to establish who Robert Mayfield is. What about David McMuldrow? Did you dig up anything on him?"

I read his name out loud again and then looked up. Sylvie was staring at me. Her sudden hesitation wasn't a good thing.

"Who is he?" I prompted.

"He's a murderer. He killed his wife and two children.

Psychologists declared him as mentally unstable, but he was allowed to walk free due to a lack of evidence."

My blood froze in my veins.

"It's so cruel," Sylvie whispered. "I've seen pictures of his children and the abuse they endured. It is too horrible to even imagine."

"It's a harsh and unfair world," I said bitterly. "Even if you fight for justice, expect to lose and maybe even be ridiculed for trying." I looked at the black book in my hands. "My sister's boyfriend Danny walked free because the judge was swayed by personal biases and failed to see that behind Danny's smiling face and charming words hid a monster. No law in the world will help if justice is swayed by a human inability to judge between right and wrong, good and evil, and that beautiful doesn't equal good."

"I know," Sylvie said weakly.

I closed the book, wishing it'd be as easy for me to shut off evil. Put it away. Hide it. Burn it. Do whatever was necessary to make the world a safer place.

"Sometimes I wish I could kill him. There were nights I wanted to see him dead for all the torture and pain he caused my sister." I laughed—not because it was funny but because the thought hurt.

I wiped a stray tear from my face, the reminder of loss too heavy, and watched the moisture on my finger. "They granted him protection. While my parents and I were threatened by Danny's friends and feared for our lives, that piece of shit spent his days cozy in a safe house. No matter how many years pass, I can't stop thinking about her and all the things I could have done to save her. People keep saying shit happens for a reason. I'd love to know what that reason is."

Sylvie's arms wrapped around me in a tight hug. In the silence of the room I knew she understood me. That she was there for me—she always was. As simple and straightforward as her touch seemed, it meant a lot more than words, which were cheap and worthless, spoken with no real intention behind them, except maybe to put an uncomfortable conversation to rest. Besides, there were no words Sylvie could say to ease the pain inside me. She knew it. I knew it. Saying sorry was simply not enough.

Time couldn't erase my memories. Time couldn't make them hurt less, but made me appreciate them more. With every day, with every breath I took, I could feel myself growing, becoming stronger—a braver me who accepted that this world wasn't just beautiful. It was cruel. It was heartbreaking, and only the strongest survived. The kind of world that had taught me the need to keep going, to continue fighting, to keep learning. To get up after falling and keep going some more, without relying on anyone, without looking back.

"I'm sorry for laying this on you. My head's a horrible

place to be in right now. I don't know when it all turned so serious," I said, feeling guilty for my emotional rollercoaster ride. I forced a smile on my face and peeled myself out of Sylvie's embrace.

"I wish you'd talk about it," Sylvie said gently.

I shook my head. Now wasn't the time. "The point I wanted to make is that we can't be sure whether the guy we're looking for, Eric Statham, *isn't* the football player. No matter how hot he is, don't let his appearance sway you, because evil people look just like you and me. An evil mind isn't always the result of bad upbringing. It's the result of bad character, and it can happen without any outside influence. There are attractive bad people, not because they were created that way. It's a matter of choice, one we'll never understand no matter how hard we try."

"I always thought the bad guys look insane." Her lips twitched. Her feeble attempt at infusing humor into a tense situation was more than welcome.

"You've been watching too many horror movies."

"You make me think twice about inviting the pizza delivery boy in. Makes me want to hide inside a room like a loony bin and trust no one."

"Is finding the book the reason why you want to go on a road trip?" I had been wanting to ask the question since Sylvie told me about her discovery. "Is running away from it all your solution?"

"Never thought about that," she admitted. "Kenny asked me before I found it. But in some way, yes. I thought if I physically distanced myself from it all, I could escape. Maybe when I return everything will be over, because right now I feel like I'm being watched. I know that's paranoia talking, but still."

"Running's not the answer to our problems." I glanced at my watch. In less than an hour, Jett would finish work, and I wanted to be home before he was back. I pushed the book and disk inside my handbag. "Gotta go." I stood and headed for the door, then stopped midway, remembering I hadn't asked about the disk. "Did you check out the disk as well?"

"I tried, but it requires a password."

"We'll have to talk to Kenny, then. By the way, he's awesome." I shrugged into my jacket. "It took me a while to figure him out, but I'm glad you're dating."

"Yeah, me, too. Who knew Italy would turn out the way it did?" Her cheeks flushed a little bit, which never happened when Sylvie talked about a guy. "Speaking of Italy, I forgot to ask. Have you by any chance seen my tennis bracelet? I remember I still had it when we came back."

I shook my head. The tennis bracelet was one of Sylvie's favorite pieces of jewelry. "It's probably in the bathroom. If it's not there, I'll stop by later this week to help you find it."

"It's okay. For all I know it might be somewhere inside the suitcase. I haven't unpacked yet." She laughed and accompanied me to the door, hesitating. "Want me to come with you?"

"No. I'll be fine." I hugged her briefly.

"Are you sure?"

I heaved an exaggerated sigh. "I'm not afraid. I stopped being afraid of bad people a long time ago because I don't care what happens to me. What scares me is disappointing Jett, so right now I really want to get this over and done with."

She leaned against the doorframe and crossed her arms over her chest. "It's called being in love, I guess. You simply treasure what you want to keep. If he doesn't forgive you, he doesn't feel the same way about you. You deserve someone who stands by you in every possible way. If he truly loves you, he'll walk the extra mile just for you."

"Thanks for the insight, Oprah." It was our favorite line. "I'll call you later with an update on the Jett situation. Wish me luck, and make sure to lock up."

"You know I always do." Which was a lie. She always forgot.

Sylvie didn't move out of the way, and in spite of her encouraging smile, her gaze implored me to stay. I wanted to so badly I almost caved in. But I needed to talk with Jett.

"I'll see you when I see you." I walked past her, eager

for some alone time to sort through my thoughts.

11

OUTSIDE, THE RAIN had stopped, but the sky was still a palette of gray. The air carried the scent of fumes and damp earth, and a faint promise that fall would soon be coming, coloring the streets in hues of copper and orange. I forced oxygen into my lungs and headed down the road in search of a taxi, minding the puddles at every corner.

I reached a crossing and stopped. A black limousine passed by and turned a corner, heading for Sylvie's building.

The lights changed to green. I was about to cross the street when I noticed a guy walking toward me, waving.

"Excuse me?" he said in a strong foreign accent I wasn't able to place. "Can you help me?" Dressed in jeans and a T-shirt with the logo "I love NY" slapped across his chest, he looked like a tourist. And a lost one at that. I smiled.

"Sure. Where are you heading?" I asked.

He inched closer. His arms brushed mine casually as he showed me the map. He didn't seem to mind, but I leaned away to put some inches between us. It happened before. People who didn't know when they were in my personal space.

"Sorry." He smiled apologetically and pointed to a spot on the map. "I need to get there."

"You should get a taxi. It's way too far to walk." I had looked up to make sure he understood when someone grabbed me from behind and covered my mouth with such force it knocked my breath out of my lungs. My handbag was yanked off my shoulder. For a moment my mind went blank, unable to put a meaning to the situation, and then awareness kicked in. My heart almost froze in my chest as I struggled against the iron grip dragging me to a nearby car I realized was the black limousine.

"Let me go!" I screamed, but no sound escaped my throat. I bit as hard as I could on the hand clamping my mouth shut, my teeth piercing through skin.

"Bitch," a male voice hissed a moment before I was pushed flat on my knees and the car door slammed, bathing me in pitch-black. In spite of the sharp pang of pain shooting through my left knee and carrying through my thigh, I dashed for the door and yanked at the handle. It didn't open.

I was trapped.

Fuck!

My breath quickened as countless thoughts began to race through my head. I was being abducted, and nobody knew where I was. If I didn't alert someone now, I might never make it out alive. Slamming my fists against the window, I screamed for help. My voice echoed in my ears, but nothing stirred and no one came to my aid. The windows weren't just tinted, making it impossible to peer inside—or out; the car was probably also soundproof. The engine whirred to life, and then we began to move.

Think, Stewart.

I took a deep breath and let it out slowly to calm my frayed nerves. Maybe if I were lucky enough, my abductors might make do with my handbag and the valuables inside, and dump me back on the street. I knew I was holding on to foolish hope, but I couldn't let reality kick in just yet.

I figured I could write a note and throw it out—if the window opened. Someone might find it and call for help. I always carried paper and pen in my handbag, and my mind already came up with a message: Help me. I was abducted in a black limousine by two guys, one with an accent. Thanks and don't always trust a tourist.

I laughed bitterly at my own horrid joke as I sank back to my knees and brushed my palms across the floor in search of my handbag and a miracle. If only I could get my hands on my cell, the first thing I'd do was call 911, and they'd track the car. Or send a text to alert Jett of the situation.

And then someone switched on the lights. I blinked several times until my eyes adjusted and I took in the figure sitting on the other side.

No shit!

My mind placed a name to the face, but it couldn't be. I was either hallucinating or going crazy. But he looked pretty real and there was no mistake he was the same guy I had seen in all the pictures at the funeral. In front of me, his fingers interlaced, bent forward to regard me intently, was Robert Mayfield. And he was very much alive.

12

"YOU'RE PROBABLY looking for this." Robert Mayfield tossed my handbag my way, and it landed at my feet. I snagged it, thankful he hadn't opened it to check its contents. While I didn't know for sure what he wanted from me, or why he was alive, I had a pretty good idea. For a moment, I was tempted to retrieve my cell, but I couldn't risk him discovering the black book and disk. I needed those in case I had to haggle for my life.

"I know you have a cell phone in there. Don't even think about trying to call anyone," he continued, reading my thoughts. "In fact, hand it over."

"I wasn't going to call anyone," I muttered. I opened the zipper just enough to squeeze my hand through and rummage for the phone. When I found it, I passed it on to him, making sure he didn't glimpse the side compartment where I had hidden the book and disk.

He motioned for me to sit down opposite from him. "Can I offer you a drink, Brooke?" Without waiting for my answer, he poured whisky into two glasses and handed me one. I sat down in the leather seat and took the glass from his outstretched hand but didn't drink. "I have to apologize for the way my two guards treated you. It's not standard procedure with our employees."

"I thought you were—" I began.

"Dead?" he finished for me. "That's what everybody's thinking. It's what I want them to believe."

He pointed at my drink invitingly. I watched the golden liquid like it was poison because I didn't trust him. People who want a friendly chat don't abduct you. They usually invite you over for coffee instead of making you think you might be about to be smuggled to Mexico.

Alarm bells began to ring in the back of my head, and my throat felt parched.

"I don't understand. Why would you want your sons to believe you were dead?" I whispered. "Why would anyone put their children through so much pain?"

"Drink. It's safe."

I didn't follow his command. My fingers clutched at the glass as I watched him for a few seconds, waiting for his explanation. It never came.

Robert Mayfield raised his eyebrows and gestured at the

glass again. He wanted me to drink up. I figured it was some sordid power game, and if I wanted to survive and escape, I had to play along. Judging from the expression on his face, he knew it just as well as I did. Maybe if he thought I was being cooperative, he might consider letting me go. I lifted the glass to my lips and took a sip, then let the whiskey burn its way down my throat.

Pleased with my action, he took a sip and leaned back with a smile, swirling the golden liquid in his glass.

"To answer your question, it's complicated," he said at last. "I'm doing them a favor."

I hoped he'd elaborate. When he didn't reply, I realized that was all I'd get out of him. As much as I wanted to probe, a more important question lingered in my mind.

"What do you want from me?"

"So many questions, Brooke." He shook his head slowly, as if he had to educate an ignorant child. "Jett didn't exaggerate when he said we should hire you because you were feisty." He refilled his glass and leaned back again, his green eyes assessing me. Even though they were the same shade as Jett's, I didn't see any warmth in them.

"Are you going to hurt me? Is that what you want?" I asked quietly.

His smile disappeared. I couldn't suppress a light tremble as a cold shudder ran down my spine. Whatever he had to say, I was sure I wouldn't like it.

"Quite the opposite. I have a proposition for you. Let's call it a chance to start over. A new life, Brooke."

His fingers moved inside his pocket to pull out a check he slid over toward me. Seeing all the zeroes, I almost toppled off my seat.

Holy hell!

Two million!

"Move to Portland, Oregon, and the money shall be yours."

"Why?" I narrowed my eyes. No one gifted so much money unless they received something in return. Robert Mayfield wanted something. Guys like him always did.

"I want the book. You still have it, don't you?"

Deep inside of me, I'd seen it coming.

Of course he wanted the book. The fact that it had laid buried in a basement showed its true value. I pressed the bag to my chest.

"It depends," I answered. "What else do you want?"

"I want you to stay out of my son's life." His voice was cold, just like his icy stare that never shifted from me as he spoke.

I blinked several times, unable to grasp the meaning of his words.

"You—" My voice failed me.

"You understood right, Brooke," Robert Mayfield said calmly. "Tomorrow you'll leave New York and Jett. You'll disappear—just like me. You won't get in touch with my son, nor with your family or friends. Everybody you ever knew will believe you disappeared without a trace." His voice dropped to a whisper as he leaned so close I could smell the alcohol on his breath. "Don't even think about running or not accepting my offer. I'll make sure no one will ever find you. My people will watch you to see if you follow the rules."

"No. I don't want the money." I shook my head vehemently. "And I'm not going anywhere. You can't stop me from seeing Jett or my family. People mean more to me than financial gain." The thought of losing Jett, my family, my old life, scared and angered me. "You can have the book, but I'm not leaving my old life behind. I'm declining your offer." My legs were shaking so badly I feared they might buckle beneath me, but my voice was surprisingly composed.

"You will want it." His voice was so forceful I flinched. "You don't understand, Brooke. If your family, friends, or Jett mean anything to you, *anything* at all, you'd better do what I say, or I'll make them go away. Just like that." He snapped his fingers. His lips curled into a smile, but his eyes betrayed his real emotions. "You have no choice. If you want them alive and safe, you'll bring me the book and leave your life behind without telling anyone."

I interlaced my hands in my lap to stop them from

shaking.

"You wouldn't." For some reason I felt the urge to appeal to the human part of him because, in my stupidity, I thought there had to be one.

"Leave me no choice, and I will," he said, misinterpreting my gesture, and retrieved a jewelry box the size of his palm from a compartment, then opened it and handed it to me. I stared at the piece of jewelry in silence. Of course it could be anyone's but I knew it was Sylvie's missing tennis bracelet, and the thought scared the crap out of me.

"She was asleep. Didn't even notice the two men breaking in and unclasping it from her wrist. I know everything about her. The places she visits, the people she meets. Let's say, one Thursday evening she visits Vixen's into the early morning hours, the way she always does, but this time she's not making it home, and no one will ever know what happened to her.'

The threat hung heavy in the air. I swallowed hard to get rid of the bile rising in my throat. My head felt heavy and tired, and my lungs burned, as though I had been underwater for too long and couldn't come up for air.

"If I do what you say, what guarantee do I have that you'll keep your word and not harm them?" I raised my brows. "Or me."

"None. My word should suffice." His eyes were probing

mine, challenging me, observing. They reminded me of a hawk—ready to catch his prey. The limousine came to a halt, but the engine continued to whirr softly. A traffic light, I assumed. People and cars all around us. And yet no one could peek inside, no one could be alerted to this most bizarre situation.

The car began to move again, rolling slowly, then picking up speed. In the silence of the car, I watched him adjust his tie. It was just a tiny movement but enough to tell me he was getting annoyed with me.

"A rented apartment's waiting for you in Oregon," Robert Mayfield said. "Tomorrow my driver will pick you up from the underground parking garage at eleven a.m. Don't take anything with you except for your handbag with the book. You'll be provided with everything you need for your new life, your flight tickets, and your new passport. The money will be in your new bank account. I'll get in touch with you once you're in Oregon. I'll do whatever it takes to keep you away from Jett. If you break one rule, your friend is the first one to go."

His tone was serious. Something rose within in me— despair; hopelessness at the prospect of abandoning Jett, my family and Sylvie; fury that Robert Mayfield hated the idea of Jett dating me. This was my last chance to change his mind. If I didn't try, I'd regret it.

"Why do you want me out of Jett's life?" I asked. "What

if I break up with him and give you the book? I could still stay in New York but keep away from—"

"Aren't you listening?" He cut me off. I stared at him in shock. "Let me make it clear to you, Brooke. You have no choice."

He wiped imaginary lint from his slacks before crossing his legs and leaning back, self-satisfied. "Why doesn't matter. I'd hate to see you suffer more than necessary. Your sister was a pretty hard loss." I swallowed down the knot in my throat. So he knew about my family and my past. No big news. Nothing to scare me there. What scared me was the fact I didn't know him and consequently didn't know what he was capable of. He pressed a button. The passenger's door opened, but I didn't move. Didn't call for help. Never before was freedom so close and yet so far away.

"This meeting never happened. If any word gets out or you try to seek help, I'll make you and all the people in your life pay. Don't make the mistake of thinking you can outwit me because you can't."

"I understand," I whispered. "There won't be any problems."

Pleased with my reply, his smile widened. "Good. I'm happy we've come to an agreement. This might be hard to believe at this point, but I'm doing you and your child a favor."

My heart stopped.

How the hell did he know about the pregnancy?

The only people I had talked with were Jett and Sylvie who probably told Kenny.

"Let's say I have my own resources," Robert Mayfield said, as if sensing my shock. "You've been watched ever since you entered Jett's life."

How?

And then the answer dawned on me. Emma. How could I forget her? She was always there, listening, watching. She had brought Jett's bouquet of roses and had probably read the card tucked inside. And she had dated Robert. She told me so herself when I commenced my initial position with Mayfield Realties. She was more inconspicuous than a private investigator.

"Tomorrow. Eleven a.m. sharp." He pointed at the door. "We're done for today." He nodded meaningfully, waiting for me to leave. Without a look back, I exited the limousine. With my heart pounding in my chest and my mind a blurry mess, I slammed the door shut and stood glued to the spot. The reality of what happened hit me so hard I couldn't form a coherent thought. Long after the limousine drove away, I didn't move. Minutes passed. People walked past, some cursing, some simply dodging me. A few cast curious glances my way, and still I remained frozen in place, locked in time and space—until someone stepped in front of me and squeezed my arm gently.

"You okay, miss?"

I raised my gaze to peer at a guy, late fifties, dressed in dirty pants and a jacket that had seen better days. A guitar dangled on his back, kept in place by a frayed leather strap. I nodded and he raised a plastic bottle, offering me what looked like orange juice. I shook my head and opened my bag to pull out my wallet, the way I always did when I saw a person in need.

"I have no need for it," I said, pushing all the banknotes into his hand. It was the truth. Soon I would live a different life with a new identity and spend money I didn't earn. Robert Mayfield could buy me a new identity, but he couldn't buy me love. He couldn't buy me happiness. A family or a place that felt like home.

"Please don't kill yourself." He held my arm, his warm hand not able to penetrate the cold blanket covering my heart. Even though I hadn't been thinking of committing suicide, I knew I had been close to forming the thought. So very close to it, because I felt like jumping off a cliff. Step in front of a car. Drown to stop the pictures of the happy and familiar faces flickering before my eyes.

I would raise a child on my own while Jett wouldn't stop searching for us. Eventually he'd believe I had left him, or that we were dead. I knew what death brought upon people and didn't want anyone who cared about me to go through so much pain. The guilt would kill me slowly.

Where lay the difference between starting a new life—full of emptiness and loneliness, knowing that my absence caused pain to those who loved me—or stopping it right now to enter complete darkness? A place where I could rest and forget, where something like a conscience might not exist.

I swallowed hard as I considered my options.

The outlook of forgetting was pleasing. Much more than a new life with happy memories haunting me, reminding me of all the things I had lost. Living a life that was forced upon me, rather than chosen by me, was senseless. I didn't want to go through that kind of agony.

"Don't kill yourself," he repeated, his pale gray eyes interlocking with mine. "It's not worth it."

"That wasn't entirely my intention," I whispered, "but thanks."

"Well, in that case new cannot always replace the old." He let go of my arm.

I frowned. Did he think I was involved in a love triangle and couldn't decide? I opened my mouth to set things straight when he cut me off. "Whatever you decide, never choose the most straightforward option. Believe me when I tell you this: the easiest choice is *always* the wrong one. Choose the path that matters in the long term, the choice that would never hurt others. It might seem difficult at this point, but the right choice is the one that takes the most courage. It's the one that seems impossible at first."

He pressed my money into my palms and then he cupped my hands in his, the roughness of his fingertips chafing my skin.

"Please, keep it," I said, weakly.

He shook his head but didn't let go. "Even the best of us have bad days. We fall, we climb. That's life. I can promise you, your worst day is never your worst. Your worst day's the day you realize you gave up too soon and you can no longer rectify your mistake." He scanned my face, waiting for his words to sink in. My throat was tight from the knowledge he was right despite not knowing me. He was so close to the truth.

"What if I have no choice?" I asked. "What if that choice was taken from me?"

"There's always a choice. Maybe not now. Maybe not tomorrow. But life never stays the same. Sooner or later, maybe in a few days or a few weeks, something you never thought possible will happen. That's the beauty of fate."

I nodded, overwhelmed by the fact that of all the people who had walked past me, it was the poor and probably homeless man who showed compassion still existed.

"You'll be okay, kid." He smiled gently. "God would never give you a situation you didn't possess the strength to handle. You have everything you need to deal with that situation within you. The only thing missing is courage."

"Thank you," I whispered, meaning every word. "Please take the money." I gently pulled my hands away from him.

"No." He shook his head again.

"But I insist."

"Then let me play a song for you so your generosity makes sense." He sat down on the pavement, back pressed against the dirty wall of a building, and began to strum the chords. I recognized the song. Tears formed in my eyes as I listened in silence to the old man's soft voice as he sang *Tears in Heaven*. When he finished, I realized I knew what to do.

"You have a gift," I whispered. "You touch people."

With a last smile at him, I started to walk slowly as my mind kept circling around his words.

We were two random strangers, and yet he decided to listen. Even when he had no idea what I was talking about, he was right. I couldn't do what I wanted. I couldn't stay with Jett just because I loved him and couldn't bear to be without him. I had to stop thinking about myself and to start caring for the safety of those who mattered. It would be hard to leave them behind, but it would also be selfish of me not to.

Maybe Robert Mayfield was bluffing, but at this point I couldn't risk not believing him.

It would be the hardest decision I had ever made, but it

was the right choice. It would be the choice that would come with the smallest risk—a broken heart. I could deal with that, but I wouldn't cope with fear and regret keeping me awake at night, knowing their lives might be at risk because of me. And if this man was right, maybe sooner or later, hopefully not too late, the tides of life might turn in my favor.

13

THE WALK TO Jett's expensive neighborhood was long but gave me enough time to understand what had just happened. By the time I arrived at Jett's apartment, the sun was long gone and my mind had settled, accepting that fate had made my decision for me, which meant this would be my last day with Jett.

I greeted the concierge in the foyer and rode the elevator up to Jett's penthouse, my gaze shying away from the mirror. I couldn't bear to look at myself because my image reminded me that soon I wouldn't be Brooke anymore. I pulled the keys out of my handbag and let myself in. For the umpteenth time, I wondered how Jett would react if he knew his father was still alive and that he was the threat Jett feared. Would he believe me?

Feeling tired and defeated, I opened the door, expecting

an empty apartment since Jett spent much of his time at the office lately—until I saw the lights switched on.

"Where have you been?" Jett was standing in the doorway, his hands buried in his pockets, a frown on his face.

"I grabbed a coffee with Sylvie." I avoided his gaze as I kicked off my high heels. "We had a girl talk. You know Sylvie. She couldn't wait to tell me all about her relationship with Kenny and her new job offer, so I stayed a little longer than anticipated."

I peered up at him and instantly noticed the dark shadows under his eyes and the soft line on his forehead. As much as I wished to hug him, I couldn't because I was afraid I'd break down in tears if I did.

Change the topic. Don't think of tomorrow. Don't go there.

"How did your business meeting go?" I asked casually. "I didn't expect you to be back this early."

"It's been delayed." He hesitated. "Nate has decided to stay with us for a while to help me go over the data. If we're lucky, we won't have to sell shares in the company. As soon as everything's sorted out, I hope we'll have more time for ourselves." He walked over and wrapped his arms around my waist, pulling me against him.

My heart felt as though it was being ripped apart. I cast my eyes down and leaned my head against his chest, the reminder we would not spend any more time together too painful.

"Today all I could think of was you. Naked. In my bed. I've missed that. I've missed you. Like fucking crazy," he whispered and kissed my neck.

"I'm grateful my brother's staying because it makes things so much easier. I'm looking forward to spending more time with you, Brooke."

I couldn't help myself. Tears started to roll down my cheeks. I buried my face against his chest in the hope he wouldn't see them as I fought against the tornado threatening to rip my chest apart. My fingertips brushed his neck. Hearing the sound of his voice and the steady rhythm of his breathing, smelling his scent and feeling the warmth of his body—was just too much. I couldn't bear it.

They reminded me too much that in a little more than sixteen hours, our time was up. I swallowed hard to get rid of the bile in my throat, which only made my tears fall harder. I could feel the first wave of sobs rippling through my chest. If he kept going like that, I'd break down. I couldn't afford that, so I stepped back and turned away hastily, heading straight for the bathroom as fast as I could and locking the door behind me. Pounding steps followed right behind. A moment later, he knocked.

"Brooke?" His tone sharpened with a layer of worry. "Are you okay?"

My heart pounded painfully hard, the tiny movements piercing me like knives. I wiped the tears away with my sleeve and drew slow, measured breaths to calm myself.

"I'm fine." My voice shook.

"Did I say something wrong? I didn't mean to upset you."

How could I tell him that, yes, he had done something wrong by saying all the right things?

"No. It's me." I inhaled and held my breath as my heartbeat spiked again. "I'm tired, emotional, and a little bit sick. My hormones are acting up, which is normal."

That part was true. My gynecologist had told me when I went to see him to confirm the pregnancy upon my return from Italy.

"Want me to get you anything? Maybe order dinner?"

"No." I shook my head even though he couldn't see me. "I won't be able to keep anything down."

God, it was so hard to pretend in front of him but so much easier to lie behind closed doors. I'd never let him see how broken I was.

"I'm going to take a bath and go to bed early." I paused for his answer. When it didn't come, I continued, "Don't worry about me. Just give me a little time alone, Jett. It's been a long day."

We fell silent, but I knew he lingered outside. Inches separated us, and yet they felt like miles of sand-covered dunes ready to pull us apart if we tried to get near each other. He might not know me well enough, but he was an expert in reading body language. If I opened the door, I feared I might confess. I had to stay strong for myself, for him, for our baby's sake.

"Brooke." His voice was like silk caressing my senses.

"Yeah?" I held my breath.

He let out a sharp breath. "I know I've been neglecting you—us—those past few days." His hand brushed over the door. Or maybe he was leaning against it. I couldn't tell, but I imagined him out there, sensing something, worrying, and my heart broke just a little bit more. "I'm sorry I didn't spend as much time with you as usual. I just didn't want to stress you out with my problems."

My eyes moistened again. I wanted to assure him that I understood because I knew that losing his father had been hard on him, but didn't. Instead I said, "You don't have to explain."

"Let's go out for dinner tomorrow after work. I'll book us a table wherever you want. You pick."

Too late.

By tomorrow evening, I'd be in Oregon and Jett would be waiting for me, wondering where I was. He'd call my cell, then Sylvie's, after which his worry would magnify. How long would he wait before filing a missing person report? Would he hire Kenny again to find me? Probably, only this time there would be no credit card purchases and no flight tickets to show me boarding a plane. Tears ran down my face. There would be many more in a future that seemed blank and depressing without him.

"Baby?" Jett said, jerking me out of my depressing thoughts. His tone was pleading, and I realized he had misinterpreted my silence. "I want to make it up to you. Maybe this weekend. No phones. No work. Just you and me, white beaches, and good food."

"I'd love that." I smiled bitterly, meaning every word. Now was the time to tell him all the things I wouldn't get the chance to say to him in the future. I thought of the one thing I could say without raising his suspicion. "I couldn't wish for a better boyfriend than you, Jett. Thank you for always being here for me and for loving me the way I am."

Thanks for everything.

I walked over to the huge corner bathtub and turned on the cold-water stream, and shrugged out of my clothes.

"I'll be in my office," Jett said softly. "Call me if you need anything."

I waited until he walked away. Only when I was completely sure he was gone did I step into the freezing water, knowing that not even the cold could numb the pain. Pulling myself under until my body was submerged with the only sound the beating of my heart drumming hard in my ears, I let my tears flow freely.

14

I CONSIDERED MYSELF blessed. I truly did. I had experienced love. I had met that someone special who made my heart flutter and, most importantly, reciprocated my feelings. I had a best friend who'd always be there for me. I was blessed, because I had lived.

Better love and lose than never love at all.

I kept telling myself that every single second of every hour that passed. So why was it so hard to let go when time demanded that we part? Life didn't always warn us when we had to say goodbye. If we knew when it was time to leave, maybe we'd make more of an effort to spend as many moments as possible with the people we loved. And there lay my problem—even though I knew my moments were counted, I couldn't deal with it.

I sat in a dark place, on an unknown road, with

absolutely no clue where I was headed. Desperation washed over me as I realized I might never experience this kind of happiness again. I'd never meet someone as great as Jett. Knowing I'd lose him brought out the worst in me. A part of me wanted to write a letter to tell him how truly happy I had been with him. I wanted him to know just how much I had looked forward to a future full of happiness. And yet I couldn't. If Jett thought I had died, this letter would never bring him consolation; it would bring him guilt. I decided to do it the hard way—no letters, no hints, nothing to trace back to this one moment.

By the time Jett finished up work, it was past midnight. Apart from a sliver of moonlight falling in through the pulled curtains, the bedroom was bathed in darkness. The mattress groaned under Jett's weight, as he lay down gently, careful not to wake me. My eyes remained closed, but I could sense his gaze on me. His arm wrapped around me, barely touching my skin, and his warm breath tickled the nape of my neck. Eventually his breathing slowed down.

Even in the darkness of the room with nothing but the feeling of his arms around me, my mind continued to seek him, as if he was already far away. I lay awake facing the digital watch. With every minute that passed, with every hour that went by, my dread intensified. At 3.15 a.m., Jett stirred and I turned to regard his sleeping features. My heart broke at the sight. Careful not to wake him, I let my fingers trace the contours of his face. But Jett had always been a light sleeper. He opened his eyes groggily and pulled me to his chest.

"Trouble sleeping?"

My throat was so choked with emotion I couldn't reply. Instead, I just nodded. There were no more words to say, so my lips touched his mouth gently. It was just a brief kiss, but enough to wake him up instantly.

I smiled. It was a bitter kind of smile as my fingers touched his naked chest, marveling at the smoothness of his skin and the warmth seeping into my body. It took him only a second to process where I was heading, and then his hands slid around my head as I kissed him again. I thought crushing my lips against his would help subdue the pain. That it'd bring me relief by stealing that one last kiss. Instead it ate me up from the inside. Breaking me apart.

"I need you," I whispered against his lips, and climbed on top of him. "Deeply. Whatever you wish."

"You're asking for it? In the middle of the night?" He sounded unconvinced. In the moonlight his green eyes shimmered dark, every trace of sleep gone.

"Yes," I whispered.

I had been wrong. The pain wasn't breaking my heart; it was killing me. I wanted to have it ripped out of my body. Fucked out of my system. Tomorrow had become today, and I didn't want to think about it anymore.

"I want it rough," I said. "I want you to fuck me like you don't care about me. Like I'm just a stranger."

The air between us was charged with questions unspoken. I could feel Jett's hesitation, his doubts, his confusion.

"I can't do that." He sat up and pushed me away gently but definitely. "I don't want to hurt you."

Rejecting me when I needed it the most was the last thing I expected.

I was so furious, I slapped him. Not hard, but hard enough to make him look up. I tried slapping him again, but this time he caught my wrists, pulling me close to him.

"Brooke, no," he said, determined. "I'm not that kind of person."

I yanked my arms away, but he didn't let go.

"I need you, Jett. I need you right now," I whispered. I bent forward to kiss him again but he withdrew with a confused expression on his face.

"Back in the Hamptons you said you're not into rough sex."

"I've changed my mind," I whispered. "It's what I need now. Please. Don't you see that I'm asking you? I want you to fuck me hard." I rocked my hips against his groin, not wanting to give up. "Please." He didn't pull back, which showed me his resolution was weakening.

I inched closer again to kiss him, and this time he

responded the way I expected him to. He let go of my hand and flipped me back on the bed, positioning himself on top of me. His mouth hit mine with such ferocity, it knocked all the air out of me. I looked up, suddenly scared. His eyes shimmered with a dangerous glint, and there was just the hint of a smile on his lips.

"You want it rough, baby? If that's what you need, you'll get it." His knees squeezed between my legs, parting them. "But I'll have it my way."

15

JETT MAYFIELD WAS the first one to reciprocate my love and set my heart on fire. He was my summer love, and my feelings for him were real. I knew because I couldn't stand the thought of him being with someone else. My mind kept seeking him whenever he wasn't with me, and my heart trembled just hearing the sound of his name. Intermingled with my love and the happiness I felt around him, there was sadness—a black heavy sadness coming from a sudden but ugly awareness that not everything in life is meant to last. To taste happiness in pieces and then have it taken from you, leaving behind nothing but jaded memories that are like bullets, tearing you open, wounding you, scattering you into a million fragments—I wasn't sure I was ready for that just yet. I wasn't sure if I could face a future without him.

I stood in front of the bathroom mirror and stroked my hand over my belly, as if the motion could protect my unborn child from the knowledge that I was about to break the trust of the one I loved. I was doing it for us. It was better for us. If he *knew* what I was about to do today, that I'd break my promise and leave him, he'd try to stop me. I just knew. I couldn't risk anyone hurting him. I'd rather it was me who ended up hurt.

At five a.m., I dressed in the bathroom, grabbed my bag, and left. I didn't even bother to take a shower or put on makeup. Fuck my appearance. There were more important things to take care of.

It was a new dawn—a dark dawn—as I took a taxi to Mayfield Realties and told the driver to stop a block away. He wasn't thrilled to let me walk the distance but didn't argue. I paid and stepped out into the chilly morning air, wrapping my jacket around me as I headed in the opposite direction. In a little more than five hours I'd be driving to the airport. If I wanted to initiate changes, I had to do it before anyone noticed.

Maybe Robert Mayfield thought he could remove me from Jett's life, but he couldn't take away my dignity or sense of justice. He'd get the book he desperately wanted, but I had no intention of giving him the disk, and I sure had no intention of making him aware of its existence.

I stepped into the self-service kiosk of a hotel lobby and

jotted down Sylvie's address on a prepaid flat-rate envelope and sealed the disk inside. Angered by the ugly awareness that I could never tell Sylvie what really happened, nor include a letter, I paid with the only prepaid credit card I owned and left the kiosk, hoping the envelope would arrive safely; hoping that somehow Sylvie would understand the silent message. I knew she'd feel the urgency. She'd know what to do. They might never find me, but with Kenny by her side, maybe they could still unravel the secret of the Lucazzone estate.

Leaning against the cold wall of the building, I felt better. Hopeful almost. Not about my future, but about the fact that Robert Mayfield hadn't won. I wondered what would happen to the beautiful Italian mansion once the lawyer realized the heiress was gone. Would Alessandro Lucazzone sell? Would Jett still be inclined to buy?

With the sun rising, the streets began to fill with life. I walked the short distance to my office and let myself into the foyer. The morning security guards exchanged glances as I showed them my ID.

"Busy day," I mumbled by means of explanation. I ignored their chatter and headed for the elevator, ready for the second part of my plan.

I had every intention to make my last day in my job as painless to everyone as possible—even if that involved keeping people at a safe distance and, in Jett's case, breaking up with him. It was a necessity, and the only way he'd move on with his life sooner rather than later. If only I could find a way to make him believe I didn't care about him, I knew I'd feel better knowing he wouldn't be hurt by the way I'd suddenly disappeared from his life forever.

***

I was about to finish sorting through the papers for the first conference meeting and placing files back in the cabinet when I heard Jett's voice down the hall.

"Is Brooke inside?"

Someone answered, and within seconds the door was thrown open without so much as a knock. He was angry, and he made no secret of it.

"Why did you leave?"

I remained silent. He moved around the desk and stood in front of me, arms pressed against the cabinet, inches away from my face. His impressive stature blocking my sight, I had no choice but to meet his gaze and answer his question.

"I couldn't sleep, so I came to work early." I pretended to search through the folders, trying to find the one I needed.

"What's wrong?" His eyes scanned me up and down, noticing, analyzing. I had been stupid to think Jett wouldn't pick up on my emotional undercurrents.

"Nothing." I shrugged. "It's not even a big deal. You were asleep, and I didn't want to wake you. Don't blow it all out of proportion."

His voice dropped to a whisper. "Did I hurt you last night? Is that why you're mad?"

"No." I frowned, thinking back to our lovemaking session. He had been rough but not to the point of hurting me. "I wanted it. Remember?"

His eyes continued to scan my face, my business suit, and then he noticed the dark bruise on my arm—the result of my unfortunate encounter with Jett's father. I almost stopped breathing when he grabbed my wrist and held it up. I had seen it the previous night while soaking in the bathtub, but he hadn't.

"What's this?"

I shrugged. "I fell. No big deal."

His eyes narrowed on me as he considered whether to believe me. Something flickered in them, and I knew I had to come up with a better lie.

Damn!

He was being suspicious, and I had never been a good liar. I walked over to the window, putting as much distance as possible between us, and turned away. In a little more than half an hour I was expected to get into a car and leave everything behind. Now was the time to release him.

"This isn't working, Jett. I don't think it's a good idea we're dating." The words flowed so fast from my lips, I could barely think. I held my breath and bit my lip hard to keep myself from looking at him. The room was so quiet my heartbeat sounded like a drum counting down the seconds in my ears.

"Why not?" he finally asked. His tone was cold, any trace of his love for me gone. I shuddered and pushed my hesitation to the back of my mind.

"We rushed into this and I—" My voice failed me. Even though we weren't touching, I could feel him all around me. He was beautiful and so very angry. The pressure behind my eyes grew stronger. I lowered my head so I wouldn't give in to the magnetic pull urging me to look at him just one more time. "I think we should take a break."

He inched closer. His fingers clasped around my shoulder, and I had no choice but to turn and face him. I expected anger, sadness, indifference, anything but—

Gentleness.

"What are you afraid of, Brooke?"

My eyes filled with unshed tears before I could stop them. I didn't see this reaction coming and had no idea what to say to him. That I worried for everyone's safety because I wasn't welcome in his family?

"Maybe I'm afraid of the fact that you mean more to me than any other person ever will," I whispered. "I'm not used to having such feelings. They scare the hell out of me."

His fingers settled beneath my chin and pushed lightly, forcing me to meet his gaze.

"I'm scared, too," he said. "But that's not why you'd break up with me. What's the real reason?"

His words didn't manage to settle the storm inside me— they made it worse because they reminded me just how much I believed him.

"Maybe I don't have a choice," I said before I could stop myself. "Maybe I want to, but that's not an option for me."

He stared at me confused. "What the fuck are you talking about? We always have a choice, Brooke." I had heard it all before. Everyone seemed to mention choices lately. I should never have started, because Jett wouldn't understand. No one could.

"I'm not afraid of loving you, Jett. I'm afraid of what it might mean for us...and my child." His eyes narrowed on me, and the glint of anger from before resurfaced. I swallowed. "I don't think what we have is healthy. I just think—"I stopped in mid sentence, lost for a moment in the magic of his green eyes rimmed by dark, long lashes. "There's no assurance in life that'll last. I want to get away from you before we collide. Just because we were meant to meet doesn't mean we're meant to last."

He stared at me with a look that said he couldn't understand me, that I was crazy. Maybe I was crazy to give it all up, but he didn't know my dilemma, and his drawing at straws and trying to understand when I was running out of time made me desperate.

"Damn it, Brooke!" Glowering, he wiped his hand over his face in fury. The intensity in his eyes made me flinch. "I thought we had left all those fears and insecurities behind us. I thought you had learned to trust me that I'm not going anywhere after the baby's born—if that's even what you're so worried about. Obviously, I don't know, because I've no idea what you're talking about." His shoulders slumped, the tense expression on his way giving away his disappointment.

"I'm sorry," I whispered.

He shook his head. "No, you're right. There's no guarantee it'll last. But there's one truth, Brooke. A simple naked truth that I'd do anything for you. Do you know why? Because I don't care about anyone but you. I don't care that you have issues. I don't care that you don't trust me. My feelings for you will never change."

The heaviness in the air was oppressing—the sea was about to crash upon me. I smiled to hide my tears. He didn't return my smile, and his voice was cold as he spoke. "The baby's not yours, it's *ours*. There's no way I'd let you raise her alone. Maybe we'll collide someday, but you know what? We'll make up, because what we have isn't something that will crumble easily."

A knock on the door, and Emma's head popped in. Jett's expression changed to an angry frown at the disruption.

"Miss Stewart? Your meeting's about to start."

"Give us five minutes," he barked.

"I'll be right there." I turned my head from Emma to Jett and whispered, "I'm sorry. Gotta go."

The door closed behind Emma. Grabbing my handbag, I stopped and shot Jett a smile. "Let's talk over dinner."

A dinner that will never take place.

"Okay." He hesitated. My body burned to touch him one last time. Run my fingers through his hair. Kiss him so I'd remember the taste of his lips forever. Instead, I bit my lip hard until I drew blood, grabbed my handbag and a folder, and walked past. His hand gripped my arm, stopping me.

"Brooke?"

I froze to the spot, unable to respond, unable to turn around as an electric shock ran down my spine. There was no point in saying anything else. No point in trying when I had failed. He wasn't released. He wouldn't be for a long time.

"You can't break up with me. I won't let it happen," he whispered. "If you don't want me, I understand, and you're free to go because I want to see you happy. But if you love me the way I love you, I won't let you go. I'm not giving up on us. I can't force you to love me just as you can't force me to stop loving you."

And then he let me go. I walked out of the door, away from him, away from his promises and the future I had looked forward to. My feet carried me so fast I barely acknowledged the people in the corridor and in the elevator.

Walk. Walk. Walk. Do not think. Do not feel. Do not look back. Just walk.

Never in my life did I force myself so hard to get away from the one person I loved the most.

My cheeks were damp with tears, and I wiped at them angrily. Life sucked. Absorbed in my thoughts, I didn't notice the guy around the corner—until I bumped into him and his soda can dropped to the floor.

"Whoa." Nate's arm went around my waist, steadying me.

He was standing in front of a vending machine. I picked up his soda can from the floor and gave it back to him. "Sorry."

"Are you okay?" He pointed at my lip. "You're bleeding."

"I'm fine." I wiped away the blood with the back of my hand and ran the tip of my tongue over my lip to stop the flow. "Just having a bad day. That's all."

The excuse came out effortlessly, probably because it wasn't much of a lie. I wasn't just having a bad day; I was having the day from hell.

As I met his gaze and smiled, something passed between us.

"Don't we all." He smirked. "Want to tell me about it?"

I shook my head, wishing I could tell him.

"I'm not sure my brother told you, but I'm staying for a few weeks to sort out the issues my father's death caused," Nate said. "We're researching a new brand image."

My brows shot up. *Mayfield Realties* was huge and successful already. Why would anyone want to change anything about the that? "What's wrong with the company as it is?"

He shot me a quizzical look and lowered his voice. "I assumed you already knew we've been in trouble for a while. Internal changes have been initiated." He opened his can and took a sip, his eyes never leaving mine. "Jett's been working around the clock the past few days to save what's left before the media get hold of it. We've been looking into ways to transfer all our employees and their positions to other branches, but—" He clicked his tongue, leaving the rest open to interpretation.

He took another sip and then pointed at the vending machine. I shook my head, declining his silent offer. Too many thoughts kept swirling inside my head: Jett working around the clock...new company...people being transferred.

His eyes focused on my lips, and I wondered whether I was still bleeding.

"Are you sure you don't want to talk about it?" Nate's voice pulled me out of my trance. I peered at the analog clock above his head. It was almost eleven a.m. The red pointer scared me the most, because with every second that passed it kept making a ticking sound reminding me of TNT ready to blow up.

"Maybe another time." The words stumbled out all mumbled. "Nate, my conference meeting is starting in a few minutes. Do you mind taking notes for me? Just for a few minutes. I need to use the restroom. Everything you might need is in there." I pressed my folder into his hands.

"No prob." He smiled, the smooth skin beneath his eyes crinkling a little. "You can repay me later."

I pointed at Conference Room 1, and we walked the short distance together. Through the glass partition I saw my team had already gathered and were chatting animatedly.

I squeezed Nate's arm. "Thanks."

"Anytime," he said.

Nate entered and waved, then said something and the meeting started, the voices of my colleagues not able to penetrate the chaos of thoughts flooding my mind. They were an effective team, and I was thankful for the opportunity to have worked with them.

With a twisting sensation in the pit of my stomach, I checked that the book was still inside my handbag, just as ominous as before, and just as cursed for ruining my life.

The clock ticked.

It was time.

Fighting the nausea bubbling up inside me, I made my way to the underground parking garage. The air was cold down here and a shiver ran down my spine, but my mind spun in a feverish trance, my stomach twisting like an evil snake. I reached the first level and stopped, realizing Robert Mayfield had never told me where to meet him. That's when I recognized the guy with the "I love NY" T-shirt peering from under a suit jacket. His blond hair was combed back in a slick style, revealing the smooth face and stony features of someone who I guessed never smiled. When he noticed me, he gestured at a black sedan with tinted windows.

I scanned the area even though I hadn't really expected Robert Mayfield to turn up.

"Get in," tourist guy said.

My heart pounded hard against my chest as I slipped into the back seat and he slammed the door shut, locking me inside. He jumped into the driver's seat and started the engine, but didn't drive off.

"Do you have the book?" His English was perfect, not even a hint of an accent to suggest he had ever lived anywhere but in New York. I had been an idiot to fall for his trick, believing he was a foreigner. My glance met his in the rearview mirror.

"Yeah." I reached into my handbag and retrieved what he wanted, then handed it to him.

"Did you tell anyone about this?"

I shook my head.

"I've kept my part of the bargain," I replied through gritted teeth.

"Do you see the black leather briefcase?"

It was at my feet—a huge ugly thing—the sort you see in movies with money in it.

"Everything you need is in there," he said. "Open it."

I lifted it. It was heavy and locked, and something I didn't want to touch. "I don't know the number combination."

"Put in the zip code of the Empire State Building." He smiled, self-assured, probably thinking I wouldn't know the zip codes of the only five buildings that were large enough to have their own codes.

My jaw jutted up. "That would be 10118." I typed in the number, and the case opened with a click. Robert Mayfield hadn't lied. Stacked inside were documents and a new passport, as well as cash and a few credit cards. I opened the passport and stared at the photograph I had provided to get my staff ID card. The name read *Carol Laura Harley*.

Was that supposed to be my new name? I scanned the rest. Even my birthdate and birthplace were different. In my new identity I was two years younger and born in Oregon. I turned the passport around. It looked old and genuine, and the corners were slightly flaked as though it used to belong to someone else and my picture had somehow been inserted inside. Robert Mayfield wasn't the clean and genuine guy everyone made him out to be.

Judging from the driver's impatient glance, we were on a schedule. I put the passport away and folded my hands in my lap, unsure what to do. The driver kept watching me, and for a second I thought I detected pity in his expression. Maybe his job was more demanding than I thought. Being Robert Mayfield's driver probably also included the duty of beating the crap out of people—or worse.

Don't go there. Don't even think what this guy could do to you.

"Ready?" he asked. "Your flight leaves soon."

"Yeah." I buckled up the seatbelt. He started the engine and pulled out of the parking lot.

That's it, Stewart. Say goodbye to your life.

From the periphery of my eye I caught a dark blur heading toward us. I turned but too late. The car hit us sideways with a loud thud. My head banged against the window. In the same moment the seatbelt tightened across my chest, crushing all the air out of my lungs.

It all happened too fast. I peered around me, too shocked to fully grasp the situation, when the front door was yanked open. Hands pulled out the driver, and a stifled gunshot echoed. I froze, unsure whether to jump out of the car or hide. In the two seconds it took me to decide a guy slumped into the driver's seat. Our eyes connected in the rearview mirror. In his oversized sweater and ripped jeans, he didn't look like anyone Robert Mayfield would employ.

I snorted. Seriously? I was being car-jacked? I opened my mouth to scream for help when the front passenger door opened and a guy jumped into the passenger seat, pointing a gun with a silencer at me. I whimpered, but the sound remained trapped in my throat.

"We got her," he said slowly into his phone.

My heart began to race against my ribcage at the realization this wasn't a random car-jacking, or an accident. They were after *me*. Judging from the guy's smug grin, they had planned this move.

PART 2

PROLOGUE
JETT

IT ALL SEEMED like a memory, a dream, hard to grasp and to explain, and so difficult for her to accept, as if she couldn't allow happiness to happen to her. Right from the start, I knew Brooke would have trouble trusting me. But breaking up with me when things were going well made no sense.

For the past few hours I had been trying to focus on the spreadsheets on my computer screen. At some point they had become nothing but a big smudge of unrelated numbers because my mind kept circling around the thought that Brooke was hiding something. I had seen it in her face, heard it in her voice. She wasn't a particularly good liar. In fact, she couldn't lie if her life depended on it. She might fool the people around her, but she couldn't fool me, and I had every intention of making it clear tonight at dinner. I'd put a stop to her nonsensical fears because she was my woman, and if that meant literally forcing her to sit down and talk, then so be it.

"Please take a seat, sir. Mr. Mayfield will be with you shortly," one of my assistants said to a board member in the hall. "Would you like a cup of coffee?"

I glowered and wished I had closed the damn door and pretended I wasn't available instead of having to deal with yet another client who was afraid he'd lose his money once the shares crashed and burned. Ever since the news broke about my father's death, people had started to question the credibility of the company, as though it hadn't been I who'd brought in most of the major deals ever since I joined Mayfield Realties.

In the past few weeks I had been working on setting up my own company. I had invested everything I had—my money, my apartments, my shares in Mayfield Realties— and was ready to start transferring the staff I wanted on board when a routine check came back with devastating news that could cost me both the new business venture and my credibility. Infusing confidence into the new company and my abilities to build an empire away from my father's influence would have been an easy task, were it not for the fifty million dollars missing from the Mayfield Realties accounts.

I squeezed my eyes shut and rubbed my forehead to get

rid of the pressure building inside my head. The last thing we needed was board members and shareholders panicking and demanding to see the financial reports. I couldn't make the books public until I figured out what was happening. The spreadsheets on my screen were supposed to shed light on where the money had disappeared to, only I couldn't focus with Brooke occupying my mind.

"Mr. Mayfield? You—" My receptionist's voice echoed through the intercom. I pressed the response button to cut her off.

"Send him in."

"Right away, sir."

A knock on the door, and a man in his fifties entered. One of the assistants placed a file on my desk and then closed the door behind us.

"Take a seat." I pointed at the seat opposite from me and read the name on the file:

Clarence Holton

The name sounded oddly familiar. I pondered for a moment, and then it hit me. I had read the same name on the hit list in the black book. There had been a Holton, no doubt about it. I just couldn't remember the first name.

My gaze brushed his salt-and-pepper hair and tanned face before settling on the sleeves of his tailored suit. My father had told me that all members of the elite club wore special cufflinks to recognize each other. They were silver round buttons engraved with a symbol that looked like leaves growing over circles and ended in a sharp "V"-split tail in the form of a lizard's tongue—the symbol of parasitic animalistic power growing over physical matter.

"Thank you for seeing me," Holton said. He lifted his hands, then crossed them on the desk. My gaze fell on the cuffs. They were smaller than I remembered, but the spitting image of those my father showed me.

I looked into his eyes, my face a stony mask.

"I'm a busy man." My voice betrayed a mixture of boredom and annoyance—a winning combination in the business world. It was the kind of voice I had learned to use during my time in a gang; the kind of voice that always earned respect and let people know they couldn't mess with me.

"I never got the chance to tell you how sorry I am about your father's demise."

"Don't worry about it." I drew in a sharp breath and let it out slowly—another one of my tactics to signal to get to the point. The spreadsheets were waiting, and then there was also my tiny problem with Brooke. I had no time for small talk, and particularly not with someone like Holton.

"Your father and I were very close," Holton said. "Now that he's no longer with us and you're in charge, I hope we'll become friends."

The way he said the word "friends" made me recoil with disgust. I had no intention of being his friend, not even an acquaintance.

"I'll think about it," I said. "If there's nothing else—" The invitation to leave hung heavy in the air. I knew he could feel it by the way his eyes narrowed a bit, which he downplayed with laughter.

"Like father, like son. *Triad* magazine's having its annual September issue party." He raised a brow meaningfully, like I was supposed to know what the hell he was talking about. When I remained silent, he continued, "We'd love to have you as a guest of honor. You're single, as far as the world knows. Plenty of attractive models will be attending. Maybe one will catch your eye."

"I thought you were a magazine, not an escort service."

My statement caught him off-guard. His eyes shimmered with annoyance, and in that instance I realized Clarence Holton wasn't here because he was worried about the company or his shares; he had been instructed to recruit me. Maybe my father had left the club, but Holton was still an active member.

"I'll think about it," I said, standing. He followed suit, and I accompanied him to the door. For obvious reasons, I couldn't kick his ass out of my office. The shareholders couldn't sell or the shares would plummet to an all-time low. His connections to the media prevented me from making rash decisions. And I hated it, because it felt as though I supported his dark and twisted secrets and lifestyle.

"Thanks for stopping by." I held the door open and gestured for an assistant to accompany him to the lobby.

"One more thing, Jett." He turned to face me, his face an ugly mask of pretense. "Please stop by. You'll enjoy it."

I closed the door before I smashed his face in. For the hundredth time a surge of anger pulsed through me as to why my father had brought this mess upon us. I shouldn't have refused to talk to him before he died. If I had listened to what he had to say, maybe I'd know what was going on and figure a way out.

Taking a deep breath, I sat in my chair and retrieved the spreadsheet files. I had too much on my plate, and I couldn't afford another distraction. The company and my relationship with Brooke came first. I'd deal with the club later.

***

Brooke was late and a workaholic. I wouldn't have been surprised if she had forgotten about our date. My phone cradled between my shoulder and my ear, I waited for her to pick up her cell phone. The line went straight to voicemail—like it had for the last few hours. I should've checked on her after her conference, but shareholder calls kept trickling in and I had no time. Besides, I figured she'd be busy and we'd talk over dinner anyway.

"Fuck." I slammed my phone on my desk and turned to look out the window. Clearly she was pissed, and I had no idea why. I'd probably gone too far by telling her she couldn't break up with me. Brooke didn't like to be told what she could or couldn't do. But damn it! The woman had issues.

"Can I get you anything before I head home?" Emma asked from the doorway. I turned, realizing I hadn't even heard her walk in. She was dressed in a fitted trench coat and was holding a briefcase in one hand. A handbag dangled from the other arm. I wondered how much they had cost her. My father hadn't been known for his generosity with his mistresses. Maybe he had been more smitten with this one than the rest, even though they all sure looked the same, albeit they were getting younger with each new conquest.

"No. You can go," I said. "On second thought, have you seen Brooke?"

"She left during her meeting. I haven't seen her since."

I frowned. "Which meeting?"

"The one that started at eleven a.m. She didn't return for the afternoon acquisitions talks. Your brother jumped in." She smiled. "Want me to call him? He might still be around."

"I'll do it," I said to get her to leave. Even if I called Nate, he probably wouldn't know more than I did.

Emma's gaze lingered on me as if she wanted to say something else, and then she settled on, "Have a good weekend."

I mumbled a "yeah, have a good one, too" and turned my attention back to my cell phone. After she closed the door behind her, I sank in my chair, my fingers tapping on the huge desk in annoyance as I recalled my conversation with Brooke. I was sure I'd heard her correctly when she agreed to talk over dinner. Why would she do that and then leave without telling me? I always thought of her as responsible, which made me assume whatever issues she had wouldn't encourage her to run from me. It wasn't like her. Or maybe I didn't know her as well as I thought I did.

At 7:30 p.m. and countless calls later, I realized she wasn't going to pick up, and I dialed Sylvie's number. The line rang a few times before she replied.

"Where's Brooke?" I asked by means of introduction. The television was blasting in the background. A brief pause ensued, during which she lowered the volume.

"Jett?" She sounded surprised, probably not expecting to hear from me. "I saw her yesterday." She hesitated. "Is everything okay between you guys?"

Sylvie probably knew we weren't okay, but I wasn't ready to go into that.

"We're good. She told me you met," I said. "Apparently she left work early, and I thought she might be with you. We were supposed to meet for an early dinner. I got us a table at *Le Bernardin*."

"Wow. That place is booked months in advance. Wish I could come along." Sylvie let out a sigh of relief. "I'm so glad things worked out. I was worried she might be too scared to tell you."

Tell me what? I frowned, realizing I was missing a part of the picture. Brooke hadn't been particularly talkative the night before. In fact, I had never seen her so quiet. The following morning she had been even more cryptic.

"So what do you think?" she asked.

"About what?" I asked cautiously.

"About how I found the book with the disk tucked inside my handbag," she said. I froze. "I swear it was an accident, but I'm taking the blame even though Brooke's adamant she put them inside my bag. Don't listen to her, though." She laughed.

"What the hell are you talking about?" I rubbed my temples as I tried to make sense of her drivel. "What book?"

The line remained silent for a moment.

"She didn't tell you, did she?" Sylvie whispered

eventually. "Oh, shit." The line went dead. Without a second thought, I redialed her number because no one hung up on me. This time Sylvie picked up on the first ring.

"Sorry, Jett. I got disconnected. Bad signal." She laughed. What was it with people and laughing when they were lying? "So, Brooke's not there?"

Ignoring her question, I decided not to beat around the bush. "Are we talking about the same book and disk that were stolen in Bellagio?"

"Yep. Unfortunately or fortunately, depending on the way you see it. They were not stolen, just—" she paused "—misplaced."

I took a deep breath and let it out slowly as I sorted through my thoughts.

"Where are they now, Sylvie?"

"With Brooke, of course," she said, and then she started to chat away. Her words flew so fast it felt like a sledgehammer was pounding inside my head. "Honestly, I thought she had told you already. She wanted to do it last night because she knew you'd be angry and she wanted to get it off her chest."

"Whoa, slow down." I pinched the bridge of my nose. "First, why did Brooke assume I'd be angry? That's crazy."

"I don't know. Maybe because you could blame her for your father's death?" She made the question sound like a statement.

"Bullshit." I was so angry I felt like I could hit a wall. "I'd never blame her for anything."

"Brooke told me how guilty you feel about your father's death. She thinks that since the book was never stolen, she might have caused his death."

"What the fuck?" For someone so clever, Brooke's reasoning sucked. "That's the most fucked-up thing I've ever heard. She knows Robert and I never had a close relationship. I stopped grieving about my father a week ago." Right after I found out about the missing fifty million dollars.

"Right. The way you say it makes it all sound really stupid. Brooke was convinced you blamed yourself."

"I do." My voice dropped to a whisper. "But for different reasons than you think." I stood and began pacing the room up and down, my anger coursing through me. "Look, I'm worried about the company. I've kept us from drowning for years, but my father's legacy is a huge financial hole that could swallow half of New York City. The books don't make sense, and I can't tell anyone about it without risking the shares taking a dive. I know you have a business degree, so you can imagine what that would mean." My glance fell on the clock on the wall. "It doesn't matter now. I need to talk to Brooke. Do you have an idea where she might be? Coffee shops she frequents? I'm not comfortable with her being alone. Not when she has that damn book and she's in a conflicted state of mind thinking I'm the enemy."

"Have you tried calling her?"

"Yeah." I cringed inwardly, not stating the obvious. "It's switched off. I wouldn't have called you if it wasn't."

"Switched off as in 'you can't reach her because she's blocking your calls' or switched off as in 'switched off'?" she asked.

"Seriously?"

"Sorry." Sylvie continued in her annoying "sorry for even asking" voice. "I just can't believe she would switch off her cell. She never does. Maybe the battery's dead or she left it somewhere. Did you guys have a fight?"

"Sort of." I breathed out. "But, like I said, the only thing that matters is finding her."

"I know a couple of places she could be. Are you at work?"

Finally.

"Yeah."

"I'll be there in twenty minutes," she said. "By the way, Jett, I'm really sorry about your father. Not just because he's dead, but also…you know…" She trailed off.

"Thanks."

I hung up and looked out the window at the last rays of the setting sun coloring the sky in dark copper. I didn't like the fact that Brooke hadn't told me about the book. I could deal with the fact that she had tried to break up with me because I could see her possible motivations. Maybe she thought she was protecting me; maybe even protecting herself from whatever she thought I'd say to her. I could deal with that, but I couldn't deal with the fact that she kept secrets from me that might risk her life.

I peered at my cell phone for the hundredth time. The whole story sounded too far-fetched. My gut feeling told me I was missing something. Even though Brooke didn't trust me, she had promised she'd stay, so what made her change her mind?

Speed-dialing the one person I knew would never fail me, I pressed the cell to my ear and whispered, "Kenny, I need you to track down Brooke's phone right now. I need to know where she is and who's with her."

"Stalking her much?" Kenny laughed. "You got it."

16
BROOKE

SOMEONE SLAPPING ME was the first sensation I had upon waking up. The second was the overpowering smell of decay and excrement. Bile rose in my throat and my stomach turned, urging me to vomit. I bit my tongue hard to fight it and tried to pry my eyes open, but everything around me remained dark. At some point a chill must have crept into my limbs because my legs and arms felt numb, and I couldn't stop shivering. I was so cold, it felt as if I had been shivering for a long time in the darkness where I now resided.

Another slap—this time it was so hard I knew it was across my face. A pang of anger flickered to life inside me, giving me enough strength to stir from my uncomfortable position. The left side of my face tingled and burned, as if someone had used a whip on me. I pried my eyes open groggily, and a strangled gasp escaped my throat. The cold sensation I had assumed was inside me actually came from the cement floor underneath me, penetrating my business suit. Through the hazy curtain before my eyes, the picture before me didn't make much sense. The whole room seemed cloudy and filled with light mist that was spinning so fast it took my eyes several seconds to adjust, but I could smell the putrid, sickeningly sweet air.

Sitting up, I tried to kneel and stumbled forward. My palms caught my fall, and I realized both hands were bound in front of me in some kind of praying position. I waited until the spinning slowed to a bearable level and opened my eyes again to take in my surroundings.

I was in a room the size of a cell with dirty gray walls and a naked light bulb hanging from the low ceiling. The floor was cold and showed brown spots I assumed were dried dirt and God knows what. Behind me was a dirty mattress with yet more brownish stains. My head hurt like a bitch, but that wasn't my primary concern. All I remembered was the car-jacking, Robert Mayfield's driver being shot, and a guy pointing his gun into my face. Another guy got into the back seat and pressed a cloth against my mouth, the sickening sweet smell of chloroform still embedded in my mind. Nothing after that.

Where was I? What had happened?

"Good. You're awake," someone said. His voice was

familiar. I turned toward the door and narrowed my eyes to focus on his height, age, or anything I might catch through my blurred vision and use to help me identify him later.

He walked in, and the door closed behind him. As he inched toward me, his features became clearer. It was only when he squatted that I recognized him.

Years had changed his face and body. He had put on weight. His nose had been broken and there were scars on his cheek and on his left eyebrow, but the resemblance was uncanny. It was the face that still haunted my dreams.

"Danny?" My question was barely more than a hiss, or maybe I couldn't hear my own voice through the drumming in my ears. My heart pounded so hard against my chest I was sure he could hear it. "What are you doing here?"

"I'm working, that's what's happening." His voice was nonchalant, unaffected, lightly mocking. He licked his lips as his dark brown eyes assessed me.

Seeing him brought back the memories I had been trying to bury for more than ten years: the time my sister fell in love with him, the days after she died, and the way he smiled when he was allowed to walk free. Danny must have seen my shock and felt my thoughts because he started to smile, and a shiver ran down my spine.

"You thought I forgot the troubles you caused me?" His tone had a warning undertone to it. "You really thought you could get away?"

I stared at him, barely able to swallow the bile in my throat. My mind was chaos, completely overwhelmed by his presence. I thought I had put enough distance between us, both physically and emotionally. Of all the people in the world, how could I meet Danny and under those circumstances? My body was burning with repulsion and hate. So much hate and disgust. In spite of the cold, I was burning inside—burning so hot I wanted to push aside anything that stood in my way of hurting him. I wanted to claw at his face and eyes. I wanted to see him bleed, like Jenna had bled—slowly and with no compassion.

"You seem surprised I still remember Jenna," he said. "It's not easy to forget a pretty girl like her. She was a gold mine."

"You son of a bitch, you killed her," I spat out. I pushed up on my elbow to kick him, smash his face in, but the ropes kept me bound in place. Angrily, I spat in his face. "I wish I could kill you."

"I'll admit I deserved that." He wiped his face, amused. "But it's not my fault she was weak and took more than she could handle."

"You hooked her on your shit," I whispered. Jenna was drugged that fateful night, but the coroner report clearly stated she died of internal bleeding, not of an overdose. "You shared her, you piece of filth. You passed her along like merchandise."

"Business is business. Besides, it's in the past now, isn't it?" He shrugged. "For what it's worth, I have to thank you. Without you, I'd never have met your sister. I wouldn't have received good money for a good time. For old time's sake, I'll make you a gift, Brooke."

I flinched at hearing my name roll off his tongue. He leaned forward, and his voice dropped to a whisper dripping with fake secrecy. "Do you want to know what it is?"

"Go fuck yourself. I don't want anything from you."

He smiled again, only this time his expression betrayed his feelings. My words had displeased him. I tried to move a few inches back, but it was too late. He moved so fast I barely had time to blink or flinch. He grabbed my bound arms and twisted with such force I feared my bones would break. Pain shot through me, and I winced as his other hand forced my chin up hard.

"I don't usually take secondhands but on the off chance you're lucky and make it out alive, I'll make an exception. I'll even be generous and grant you release."

"I'd rather die than—"

He twisted my arm again. My words died in my throat as my vision blurred from the excruciating pain shooting through my shoulder and spine.

"When he's done with you," Danny whispered, "you'll wish I were your first." He let go of me, and I stumbled forward, tumbling to the floor. I turned warily, watching his every move. "I'll give you a good fuck, Brooke. One you'll never forget. I will fuck your brains hard until you break—just like I did with your sister."

"You're sick." I fought to sort through my thoughts, picking out all the things I wanted to say to him, but my hate blinded me, rendering me unable to speak.

"Save that for the one who wants you first."

He walked to the door and knocked, then turned back to me as he waited. His smile was gone, and I realized his eyes shimmered with pity as he stared me down.

"I don't see why they wanted you. You're far too old," he said. "I can only imagine that it's either a personal preference, or they want the sister of the one they had."

Footsteps echoed in the corridor outside the door.

"What do you mean?" I asked, his words swirling in my mind.

"Are you really this stupid?" he mocked me. His lips curled upward and all traces of pity disappeared. "I was paid well to provide Jenna, and they were very happy with her. Even if you'd testified against me, you'd never have won. People appreciate my services. Or how else do you think I walked out innocent? Think about it."

The door opened, and Danny left without so much as a look back. Then the door closed again, and I was alone in the room with his voice ringing in my head. My mind recalled the events after Jenna's death and ventured to the man who let Danny walk free.

Danny lured my sister into a world of drugs and sold her to others for sex. I had known that for a long time; what I never understood was why a judge would let him go free. I could only imagine the reason now. It had not been Danny's charms or the way he had lied that swayed the judge in his favor. It was probably the judge's personal interest in Jenna or him playing a part in what happened to her. I was ready to bet on the latter.

17

THE LIGHT BULB above my head cast a glaring light on the dirty floor and the ropes around my wrists. The stale, putrid scent lingered in the air. At some point my sense of smell got used to it, and I dared to draw deeper breaths. I didn't know when I fell asleep, but that was all I wanted. Not thinking. Not feeling. Just sleeping—until I could forget where I was and what I'd heard. Even my nightmares were better than reality. Waking was like falling straight into hell with no escape, where the pain from the tight ropes cutting into my skin provided more relief than discomfort.

"You should deal with it, you know?" a female voice whispered. I spun slowly in a circle to scan my surroundings. There were no windows—just walls and one closed door, behind which Danny had disappeared. My only escape route was that door, only my ropes were too short to reach it. A shudder ran down my spine as I realized nobody but I was in the room. Was I going crazy?

"Hey, I'm talking to you," the same voice said. I scanned the room again, and this time my glance fell on a small vent in the wall I must've missed before. Pale skin shimmered through the grids, but the holes were too small to see behind. Craning my neck to get a better look, I ignored the nausea in the pit of my stomach and walked a few steps forward. As if sensing my curiosity, whoever was on the other side shifted and squeezed their fingertips through the openings. The nails were long and dirty, and definitely belonged to a female. "I'm in the room next to yours. Can you walk over?"

"No." My eyes remained fixed on the vent. The fingers disappeared, and finally I could see the eyes and lips of a woman. I couldn't tell her age, but from the sound of her voice, she was young, maybe younger than I was. "I'm bound." I lifted my hands to show her.

She let out a groan. "You need to stop crying, Brooke."

"How do you know—"

"Your name? They mentioned it outside," she said. "And you need to stop sleeping."

"Why?"

"Because you make it easy for them to inject you with drugs, and you won't even notice. Trust me, you'll want to keep control over your body."

"Who are you?" I crawled closer to the vent as far as the rope around my wrist allowed until I was six feet away from the opening. Up close, I could see her face more clearly.

"I'm Liz. And before you ask, I don't know where we are." She was slightly chubby and in her late teens—maybe around seventeen or eighteen years old, with a blond bob and bangs. Even with the vent obstructing my view, I could see just how pretty she was. A normal girl—were it not for the caked dirt on her face. I held my breath as I realized it probably wasn't dirt—more like dried blood.

"How long have you been in there?"

"Almost three months. I stopped counting a while back." She smiled nervously, but her eyes looked at me with such intensity I knew she'd gone through a lot. My chest felt heavy with dread. Three months was a long time. Clearly, whoever held her hostage harbored no intention of letting her go. I realized the eyes looking at me were the eyes of someone who had seen horrible things. "You have a better chance to survive if you're strong but compliant. If you want to live, you have to play along and do whatever they ask you to do—and they'll always ask just once. If you struggle or don't follow their commands, they'll ask for permission to kill you." She paused before adding. "And some of them love doing that."

I nodded and forced air into my lungs as I tried to

memorize every single word.

"They bring food once, sometimes twice a day," Liz continued. "It's usually the same thing: bread with one dish consisting of rice with meat, or steak with fries, and a glass of water. If you're lucky, you'll also get two blue pills and one little white pill. Eat the bread, drink the water, and always take the blue pills as soon as you can. But don't eat the rest of the food because it's spiked. Whatever you don't eat, find a way to get rid of it without them knowing. And remember, the better you get at playing along, the higher your chances of staying alive. Better yet, try to exceed their expectations."

"What are the blue pills for?" I asked.

"They'll keep you awake and numb the pain. I always take them."

"And the white pills?"

"Take the white ones only when you're ready to abort." She raised her eyebrows knowingly. "They tend to give Misoprostol. It's for stomach ulcers and abortion, and should not be used with the blue ones."

"How do you—"

"I heard you in your sleep. You were loud. Talking weird stuff about a disk—and more."

The disk and the baby were a secret. I couldn't blurt it all out in my sleep. Waves of panic rushed through me as I realized what would happen if whoever held us captive found out.

"How do you know everything?" I asked.

"Danny made me work on the streets until his employer noticed me and asked him to bring me here." She was cut short by the sound of a car horn. I figured we were near a street or a highway, but I wasn't sure. We kept silent for a few seconds. When nothing stirred, she continued in a hushed tone. "You can't act like this, you know? The way you did with Danny. He isn't the worst one. I mean, there are worse."

I glanced down at my hands, at the way the rope cut into my skin, the pain keeping me focused and grounded in reality while my fear paralyzed me. The whole situation seemed hard to grasp, but I knew I had to listen to Liz's advice to get out of here. It was hard to imagine that Danny wasn't the worst. He had fooled my whole family by pretending he loved my sister. He knew what would happen to her and still let her come to harm, which demonstrated he had no heart, no soul, and surely no conscience or compassion. To me he had none of the qualities that make us human.

"I don't care," I said. "He killed my sister."

"I'm not making excuses for him," Liz whispered. "He's one of the suppliers. Basically, he provides girls in exchange for drugs and money. But he doesn't take part in—" She drew in her breath and let it out slowly. The way she defended Danny, I couldn't help but wonder what their relationship was.

"Are there others like us?" I asked, almost hopeful. If there were more women, maybe we could work together and escape. There had to be a way, or else I didn't know how I could get out on my own.

"There were," she replied. "They get a new supply twice a month. The first two weeks are crucial. After that, depending on how well you behave, you have only one worth." She fell silent. Our gazes connected through the grids, and her eyes filled with fear and something else: hopelessness. Her voice dropped to a whisper, which in a way filled me with more terror than the things she had disclosed so far. "You don't want to mess with them, or else you'll be punished. If you hope that someone will help you, *don't.* It won't happen. It's never happened. We're on private property. No one's going to come looking for us here because the people who own it are rich. It's like the extreme wing of a club, or something. Danny told me, and I believe him. And honestly, it'd be a stupid idea to try to run away. Two have tried, and look where it got them."

A club?

I stopped breathing for a moment as the pieces of the puzzle slowly fell into place. Robert Mayfield had tried to protect his interests by getting rid of me. And then someone else stepped in. That was the reason why I was here, even though, according to Danny, I was older than the girls they usually went for.

"Why would you tell me all of this? If no escape's possible, then—" I shook my head as I struggled to make sense of my thoughts. If Liz knew no one made it out, why was she still trying to help me? The life she was living was no life at all. I realized I was spiraling into a dark abyss of emotions, and I hadn't even found out what was really going on.

"Because it doesn't matter," she said. Her voice sounded choked as she continued. "I want to keep you safe, even though I probably won't be able to." She moved away from the vent, out of my view. I waited for her to come back, but she didn't.

"Liz?"

When no reply came, I understood. Without hope and faith, she had done all she had thought she could. Why get attached to the "new girl" who probably wouldn't make it past the two-week mark anyway?

I sat down on the cold floor. For the umpteenth time I wondered what it must've been like for her all alone in her cell, being at other people's mercy with no one to talk to. Three months might not seem like a long time, but it was long enough to need someone near her to remind her that she was still human rather than a worthless object, someone who understood the hell she was living, someone who was there to share the pain rather than inflict it upon her.

Maybe she had found that someone.

When my limbs began to stiffen, I crawled back to my sleeping place, which consisted of a dirty mattress on the floor, and sat down. I buried my face in my hands, unable to avoid the feelings of dismay washing over me.

Jett hadn't exaggerated when he said the club was dangerous. He also hadn't lied with his statement that we were connected through a similar past. I just never realized how close he had been to the truth. How horrible would it be for him to discover his father's club kept me hostage? He'd never find out, not least because he'd probably never come looking for me after I ended our relationship, giving him a good reason to believe I had walked out on him. It had been a bad mistake. I knew it now; I had sensed it then. And I had no one else to blame but myself.

The hours ticked by, and Liz's cell remained quiet as a tomb. The light above my head kept burning relentlessly, making it impossible to sleep for longer than a few minutes at a time. It was hard to tell whether it was day or night, if one day had passed or several, but sure enough, it felt like an eternity. By the time I heard footsteps again, the fear in my mind and cold in my limbs had turned me into a shell of nothingness: functioning without reacting, or thinking. It was only when the door opened that I lifted my head and sat up, unsure what to expect.

A short guy holding a tray entered. He placed the tray on the floor and pushed it toward me with his boot, then took a step back. I looked from the tray to the gun in the holster around his waist. He remained quiet, but his dark eyes didn't stray from me. There was no warning in his eyes. Just amusement. I couldn't help but think of a caged animal in a glass house—a sick experiment, during which I wasn't considered an equal because I didn't matter.

"Thanks," I muttered, remembering Liz's advice to be compliant, even though I wanted to charge at him to get to that gun.

It seemed to do the trick because he turned away and left, locking the door behind him.

I neared the tray warily. Just like Liz predicted, the food consisted of a main course dish—chicken with rice and white sauce—and bread. Next to the glass of water were three pills: two blue and one white. What I didn't expect was that the bread was covered in a thin layer of blue mold, and the water inside the glass looked dirty. Even if Liz was right, I couldn't possibly eat any of it in my condition.

Besides, my nerves were too frayed to keep anything down. The prospect of starving to death sounded more appealing than dying by violence or drugs because at least I'd keep my self-respect. I could eat another time, once I escaped. I had to believe that a miracle was possible. But I was too thirsty to abstain from drinking the water. I took a sip and grimaced. It tasted just like it looked.

I grabbed the tray and scanned the cell to find a hiding place. On the farthest side of the door was a ventilation shaft in the floor. It was wider than the one in the wall and in the middle was a hole, which I assumed served as an open toilet. The smell of excrement wafting from it was so strong I almost threw up. I kneeled down and discarded my meal and white pill.

The thick slice of bread was too large, so I tore it into bits and threw it into the hole along with the water. I held up the blue pills, considering my next move. Liz was right. If I wanted to escape, I had to stay awake. But not like this. My mind had to remain clear, without the need of whatever those pills were.

I returned the tray to the same spot where the guard had left it, pushed the pills inside my pockets in case I needed them later, and smashed the water glass against the concrete floor. The noise of breaking glass echoed from the walls unnaturally loudly, and for a moment I was convinced someone would barge in to demand an explanation. As quickly as I could, I picked up the largest shard. It was small, but a small weapon was better than no weapon at all. If it was sharp enough to cut through skin, then it would do its job.

There was just enough time to hide it in a small hole of the mattress before footsteps approached and the door swung open, just like I knew it would.

"Don't move!" one of the two guards commanded. My heart hammering hard, I pretended to finish chewing as I watched one of them clean up the shards.

"Brooke, right?" the other one said. I nodded but didn't dare look up—or breathe. He stood so close it gave me the creeps. He held up my hands to check them before stepping away again. "You might be new, but let me tell you this. If it happens again, you won't get our fancy treatment anymore."

As if I cared.

I could feel his intent stare and almost smiled with relief when they retreated, and the door finally closed. Listening for any sounds, I waited until I was sure they wouldn't return, then retrieved the shard from the mattress and cut a hole in the inseam of my business suit, then tucked it inside.

A glance at Liz's vent told me she was there, watching in silence.

"Please don't," she whispered.

I had no intention to get her involved or endanger her life, but I wasn't going to accept my new circumstances and do nothing about them, either. Ignoring her, I sat down on the mattress and began to rock back and forth in an attempt to keep myself awake.

18

WHATEVER HAD BEEN in that water began to kick in almost immediately and an odd sense of floating and being weightless filled me. My body began to shake slightly, and then the tremors intensified and my breathing quickened. It was very similar to a panic attack, and I realized whatever was happening to me might take a long time to subside. Maybe the water had been spiked and Liz didn't know, or maybe I was indeed having a panic attack. Either way, I had to get a grip on myself.

For a long time, I just kept staring at the walls. I was exhausted, but my mind was too active to sleep, even if I wanted to. A guard checked on me at regular intervals, but he never spoke.

I didn't know how much time had passed when a click outside my cell made me sit up, alerted. Another click followed, and I realized Liz's door had been opened. Several people entered her room. The hushed voices were too low to understand.

Someone laughed.

And then a sound that made my blood freeze in my veins. I knew that sound. Maybe not *knew* as in having experienced it before, but knew as in *knowing* what was happening. I couldn't tell how many men were in Liz's cell, but I could hear their laughter, the slapping, the grunting—their bodies slamming against hers as they each took their turn. Shaking, I pressed my hands against my mouth to stop any sounds from forming at the back of my throat. That's when the whimpering and screaming began. Whatever they were doing to her didn't leave much to my imagination. A sense of powerlessness washed over me as I realized there was nothing I could do to help her.

"Are you filming?" somebody asked.

"No shit, man. You think I'd miss that?" The second guy laughed. It was a deep unnerving sound, one which I instantly recognized. It was the same guy who had threatened me after I broke the glass.

"Let's get the new one in here. What do you think?" the third guy said. His voice was deep and hoarse. A smoker's voice.

The first one spoke again. "Remember the rules? Dante wants her for himself." From the way he said "her," I realized they were talking about me. But who was Dante? Danny's words that someone wanted me first crossed my mind, and a shudder ran down my spine. Maybe he had been talking about the same guy—Dante.

"If we drug her, she won't remember. Problem solved," the smoker voice said. "No one would believe her anyway."

Shit!

My heart began to pound against my ribcage, and I forced myself to take slow, measured breaths. Panicking wasn't going to help anyone.

"No, that's not a good idea," the first one said. He sounded tense, anxious even. "Dante wants her in the condition she's in now. He was clear on that."

Laughter, then a clicking sound, like a belt buckle.

"You don't have to do it," the guy with the smoker voice said. "But I want my fun. You in, Stu?"

"Count me in," the second voice replied. "But take her to the wheel room."

The wheel room? What kind of room was that? Come to think of it, I didn't want to find out. The voices continued to speak, their words no longer reaching me because the sound of my blood rushing in my ears drowned out all noise. I scanned my cell for a place to hide and escape but, like before, there was no secret entrance. No hole in the wall I could fit through.

With trembling hands I made sure the glass shard was

still hidden in the inseam of my suit. My breathing made a whistling sound as I sat down on the mattress, waiting to see how events would unfold.

Life or death. Because if I failed, I was sure I wouldn't survive the night.

The door slammed open, and in walked two men. They were big, their expressions relentless. Both carried a gun, and I realized my chances were pretty slim. But maybe that was what the guns were for: to intimidate so a woman wouldn't put up a good fight. The blond one—the one who had picked up the glass shards—had the sunken cheeks, mottled skin, and hollow eyes of a meth addict. The other one with the smoky voice, who didn't seem to care about Dante's rules, was broad with a cropped military hairstyle and a crooked nose. I recognized him as the guy who had held the gun in my face in the parking garage.

My mouth opened to scream and closed shut because there was no purpose in screaming when no one would hear me. I wanted to fight, scratch their faces, even though I probably stood no chance against two males with guns.

The dark-haired guy pulled me up, removed the ropes, and shoved me. Weak from a lack of food, water, and sleep, I stumbled forward. But my mind was sharp enough to take in my surroundings.

The corridor was long and narrow, with doors on either side. It looked like an empty storage building with locked cells, from which a corridor led into an open space with two doors. The sound of my kitten heels resonated from the walls as I was led through one door into an adjoining parking garage with three parked trucks. On the eastern side, almost hidden by the largest truck, were a dozen adjustable shelves lining the wall. Stashed on the shelves were boxes. I craned my neck, but they were too far to peek inside.

"You go in—I'll bring the rest," the dark-haired guy said. I peered over my shoulder to see him walking over to the shelves and rummaging through the boxes.

The blond guy's hand clasped around my upper arm and urged me forward to the truck in the farthest corner, then pressed a button. A ramp descended and he gave me another shove, urging me to walk up.

Inside, the light was dimmed, but I could see that the truck had been decorated to resemble a plain room with white walls and a double bed. Cuffs and belts dangled from each bedpost, and a brown rug covered the floor. My mouth went dry as realization kicked in.

This was the wheel room—a moveable transporter serving the sick purpose of holding women captive, and probably worse.

I didn't want to die in here.

This was my chance.

Probably the only chance I'd get.

Damn it, I wasn't going to let it go to waste.

Slowly, I squeezed my hand into the seam at my waist and grabbed the end of the glass shard so tight the sharp edge cut into my skin, sending a pang of piercing pain through my nerve endings. But I didn't care. Without thinking, I turned and plunged the tip as hard as I could into the man's throat and sliced to the right, cutting through skin, flesh, and nerves. His body instantly doubled over, and his hands moved to his throat. A gush of blood covered his skin and trickled down his arm onto the floor.

"Stu!" His voice was muffled by the gurgling sound of blood. His widened eyes betrayed his panic as he raised his hands to his face.

I left the shard in his throat and ran down the ramp, in the direction we had come from—and the only door I had seen.

"Bitch." I heard the dark-haired guy let out a long string of expletives, which were quickly replaced by approaching footsteps. But I didn't care and didn't turn. All I cared about was escaping. Get out of this place as fast as I could.

Through the door, I reached the open space, but instead of heading in the direction of my cell, I dashed for the other door. It was a risk. A gamble I didn't want to take, but I had no other choice. The drumming of my heart stifled all other sounds, which only made me run faster. I charged through the door, thankful that it wasn't locked, and realized I was in a stairwell. I yanked at the emergency exit door. It was locked. A curse escaped my lips.

I couldn't retrace my steps because I had no idea where the other guy—Stu—was, so I ran up the stairs, trying each door as I passed. By the time the door opened again, I had reached the third floor and my lungs were burning from the lack of oxygen. I had no idea how long I hadn't eaten anything, but I knew I couldn't go on much farther. To my right was a door leading into the third-floor corridor. This one was unlocked. I walked through and closed it behind me as silently as I could.

The corridor looked just like the one with the cells, only the doors stood ajar. I quickly scanned one of the cells as I ran past and realized they were storage boxes, just like the ones downstairs. Whoever ran this business clearly thought big. I headed for the last door to my left, almost expecting another parking garage. Instead I entered a large open space with lockers.

The door leading from the stairwell into the corridor opened, and the pounding steps told me I had no time to lose, so I opened a locker door and squeezed in. The space was tiny but big enough for me to fit inside.

My breathing came labored. Loud, even. Trying to slow down my thumping heart, I pressed a hand against my chest. Footsteps thudded down the corridor, heading for me.

I held my breath as the room fell silent. Through the tiny slits in the locker, I could see Stu's shape. And then the footsteps departed again, and the door to the stairwell slammed shut.

As much as I was tempted to stay hidden, it was only a matter of time until Stu came back. The thought of him opening the locker and finding me after what I had done to his friend terrified me. So I stepped out of the locker, and had just headed for the other end of the corridor when someone grabbed my waist and something pressed against my mouth.

I kicked and punched as hard as I could, fighting the iron grip.

"Where do you think you're going?" Stu hissed. His breathing came heavy as he punched the side of my head, sending me against the wall. Instinctively, I curved into a ball to protect my baby, but his hands curled in my hair, pulling me back to my feet. My eyes fell on a guy I hadn't seen before and on the syringe in his hand. As if sensing my sudden panic, he smiled, and I realized there were only two outcomes.

I'd be punished by paying dearly for my out-of-order behavior. And, judging by the look on his face, he no longer cared to follow Dante's commands and leave me unscathed.

The second outcome was even bleaker than the first, so I pushed it to the back of my mind, not wanting to think about it.

My scalp burned, but the pain didn't stop me from fighting and punching the space around me. My foot connected with something soft, and Stu let out another string of curses. His hand let go of my hair, and for a moment I relished the sensation of being free. Then my legs were kicked from beneath me and I collapsed, knocking my head against the floor in the process.

My vision blurred. I struggled to get up but fingers moved around my throat, cutting off my air supply. Pinned to the ground, unable to move or breathe, I peered into cold dark eyes. Stu's face was a mask of fury and arousal as he cut off my air supply. The other guy kneeled next to him. I winced when a needle pierced through my skin.

Within seconds, the anesthetic drug coursing through my veins made my body weak. I fought and kicked hard, until I realized there was nothing I could do. The realization didn't come from fear. My body was ready to give up, slowly turning into a shell of numbness. It was as if my body had no choice. I accepted that anything could happen now—that everything was my fault and I'd brought this upon myself.

Stu's hand pulled up my business skirt and tore away my panties. I felt the air between my legs and heard the sound of his zipper. I closed my eyes to hide behind my eyelids— inside my mind. Whatever happened, I didn't want to witness it.

Not even the loud gunshot made me open my eyes. Nor the thudding footsteps around me. Nor hearing Jett's name and someone shouting, "This is how it's done, Jett. You seem to have forgotten." Then another gunshot, followed by another. It was only when I heard Jett's deep voice that I forced my heavy eyes open, and my lips curled into a weak smile. He was so beautiful. A beautiful dream. At least I wouldn't feel the pain because I was dreaming of him.

"Brooke, baby." His green eyes were filled with so much worry that I wanted to assure him I'd be okay just to take away his pain. I wanted to touch him, to see if he was here or whether his beautiful face was just an illusion, but my fingers wouldn't follow my brain's command.

"I'm sorry, Brooke." He lifted me in his arms and pressed me against his chest. Through the pain inside my head and abdomen, I inhaled the scent of his aftershave as he kept repeating, "We'll get you out of here."

"There's a girl downstairs," I whispered. "Please help her. And Jett, your father—" I fought against the overwhelming feeling of losing control. Every word was a struggle. I tried to keep my eyes open, but all I saw was darkness. "He's still alive."

The last thing I heard was Jett shouting, "Call for an ambulance, Brian." And then darkness descended upon me, swallowing me up whole.

19

I WOKE UP in a bed with Jett sleeping in a recliner to my right. I watched the deep worry lines on his forehead, the way his stubble cast a shadow on his face, darkening his features. He was dressed in blue jeans and a black shirt that built a strong contrast to the pristine whiteness of the bedsheets and the walls. His hair was a knotted mess, reminding me of the many times I had run my fingers through it, but the memories quickly dissolved in favor of reality.

The dark circles beneath his eyes painted a good picture of what he must've gone through in my absence. Even though he looked as though he hadn't slept for days, my heart fluttered. He was beautiful. I didn't dare touch him, fearing he might just be a dream from which I could wake up any moment.

To convince myself that it wasn't just a dream, I looked around the room and realized we were in a hospital. Bright rays of sunlight were spilling through the windows. The door was closed, and apart from Jett's soft breathing, no other sound disturbed the serenity around us. The pain inside my head made it all feel real, but was it real?

The room was decorated in white and muted yellow. The only splash of color came in the form of a pink calla lily bouquet in a vase on the nightstand. I could smell their faint scent and remembered they were Sylvie's favorite flowers. And then the memories slowly started to pour in. A heavy weight pinning me to the floor. A shot, followed by Jett's face and his arms around my body. People speaking animatedly. Oh, God, and the pain. I realized this couldn't possibly be a dream. I was here—for real—in a hospital bed because Jett had saved me.

Again.

I smiled in spite of the pain shooting through my temples.

Somehow he had found me. We were reunited and the baby—

My heart dropped as more memories began to take shape.

Jett's father. The arrangement. Liz. The rape. The dark-haired guy punching me repeatedly, my head hitting the floor, and the way the other guy plunged a needle into my arm, injecting some drug that rendered me unable to move and eventually unconscious. I swallowed the lump in my throat. Even if my nightmare was over, it wasn't quite over. I had no clue if Liz survived the rape. I didn't know whether my baby survived the beating and whatever happened after that.

Jett had been ready to be a father. Carrying his child inside me and then losing it would feel almost like a betrayal toward him. I had to find out if I was still pregnant, and I had to do it alone, before Jett woke up.

As I moved, I nearly tore out the IV needle stuck in my vein. I winced, and Jett opened his eyes.

"Brooke?" He stood and touched my shoulder gently. "I'm here. Everything's okay."

His eyes assessed me as if he wasn't sure whether I suffered from amnesia and wouldn't remember him. I smiled in spite of the tears trickling down my cheeks. I was overwhelmed. Just seeing him, feeling him, hearing him—when I thought I never would again—was more amazing than I had ever envisioned. I had forgotten how beautiful his eyes were, and the way he awakened butterflies inside my stomach when he just looked at me.

"Oh, God, I'm so sorry," I whispered and let him hug me. "I can't believe you found me." My throat hurt, but I didn't care. "Thanks for coming for me."

"I would never give up on you, you know that." He sat

down on the bed, pulling me with him, and gently kissed my forehead, my temples, the bridge of my nose, the corners of my lips, and finally settled on my lips.

The scent of him, his warm body—everything was overwhelming. It was too good to be true. We rested in each other's arms for a long time. Jett pulled back first and tucked a stray strand of hair behind my ear as he looked deep into my eyes. "I could've been too late, though, in which case I don't know what I would've done."

His words touched me to the point tears began to cloud my vision again. I smiled bitterly. "You would have moved on eventually." I knew my attempt to lighten up the conversation sucked, but I had to give it a shot anyway. "You would have met another girl to replace me."

He laughed darkly. I looked up, surprised.

"You've no idea what you're talking about. Maybe I don't want another girl. When I fell in love with you, I knew I'd love you at your worst. Most of all, I knew you had the power to destroy me in your absence." His dark green eyes probed mine. "You're not just any girl for me, Brooke. You're the only one who matters to me."

"Even if the baby's lost?" I whispered. Admitting it to him was painful, but it was a possibility.

His eyes reflected his emotions as he cupped my face and drew me to him. "The baby's okay, Brooke. I talked with the doctor." His voice trailed off, leaving the magnitude of it hanging between us. I breathed out, relieved, and nodded as Jett continued, "Those men won't hurt you again. They deserved what they got." His serious tone sent a shiver down my spine. I didn't need to ask if they were still alive. I'd heard the gunshots, and I knew what they meant. I didn't even care who shot them. I looked through his eyes into the depths of his soul, and that was enough for me.

"What about Liz?" I asked.

"She'll make it. The nurses put her in room 122."

A dark shadow crossed his features. He was withholding something. I watched him rub the nape of his neck, a habit he had acquired following his father's feigned death, which in turn reminded me Jett still might not know the truth. I almost didn't want to break our moment, but I had to tell him.

"We have to talk, Jett," I began, adding softly, "about your father."

"He's alive. I know." He avoided my gaze. "You told me two days ago."

Two days ago? Had I slept that long?

"My father will pay for what he did to you." A nerve twitched below his left eye. "I promise you he won't harm you again."

"No, Jett." I shook my head vehemently. Strangely, I felt defensive of his father, despite all he had done. Compared to the men, Robert hadn't tried to kill me, but then again, maybe our meeting had been nothing but the stunt of a good liar. "We don't know if it was him. The men who captured me killed his driver before taking me to that building. It wouldn't make sense. Your father wanted me out of your life but promised to keep me safe. He knew about our baby. I don't think he'd break his promise."

Jett nodded, but I could tell by his skeptical expression he wasn't convinced. I was about to recount the meeting with his father when someone knocked, and a physician walked in holding a chart. Jett stood and they both exchanged glances, before the doctor turned to me.

"I see you're awake, Miss Stewart." He stepped closer, and I realized he was young, maybe five or six years older than Jett. "I'm Dr. Barn. How are you feeling?"

"I've been better." I returned his smile hesitantly.

He retrieved a penlight from his pocket and shone the beam into my eyes. "Is your head hurting?"

"A little."

It hurt a lot, but acknowledging it would only alarm Jett.

Dr. Barn pushed the penlight inside the pocket of his robe and checked my vitals. Eventually his attention focused on the chart in his hand.

"You received a blow to the occipital lobe, which is the cause of your headache. Results show no signs of swelling, though. You have no internal bleeding and no signs of trauma." He peered from me to Jett, who hadn't moved from the spot, and then back at me. "Your blood test shows you're pregnant. Were you aware of your condition?"

"Yes." I nodded. "First term."

"It looks like you were lucky, but I would strongly suggest you see your gynecologist upon your release," he said.

"Why?" Jett asked. I took a deep breath and let it out slowly, ignoring the sudden need to groan and slap his arm. I was alive, the baby was okay, Jett and I were reunited. Basically, in spite of the bruises on my arms and the thudding inside my head, I was having the best day of my life. Yet he looked like he was about to strap the physician to a chair and commence an interrogation.

"I'm sure it's just a precaution." I squeezed Jett's arm gently, silently begging him to stop his intimidation tactic, but his intense gaze remained fixed on the doctor, staring the poor man down.

"Well." Dr. Barn shifted uncomfortably as he considered his words. "As far as I can see from the tests we've run, nothing's wrong, but of course the drugs—even the brief exposure—*could* have influenced fetal development. The chance of damage is possible but minimal. To know for sure, we strongly suggest regular checkups." He let out a breath, as though he had been holding it.

"Thank you, Dr. Barn." I shot Jett a confident smile. His face remained a stony mask.

Intense.

Possessive.

Overprotective.

My smile widened at the words my brain chose to describe Jett. Even though he drove me crazy at times, I was thankful for the fact he never gave up. It was one of the many things I loved about him.

"You're welcome." Dr. Barn shook my hand and then turned to Jett. "She'll be released today. Take her home, and make sure she sleeps off the headache. Brian is expecting you tonight. Same place as usual."

There was something strange in the way the doctor's tone had become more intimate, not to mention it was an odd thing to say. Besides, the name "Brian" rang familiar. And then I remembered someone had shouted it before I blacked out.

Dr. Barn wished me well and left.

"What was he talking about when he said Brian would be waiting for you? *What* place?" I asked as soon as the door closed.

"Long story." Jett sighed and dropped into the recliner, facing me with an expression that told me he wasn't keen on elucidating.

I inclined my head, my eyes matching his stubbornness.

"You're lucky I have all the time in the world, Mayfield. So start spilling."

"Sam—Dr. Barn—and I go way back. He's the only doctor I trust, which is why I brought you here." He gestured around him. "It's his private clinic, where no one would find you." His eyes shimmered with hesitation, signaling there was more than he let on.

"Okay, but who's Brian? What does this have to do with Sam?"

Jett remained silent. I wasn't going to drop it, and he knew it. Finally, he caved in.

"When Kenny couldn't track your GPS, we had no other choice but to ask my old gang for help to find your whereabouts."

My eyes widened. I opened my mouth to ask the million questions ambushing my mind like wildfire, but Jett's fingers pressed against my lips, stopping me. "It was the only way. Either that or giving up. So I struck a deal with Brian, the leader."

"What deal?" I whispered.

"That I return." He looked away, hesitating.

I took a deep breath, and then another, unable to speak. I remembered the few stories he had told me and knew that part of his life hadn't been a pleasant experience. After he had left, he had vowed to never return. Now he would— because of me.

"I did what I had to do, Brooke. It was the only way to find you. Do you understand?" He took my hands in his, his eyes meeting mine. "Right now you're not safe. It's only a matter of time until whoever's responsible for your abduction finds you. Hiding with the people I once trusted is the only way I can be sure no one will find you, until I can take care of everything. So tonight I'm fulfilling part of the deal." He ran a fingertip across my cheek and let out a deep breath. "There's going to be a race. Brian wants to see whether I still have what it takes. Whether I'm worthy of his crew. It's part of the deal."

"I don't like it," I whispered

"Me, neither." He smiled. "But that's not important. I don't care about anyone but you, and for you I'd do anything. Going back is worth whatever Brian will put me through to earn his trust back." His expression softened, but he couldn't hide the glint of anger in his eyes. "If we'd lost the baby, I'd have mourned. But your loss would have broken me into pieces. It would have been even worse than you walking away or finding out that my father tricked us. I would've ripped apart everything and everyone, even though it wouldn't have stopped the pain. I'd hunt down anyone responsible for hurting you. And that's exactly what I'm going to do. With the right resources at my disposal, I'll let them bleed to death slowly." He looked so resolute I knew there was no point in arguing.

Jett bent forward and kissed me. "Now, I want you to tell me everything, Brooke. I want to know exactly what happened." His gaze glinted with fury. "I'll make them all pay. I promise. There's no way in hell I'll let you down again. I won't repeat that mistake. No matter what."

You didn't let me down, I wanted to whisper, but didn't because his impatience and urgency were clear. And for a change, I was ready to listen to his reasoning and follow his plans rather than mine.

20

WE STAYED IN the hospital until late afternoon. Jett ordered lunch while I took a shower, visited Liz, and then joined him dressed in the jeans and shirt Sylvie had brought the day before. Jett insisted that I eat first. Given that I looked like shit, with dark circles beneath my eyes, and purple bruises on my body, I didn't argue.

I sat down at the tiny table and ate in silence, after which I took the painkillers a nurse brought in, even though my headache had slowly begun to clear. And then we talked for two hours straight, during which I recalled the pertinent: the day Sylvie found the book and disk, how I met his father, the car-jacking, and then finally the building. The smell of excrement and dirt lingered at the back of my mind, and for a moment it took me all my might not to break down. Jett listened quietly, his fingers clenching until the white of his knuckles shimmered through his skin when I described the three men and what they did to Liz and me.

As more memories started to flood my mind, I realized I had forgotten one very important thing that happened to me on the first day.

Danny.

How the hell could I forget about him?

Maybe my mind had the bizarre ability to erase him or I was suffering from selective memory, as if forgetting was the only coping mechanism it knew to stop me from thinking of my sister. Like someone living their entire existence in darkness and one day experiencing light for the first time, I felt the raw pain, but I couldn't evade it. So I started to remember all the things I'd rather forget again.

"There's more," I whispered. My hands were shaking so badly I had to hide them under the tablecloth as anger rippled through me. "I saw Danny. He's working for them."

Jett's eyes flickered and a flash of recognition crossed his face. I didn't need to elaborate because he knew the person who frequented my nightmares, even though they had never met.

"The guy responsible for Jenna's death." It wasn't a question but a statement. "The one who walked free and whose friends threatened you."

I nodded, unable to look straight at him. "After all those years, it was the last place I thought I'd find him."

Jett's eyes narrowed. "Was he one of the three?"

"If you mean to ask whether he was shot, no. I only saw him once—the day I arrived. He's a supplier but doesn't participate in—" I trailed off, unable to speak the terrifying truth.

"Did he touch you?" His brow creased. Even though I couldn't tell whether with worry or anger, the dangerous glint in his eyes didn't escape me. I remembered the way Danny had slapped me. It had hurt, but it was nothing compared to the pain he had inflicted upon me by talking about my sister the way he had. Would Jett understand? Probably. But this wasn't the time to burden him. He had enough on his plate already.

"It doesn't matter. That's not why I'm telling you this." I cast my eyes down to hide the shame and humiliation burning inside me. My throat tightened with hate for Danny, which brought on more shame. I hated the men who hurt Liz, but the hate I felt for Danny was different.

It consumed me.

I'd never forget his words. His face. That he seemed to think he was untouchable.

Another flicker of anger crossed Jett's face. He took my hand in his and his thumb began to draw circles on my skin, encouraging me. I cleared my throat.

"Danny said he would've walked free regardless. That it wouldn't have mattered if I had testified or found proof.

Somehow, I believe him, Jett. I believe he was protected by the club."

"We'll see about that." Jett's eyes resembled a charge of force with so much power and determination I knew that if the opportunity presented itself, he wouldn't hesitate to hurt Danny. I had seen the scars under his tattoo on and beneath his upper arm, and they surely hadn't magically appeared. He'd fight for me. And I didn't want that. The risk of him getting hurt was too big—a risk I'd never take. I felt a glimmer of hope in knowing that I was safe with Jett and wished I had trusted him instead of taking off, but at the same time I feared for his safety, now more than ever.

Jett's eyes glazed over as if his thoughts were far away. I decided to change the topic and ask him the one question that had lingered on my mind since I woke up.

"Jett?" I touched his arm to draw his attention back to me. "How did you find me?"

He pushed his chair closer to me until his leg brushed my jeans. "We checked the surveillance cameras in the garage and saw that you were dragged out of the car into a van. The license plate's registered to an old lady outside the state, so I figured it must be fake, like the one in Italy. We went to Brian, and he put us in touch with the guy who creates the best fake license plates in the state." He paused, and I leaned forward, interested. "Turns out he issued the plates a few weeks ago to a guy known for doing the odd driver job, and not of the legal kind."

"You tracked him down, didn't you?" I didn't know whether to be mortified or thankful.

"Yeah. We beat the crap out of him to find out your whereabouts." Jett smirked. "Let's just say it took us several hours to get him talking and find out where he brought you. He was a tough SOB, I have to give him that."

"That's—" All words failed me.

He cocked a brow. "Impressive?"

"I wanted to say 'scary' but yeah, 'impressive' will do." I laughed, figuring Jett definitely deserved the praise for his ego after all he'd done for me. "What about your father's driver?"

"He's dead, baby," Jett said calmly. "We found him inside the van. They didn't get to dispose of the body."

There was no "probably," no "maybe," just a definite answer. I didn't know the guy, but for some reason I thought he didn't deserve his fate.

"I don't understand why they had to kill him."

"I know you have this huge heart and tend to feel guilty a lot. But don't. It's not your fault." Jett kissed my palm gently. "They want the book, just like my father, and they'll do anything to get it."

Maybe.

I hesitated, unconvinced.

"What?" Jett probed.

"They never asked for it," I said. Worry set in as I realized I had no idea where the book was. "I gave it to the driver. It was still in the car when the van hit us."

"I know. We also found your handbag and a briefcase," he said and shook his head. "They were amateurs. Professionals would never have closed the car doors and driven off, leaving behind evidence. Like Sam said, we were lucky."

I smiled. Yes, we were, indeed. Would we be next time? I didn't know, but I was sure I wouldn't get myself into such a mess again.

"Sylvie brought the disk," Jett said.

"Thank God," I mumbled. I had been so stupid to risk that piece of evidence by sending it via snail mail. What the hell had I been thinking? I thought Jett didn't hear me, but his lips twitched.

"Are you singing heavenly praise because the disk arrived safely or because Sylvie and I worked together?"

"No!" My jaw dropped. "You did? So you've tamed the dragon?" Sylvie had made it perfectly clear she wouldn't forgive Jett for the few days of heartache he had caused me, while deep in my heart, I honestly hoped they'd be friends one day.

"She's a tough one. Anyway—" He grimaced, and his electric green gaze bored into me. The serious undertones in his voice made me fear the question before it came. "I have to ask you something and I want you to be honest with me."

My heart started to hammer hard against my ribcage. I wasn't terrified of him, but the thought of whatever was going on in his mind was frightening in the word's truest sense.

"Why did you run, Brooke?" he asked, quietly.

"Because I—" Struggling for words, I moistened my lips.

"My father offered you a deal?" At my shocked expression, he smirked. "Yeah, you talked in your sleep, and we found the briefcase. It was open."

I realized I had never closed it because we were car-jacked, meaning he must have found the fake passport, the cash, and the bank account statement. A terrible thought occurred to me—that he might think material gain was more important to me than our relationship.

"I never wanted his money, Jett. He threatened to hurt Sylvie and everyone else in my life. I feared for them," I said, slowly. "For you."

He nodded but took his time to reply. "I wish you had trusted me enough to tell me rather than run away. I could've taken care of it."

"I know, and I'm sorry."

His fingers kept stroking my hand, and I relaxed against his touch. "For what it's worth, even after finding the briefcase I didn't believe you'd take off because of two mill."

"Why?"

"One of my father's club buddies showed up at my office to invite me to some party," Jett said.

"Of course. How nice of him," I said, dryly.

"My point is that after he stopped by, I called Sylvie," Jett said. "After she told me what happened, I knew someone must've come after the book. In return, I figured it must be the reason why you had been acting strange and wanted to break up with me."

I raised my eyebrows, and Jett laughed out loud. "I'm sorry, baby, but I didn't believe you when you said you wanted to break up with me."

My lips twitched. "You have a big ego, you know that?"

"I never said I'm perfect, and I can give you two examples." He paused to think.

Wow, only two?

"First, I was wrong, Brooke," he said. "The book is not a hit list. I still have to figure out what the names and numbers are all about, but we didn't get the chance to skim through the hard drive's contents. And second, I never apologized."

I narrowed my eyes. "For what?"

"You always asked what the big deal was about this club. I told you that it's a gathering that caters to those looking for extreme sexual encounters," Jett said, slowly. "What I left out is that some members kidnap and drug women to rape them." He took a deep breath and let it out slowly— almost as if the secret had been too heavy to carry, and he was relieved to share it with me. "According to my father's account, some members are pretty harmless, but a few thrive on power. They prey on fear." I opened my mouth to speak but he held up a hand, stopping me. "I wasn't proud of my father being part of it, and I was too ashamed to tell you."

"You don't have to apologize. Even if you had told me, it wouldn't have stopped them from—" I stopped because the shock sat deep.

Getting me.

Such a stupid mistake to think I could have taken care of it myself. I pushed my thoughts to the back of my mind, where I couldn't reach them and ponder over the past.

Jett interlaced his fingers with mine and for a moment I stared at them, admiring the beauty of his hands. Strong hands. Capable.

"I'll have to admit it was a bold move, Brooke. Sending the disk in an envelope, that is," he whispered. I could tell he was trying to ease the tension by being playful. I decided to play along.

"You taught me bold well."

His lips twitched with amusement. "Good. Then you're

ready for step two."

"Which is?" I raised my brows. We were back to our playful nature, how things used to be…and I loved it.

"Living fast and dangerous. Since we're staying with the gang for a while, you'd better get used to living in the fast lane, Miss Stewart."

After what I'd gone through, I could handle whatever life threw my way. Joining his gang seemed to be the least of our troubles.

"When are we leaving?" I asked.

"You're in? Just like that?" He seemed surprised.

"Why not?" I jutted my chin out. "Your old gang can't possibly be worse than your father's club. No offence."

"None taken." A glint of amusement lit up his eyes. "Let me guess, you're thinking a few boys hanging out, drinking bears, talking about their 'biaches.'"

Had I been that obvious?

I rolled my eyes. "I know they're carrying guns and stuff."

He laughed, the delicate skin beneath his eyes crinkling, and for the first time I couldn't help but think how stupid I had been to leave him. No day would've been complete without him.

"I've got to warn you, Brooke. They're insane. I hope I won't have to tell you twice." His eyes never left mine as he lifted my hand to his mouth. I watched him kiss the tip of my fingers—slow and sensual, the motion strangely arousing.

"Insane...how?" I asked, a little short of breath. The temperature was soaring, and surely not because someone had turned up the heating.

His soft touch trailing up my arm sent a shiver through me. There was nothing more delicious than the mix of shock, lust, and the vibe of mystery and possible danger.

Yep, Jett was definitely rubbing off on me.

The possibility of seeing his bad boy past for the first time was like an aphrodisiac.

"You'll find out tonight." He gave me a wry smile. "If anything goes wrong, we're leaving. Deal?" I nodded, wide-eyed, and his voice softened. "I want you to know that if you fall, I'll fall. You belong with me, and everything we do, we're doing together."

"What about Liz?" I couldn't just go and leave her behind without protection. Not that I was much protection, but still.

"She'll be fine." Jett smiled gently as he cupped my face and kissed me, his lips barely brushing mine. His breath smelled of chocolate and coffee. Together with his mouth, it was a heady combination. "She'll be staying at the clinic for a few more days until we find the right place for her to stay. Sam Barn will take care of her even though I don't think she's the club's target, but you never know."

21

AS UNCOMFORTABLE AS I felt at the prospect of leaving the safety of the private hospital behind, I also felt a strong urgency to get back to normality. Jett's silence during the drive stifled some of my enthusiasm, though, replacing it with the growing awareness that I was about to find out more about his past.

The good, the bad, and the scary. Or maybe the sexy.

The sun was streaking the sky in shades of orange and copper when we finally left the highway and turned toward what looked like an industrial estate with warehouses. The car skidded to a halt in front of a high barbed-wire fence, behind which I could see a string of buildings. It wasn't at all how I imagined the place to be. The three-story warehouses built a cluster of rundown walls that seemed abandoned. The yard looked deserted und unkempt. And some windows were smashed in. I would've doubted Jett had the right address, were it not for the high-tech security cameras at the top of the fence, their tiny black lenses flickering. I peered into one, unable to shake off the feeling that I was being watched.

We reached a gate with an intercom. I almost expected Jett to press a button and the gate to open, but instead a tall guy with the arms of a bodybuilder appeared from somewhere to our right. He nodded at Jett and opened the gate to let us through, his glance a mixture of mistrust and resentment.

"Do you know him?" I asked as we drove through the gate into a yard the size of a football field.

"Yeah." Jett stared ahead, his hands clutching at the steering wheel so tightly I feared it might snap in two. Maybe he had personal issues with the guard, in which case it was none of my business.

Jett navigated to the back, and I realized the buildings were arranged in a "U" shape with a strip the size of a two-car lane in between and with parking spaces on either side. Some of the parked cars looked just like mine at home: old and battered. I counted them: twenty-three. Jett pulled into an empty space near the front and killed the engine.

"Why are there so many cars?" I asked.

"They're waiting for us," Jett said gravely. "Ready?"

I nodded, and we exited. Walking past the first two

buildings, I scanned the dark windows. Movement on the rooftop caught my attention, and I craned my neck to get a better view. Something—I guessed a piece of fabric—fluttered in the evening breeze. Someone was up there, no doubt about it.

"Don't look, Brooke," Jett said. "This is their territory, and we have to show respect. They don't take snooping around kindly."

"But you said they're expecting us."

He nodded, the movement of his head barely noticeable. "They are. But there are rules."

I turned back to Jett but kept watching the buildings from the periphery of my vision. Jett did the same—I could tell from the way his eyes scanned the area without him turning his head.

"Do they have anything to hide that they keep guards?" I whispered.

"They all do."

I waited for Jett to elaborate. He kept quiet. From the corner of my eyes I caught someone on the rooftop signaling something.

"They're being careful," Jett said eventually. "There's a lot of rivalry going on."

Rival gangs—I knew the stories from newspapers, though they always seemed to belong to a different world. Being here made it all seem real, and scarier than I imagined.

Jett stopped in front of the fourth building. I looked up at the dirty windows. Behind them stretched darkness. No movement. No light. No life. Just shabby old walls in dire need of renovation.

"Are you sure we're at the right place?" I asked. "It doesn't look like anybody could possibly live in here."

Jett shot me a sarcastic smile but didn't comment. Instead he said, "The people you're about to meet used to be my friends. Some of them still are, but don't trust them until I say so."

"Why's that?"

"I broke a few rules."

"Some rules are meant to be broken," I said.

"I'm not sure about that." Grimacing, he opened the door and, pressing his hand against the small of my back, he guided me inside. It was one of his overprotective gestures—a gesture that was both meant to mark his territory and keep me close. I snorted inwardly. Like anyone would start hitting on me when they had more pressing issues to deal with.

We walked through a large empty hall and reached a staircase. Hushed voices carried over from downstairs. Jett instructed me to keep quiet as we headed for them, a million questions circling through my mind.

"We're down here," a male voice echoed. Jett gave me a

knowing look and tilted his head to the left. Only then did I notice the security camera and intercom installed in the wall.

We climbed down the last flight of stairs and reached what I believed to be the basement. It was freezing cold and dark; the air smelled of chemicals. With sure steps, Jett led me through a corridor, and we turned another corner before we finally reached an open space with a bar and sitting opportunities.

At least forty people had gathered—most of them male. The moment we appeared all conversations stopped, or maybe it felt like it because it all seemed so quiet and tense. I scanned the accusatory faces and noticed Sylvie and Kenny among them. She waved at me, and I fought the urge to wave back. This was Jett's world. To fit in, I had to behave accordingly. My heart dropped when I noticed some of the people carried weapons.

We were intruders.

They didn't like intruders.

In fact, with their hard stares they looked as if they didn't like anyone. Period.

Jett let go of my hand and motioned for me to stay. At the same time, a guy stepped forward. He wore a snug, short-sleeved shirt—the kind that did nothing to hide his strong, tattooed arms. But that's not why I stared. On his left arm, reaching up to his neck, he carried the same tattoo as Jett.

"Never thought I'd live to see the day you came back, bro. That took guts." His voice sounded strangely familiar, and then it dawned on me. He was the one who had called out to Jett right before gunshots rippled through the air and Jett rescued me.

Brian. That was his name.

Jett snorted. "Neither did I."

"Is that your girl?" Brian inclined his head toward me, his gaze scanning me up and down and lingering a bit too long on the bruises on my neck.

"Yeah. Brooke." Jett's answer was barely more than an irritated grunt.

"Does she know the rules?"

I frowned. What rules? Jett hadn't clued me in on any rules.

"None of your concern," Jett replied. Yet another irritated grunt, and I realized I was seeing a new side to him.

"Just asking." Brian raised his hands in defense before he turned to me, a smile on his lips. "Come closer."

"Stay where you are, Brooke," Jett commanded. His irritation was now replaced by annoyance. I decided to listen and didn't move from the spot.

Brian laughed. "Protective of her, huh? What do you think I'd do? If I wanted to touch her, I would have done so already." His eyes wandered back to me. "I'm not that kind of guy, right?" He was enjoying the show because he loved being in control. He liked to be the center of attention. I could tell that much from the way his attention kept shifting between me and his friends, as though he sought to be admired for his show.

"You know, I've been thinking," Brian said to no one in particular. "During the race I want her to ride with you."

"Come on, man. Leave her out of this," someone shouted from the back. My head turned in the voice's direction. It was Kenny.

"It's either my way, or nothing," Brian said, ignoring him. His voice carried a warning that sent a chill down my spine. The room fell silent. Some began to nod, and more joined in.

Mob mentality.

If Brian snapped, others would follow. I didn't like that, not least because many carried weapons and made no secret of it. The cave of my mouth went dry.

"She stays," Jett said. "It wasn't part of our arrangement."

"You think you can march in and make demands?" Brian stepped forward and stopped barely a few inches from Jett. "When I helped you find her, I settled my debt. Now we're even. Seeing that you need my help to hide her ass, you either bend to my rules or you get the fuck out."

"I'm not risking her life."

Brian shrugged and squeezed his hands inside his pockets. "Too bad." He turned to his friends and tilted his head toward Jett and me, which I assumed was his way of instructing them to throw us out. Jett walked back to me, his hand clasping mine.

"I'm in," I said to Brian. The room fell silent, and countless gazes focused on me. Were it not for the surreality of the situation, I would've applauded myself for faking the kind of confidence I didn't have.

"No, you're not," Jett hissed. I whipped my hand away from him.

"This is my decision," I said, emphasizing each word. With a glance back at Brian, I repeated, "Like I said, I'm in."

Our eyes met.

"Brave!" Brian nodded once, though I couldn't tell whether he was impressed or just mocking me. He walked over slowly, his blue eyes piercing mine as he looked at me for what seemed like an eternity, probably waiting for me to change my mind. When I didn't, the tension in his face eased just enough to signal me I had almost won whatever battle he was fighting. "Sam said you were discharged from the hospital earlier today. Are you sure you want to drive with Jett?"

"No, Brooke," Jett said. I ignored him.

"I'm certain. It wouldn't be the first time I saw Jett race.

He's the best."

Brian smiled, but it wasn't humor I saw in his eyes; I could swear it was surprise, with just a little hint of respect.

"We'll get on well." At last he broke eye contact and addressed the guys around us. "You heard her. What are you waiting for? Help them get started."

The crowd broke. Jett stared at me accusingly with a look that said *what the fuck?* I shrugged and shot him my most confident smile, even though I didn't feel particularly confident. Truth be told, I had only seen him race once—back in Italy—and it wasn't so much of a race but a fight between life and death. Even then, I had been scared out of my mind and couldn't get out of the car fast enough.

I was led off into the adjacent hall, leaving Jett with Brian.

You're doing great, Stewart.

So far no one had seen through my blatant pretense. I convinced myself that it was the right choice. The only choice we had. Jett needed my support, and I would sit with him to show it. I had to establish my place just as he would establish his, because it was the only place where we could hide.

22

WHAT I HAD thought to be the basement was an open space too large to belong to just one warehouse. I assumed they were all connected, making it one giant subterranean maze. As we passed through another hall, I noticed training areas complete with numerous punching bags, weight-lifting machines, four full-sized boxing rings, and various training equipment. Jett had told me this was where he learned to fight. A smile spread across my lips as I imagined him working out all sweaty—his strong biceps flexing as he punched a punching bag. How hot was that? If we stayed for a while, maybe I could get him to work out—not that he needed it. His body was nothing but perfection. His scars, the tattoo on his shoulder, his sinfully dark green eyes—he was nothing but a god to me. However, I wanted to see this perfection in action.

The picture of us lying on the red training mattress flickered inside my mind, his sweaty hot body making love to me on the hard floor. A pang of heat gathered between my legs as I imagined all the naughty things I'd do with him. To him. Let him do to me.

Someone touched my arm, pulling me out of my daydreams. I looked up at a young woman about my age, and she pointed to a door on the left.

"Get dressed. The changing rooms are through there. When you're done, meet me outside." She pointed to another door. "Everyone's waiting, so don't take too long."

"Where's Jett?" I asked.

"You'll see your *boyfriend* soon enough."

Figuring she might need some time to warm up to me, I ignored her snide remark and shot her a friendly smile. Until I realized she might be an ex, in which case she'd never warm up to me—or I to her.

I could feel her interested gaze on my back as I headed for the changing rooms. I closed the door behind me and pressed my body against the smooth wood. I closed my eyes, fighting the urge to sit on the floor and never come out again. In all honesty, I didn't do hostility well—especially when it involved a large group of armed people. In fact, if I could hide from it forever, I would. But as a highly supportive girlfriend, that wasn't an option.

"Hey."

I opened my eyes to the voice startling me and realized it was Sylvie and Kenny. She jumped up from a bench and wrapped her arms around me.

"You've no idea how worried I was when Jett said you were gone," Sylvie said. "My first thought was that you broke up with him then went undercover to hide, which is understandable, given the fact that he can be a bit of a—"

"Sylvie," I cut her off. "What are you doing here?"

She waved her hand and laughed. "Apparently, Jett being here is a huge deal, so Kenny dragged me along. Anyway, your disappearing act was more scary than everything we went through back in Italy."

I smirked. She hadn't even seen half of it. Like the car chase up the mountain. How the heck was I supposed to stay calm, living and breathing, during another one of those?

"You were close enough," I said. "I broke up with him."

"You did?"

"When someone's threatening you, you don't really have a choice," I said. "Thanks for telling him about the book." I let go of her and turned to Kenny, who had been standing like Sylvie's shadow in the background. "And thanks for helping out, Kenny."

"I'm glad you're okay." He squeezed his hands into his pockets and exchanged a strange look with Sylvie. I didn't need to be told how I looked to others. The small purple bruise just above my left eyelid and more bruises around my neck said it all. And there was the fact that Sylvie had seen me in the hospital, while I was sedated and out of it.

"Are you really okay to race with Jett, Brooke?" she asked. "You were discharged from the hospital after just two days."

And you don't look okay.

The words lingered in the air, unspoken.

I smiled reassuringly, even though I was slowly beginning to doubt the sanity of the idea.

"I'm fine. The baby's fine. Those are nothing." I pointed at my bruises, evading her worried gaze. It was the truth. A few bruises didn't bother me when I had more important things to worry about. "Stop looking at me like I'm a victim, because I'm not. I got myself into that situation, and now it's my choice to ride with Jett. And just so you know, I didn't go down without a fight."

"I never doubted that," Sylvie whispered.

Were those tears in her eyes? Because Sylvie almost never cried, which could only mean I had caused her the shock of a lifetime.

Squeezing her hand, I looked around. On the far east side was a long rack with auto racing suits in various colors and sizes. Two benches and a table lined the opposite wall. Stacked on top of the table were several cardboard boxes. The lockers were straight ahead. I walked over. Jett's name was on the third one from left. My fingertips brushed over the faded handwriting—Jett's handwriting, which I'd recognize anywhere because it always looked hurried, as though he never had time to lose, and yet so poised and elegant.

"We never saw it coming," Kenny said behind me.

"What?"

"That he'd leave his friends. It might be hard to imagine, but this is the place where Jett grew as a person. The place he called home."

"Why did Brian ask him to race, then?" I turned to face him.

"It's tradition." His tone was defensive.

"Sounds personal to me," I muttered.

"I'm with Brooke," Sylvie said. "Besides, why would they allow her to race in her condition? It's not like she wants to join."

"To them, Jett is a changed man. He grew up rich, but after joining us he proved his worth. He was happy with who he was." Kenny's eyes fixed on me, his expression torn. "Everyone knew he despised his father and that we were his family. His choice to leave the gang in favor of his father's company came as a shock to us."

"Us?" I frowned and crossed my arms. "I thought you left with him."

"I didn't," he said, slowly. "We stayed friends."

"You helped him without Brian's knowing?"

"Yes." His reply was barely more than a whisper. "No one knows, and it's better if it stays that way. They think he came to Brian alone, when in fact Jett and I have been in touch for years. We both have built our careers benefiting from each other's help."

"Wow," Sylvie whispered. "Emotional stuff."

Either she was being sarcastic or genuinely touched—with her, it could go either way. Kenny smiled at her and checked his watch. "Let's get started." He walked over to the rack with the suits and began to comb through them. I could tell from his stony expression that he was hiding something. As much as I wanted to ask why the others never kept in touch with Jett, I didn't.

Kenny picked a suit and handed it to me.

"Now listen, today's a test," he began. "Not for you, but for Jett to see if he's gone all soft. They want to see if he still has what it takes. The best you can do is keep quiet and trust what he's doing, because Jett—" he drew in a deep breath and let it out slowly "—was our best driver, and many of us want him back."

There was more to the story. It was all over Kenny's face. It was in his eyes and the way he considered his words carefully.

"What happened?" Sylvie asked, as though reading my mind.

Kenny pointed to a box on the table. "Make sure you wear gloves, just in case."

It was an obvious maneuver to avoid answering Sylvie's question. I decided to rephrase.

"What if he wins and we stay? Will there be any problems?" I asked.

"After what happened, maybe," Kenny said. "Better ask Jett."

I bit my lip, wondering what he meant. So much of Jett's past was in the dark, and while it didn't bother me because I knew he'd open up to me eventually, I sensed the magnitude of the situation.

"You have five minutes left," Kenny said and then walked out, leaving Sylvie and me alone. In the privacy of the room, my walls of confidence began to crumble.

"This is such a mess. What if we lose?" I whispered.

She clicked her tongue and sat down beside me. "Back in Italy you said he was good."

"We were chased and made it out alive. Everything is a big blur infused by panic." I shuddered as I remembered the winding mountain roads. "I was scared out of my mind, Sylvie, and can't remember much. This is different, but just as scary. God knows I hate when people speed, particularly when I'm inside the vehicle."

"Is it strange that I have faith in him?" Sylvie asked. "I know he wouldn't do anything reckless and risk your life."

I didn't know if her words were meant to reassure me, or if she meant them. It didn't matter either way.

"Thanks. But I'm not worried about Jett doing anything reckless," I admitted. "I'm worried that if we lose, he won't be able to accept failure."

I could see my own fear reflected in Sylvie's eyes. Truth be told, I had never seen Jett losing at anything. So how would he deal with it?

"Just believe in him, Brooke," Sylvie whispered.

"You're right," I replied. "What's the big deal, anyway? It's probably just a stupid race on some training ground, right?"

"I have no clue." She checked her watch. "But Kenny said you have only five minutes left, so get dressed before someone barges in here and drags you out there. That Brian guy looks like he's capable of it."

"He does, doesn't he?" I closed the door behind her and changed into the suit. It was loose on me, but not to the point of being unwearable. I grabbed some gloves, and left the sanctuary of the changing rooms.

The woman from before wasn't outside, but the door to my left was open and animated voices carried over from inside. I walked in and stopped in my tracks. In front of us were eight sports cars, four on each side—the kind of vehicles I only knew from car magazines. My jaw almost dropped as my eyes swept over one luxury model after another. They looked like they had just been imported from the manufacturer, and if it wasn't for their registration numbers, I would have believed they were.

Some of the drivers had already taken their places behind the wheel. Jett hadn't arrived yet, and the agitated murmurs showed his arrival was highly anticipated.

I spied Brian leaning against a shiny blue Ferrari, and he smiled when our eyes connected. His confidence was overpowering, and while he wasn't my type, I couldn't help but be aware of his masculinity from the way his probing glance lingered on me. He was assessing me, probably wondering why Jett would return for me to the place he once left. I raised my chin and smiled back. But it was a cold smile, one that was supposed to say, *You don't know me, and you'll never figure me out.*

The door opened, and Jett entered trailed by a dark skinned guy. The room fell silent. Like me, he was dressed in a black racing suit. I had no idea when or where he had changed, but he looked so hot my knees turned weak in spite of my better judgment. The fabric sat snug around his broad shoulders and narrow hips. The zipper at the front wasn't fully zipped up, revealing a bronze patch of skin just below his neck. I fought the urge to rise on my toes and place a kiss on it just to see whether he tasted as delicious as he looked.

His gaze barely brushed me as he inched closer. I knew

when he was angry—and right now he was fuming.

Brian threw Jett the keys, and Jett caught them in midair.

"We kept your baby. Thought you might feel more at home," Brian said. "If you need time, you know, to check your tires or whatever, let me know and I'll tell Doug."

"No need. My guys know how I like her," Jett said.

Her?

His car was a "she"?

What did you expect, Stewart?

I suppressed the urge to smile. It was a male thing—like getting all worked up about a bunch of guys running across a football field for hours—but the knowledge didn't make it less sexy.

Jett's fingers settled firmly on my lower back as he guided me to the dark red sports car to our left. He opened the passenger door and motioned for me to get in. I followed his unspoken command and watched him drop into the driver's seat, then fasten his seatbelt.

Engines began to roar, and the crowd dissipated. The wall opposite from us shifted and slowly opened, giving a view of the street and the parking lots. Most of the people got into their cars, and I realized they were spectators.

Jett pushed the key into the ignition and turned on the engine, then drove outside slowly, past the parked vehicles and onto the main road. Hundreds of questions swirled around in my head. Who was Doug? Was he the guy who'd be racing against Jett? Where were we heading, and what exactly was going to happen?

I stole a glance at Jett. His eyes were focused on the road, and I decided to postpone my interrogation. His strained expression worried me even more than not knowing what to expect.

In the rearview mirror, I saw several cars trailing us. Jett changed lanes. A blue car cut in front of the others and drove next to us. I didn't need to look at the driver to know it was Brian. Jett's foot remained on the accelerator, and for a moment I thought he wouldn't let Brian pass. And then our car slowed down, and Brian cut in front of us, and his taillights blinked once.

He was mocking us. Putting on a show.

Seemingly unaffected, Jett followed the blue Ferrari at a leisurely speed to God knows where.

23

THROUGHOUT THE DRIVE Jett kept quiet, and I didn't speak in case he was tapping into his inner powers, or planning his strategy, or whatever professional drivers did. It was only after we'd left the city behind that Jett broke the silence.

"Why did you have to intervene, Brooke?" His voice was calm but angry.

Holy cow.

That hint of a southern accent of his was even more sexy when he was angry.

So he had been giving me the silent treatment. I raised my chin defiantly and turned to look at him. The way his elbow rested against the window and his other hand was relaxed on the steering wheel, he gave the impression of being bored—were it not for the pulsing nerve in his temple and the way his eyes stared ahead at Brian's taillights.

"We need to hide somewhere," I stated the obvious.

"Fuck, Brooke. You have no idea how dangerous this is." All the anger he been hiding seeped through— gradually, like a rivulet turning into a river. "Brian and I had an arrangement. If Brian wanted to bend the situation, to hell with that!" His fingers clenched at the steering wheel until his knuckles shimmered white beneath his bronze skin. "This is exactly what I've been trying to avoid. I had it under control until you intervened."

Talk about accusing.

His sudden need to play the blame game made me angry.

"It didn't look like you had anything under control," I said quietly. "It looked like you were about to get us kicked out."

He pressed his lips in a tight line. Had I gone too far? I didn't care.

"What did you expect, Jett? That you could come back and pretend you never left them?" His silence told me that I had hit a soft spot.

"I've no idea what the big deal with you guys is, but they don't trust you, just like you don't trust them," I continued, softer. "But they want you back."

"Who told you?" he asked. I met his glance before he

turned his eyes back on the road.

"Kenny. And the fact that they kept your car and the name on your locker."

He nodded, nonchalant.

"There's something I haven't told you about my past." The ominous tone in his voice sent a chill down my spine. I straightened in my seat and turned to him until the seatbelt tightened around me. "There's a reason Brian wants me to race. Last time I did, there was an accident and somebody got killed. It was the reason why I left. Did Kenny tell you that, too?"

My heart dropped in my chest.

Holy shit.

Someone died?

"No," I murmured. "We didn't have much time to talk."

"Or he left it out on purpose."

I held my breath as I waited for him to go on and explain, but when Jett didn't continue, I realized he wasn't going to say more.

Either he *still* wasn't ready to disclose the whole story, or he didn't want to be distracted. The past was nothing but a shadow with the ability to create emotional upheaval. Maybe Jett didn't want to talk about it because it was too upsetting. I made a mental reminder to ask him later—if we survived the race—and decided to change the subject.

"Where are we going?"

"I don't know," Jett said, flatly. "Brian chooses the location."

For a few minutes we drove in silence. Finally, Brian's brake lights lit up and the vehicle slowed down to take a right onto open terrain. We stopped—in the middle of nowhere. Jett's face was emotionless as he switched off the engine and we exited the car. A half dozen other vehicles followed and parked behind us. I was sure more would arrive soon.

The moon hid behind thick rainclouds that promised a heavy shower. The only light came from Brian's taillights. A gust of wind whipped my hair against my face. I wrapped my arms around me as I watched the scene unfold.

This is it.

I didn't need to ask. My gut feeling told me.

Jett's face remained an impenetrable mask as we waited for the games to begin.

"How does this work?" I whispered.

"Three rounds with various checkpoints to make sure no one's bluffing," Jett whispered back. "The first round's always bumpy. The second is all about speed. The third's unpredictable. Whoever makes it back first wins. That's about it."

I nodded, even though I hadn't caught half of what he said. Judging from the tense lines around his mouth, he was nervous. I didn't like it, because Jett was never nervous.

A guy approached and began to talk so fast I barely caught more than a few words. Something about speed points and variation in road conditions. And then he departed again, and Jett opened my car door so I could enter.

"Hey, Jett, good luck, man," someone yelled before Jett slammed the door and I felt suffocated by the smell of the expensive leather seats and blinded by the dashboard lights I would have admired under different circumstances.

Slumping into his seat, Jett closed the door and leaned forward to whisper in my ear, his fingers fastening my seatbelt. "If we crash or the car flips, you try to get out as soon as you can."

He opened the passenger seat drawer and showed me a safety emergency hammer. "If the door's stuck, smash in the windows. Under no circumstances stay inside, or near the car. Do you understand? You have exactly twenty seconds to leave. Now repeat."

His eyes probed mine with an intensity that scared me.

"If anything happens, I'll get out of the car as soon as possible."

He nodded.

But how could I possibly leave him inside? That was when I realized what he was actually saying.

Save myself, leave him to his fate.

I grimaced. "In other words, if something happens to

you, I'm to leave you behind? I can't do that, Jett."

"You have to," he said, quietly. His eyes shimmered with a silent plea. "This car is fueled with high-explosive gas. If we crash and any of it leaks, it'll explode. There won't be time to save me. You do whatever saves you and our baby."

Hell, no!

"It doesn't have to be that way, you know?" I said. If anything happened, I knew I wouldn't leave. I'd stay with him, no matter what.

"I'm just saying. We have to take the worst into account," Jett said, misunderstanding me. He peered out the window as more cars arrived.

"Jett?" I touched his arm gently, trying my best to infuse confidence in him. "You're the best driver I've ever met. We'll be all right. I know it because I saw it in Italy. There's no reason to think about risks and what could happen when I know what you're capable of."

"It *is* a risk, Brooke," Jett said, slowly. "When I made that deal with Brian, I agreed to compete against his best man, but the truth is I haven't been involved in this kind of driving for years. And he knows it. Compared to Italy, this is nothing."

That didn't sound at all like Jett. His doubts about himself didn't make sense to me.

"People don't unlearn their talents," I said, softly.

245

"Look." He let out a long impatient sigh. "I know you mean well, Brooke, but you don't know Doug. Everything he knows, he learned from me. He knows all my tricks, my moves. And the fact he wasn't retired these past few years gives him an advantage over me. Do you now understand why I didn't want you to come along?" I nodded. "He's better than me."

"You don't know that," I protested. Jett *was* the best. Kenny had said so himself, and even without Kenny, I knew it in my heart. "Besides, it doesn't matter. I still would have wanted to ride with you."

No matter what.

He shook his head. He hadn't just inherited the hotness gene; he had also inherited the stubbornness one.

"Even if I were the best, I wouldn't want you in here. Your safety isn't worth taking the risk."

"What about my opinion?" I asked. "You never asked me."

"Everyone has to make choices at some point," Jett said. "I do what has to be done, not what I feel you want."

"Look, this has nothing to do with want." I raised my chin defiantly at the stubborn glint in his gaze.

We weren't going to see eye to eye on this one, and that was fine. I didn't *have* to agree on everything. But it would've been so nice.

"For me coming with you is the right choice, because it

means we're creating a new memory together regardless of the outcome." I sucked in a deep breath as I struggled to find the right words. "Like you, I *need* to stay by your side because you mean everything to me. If you fall, I fall," I whispered, repeating his words. "And if we fall, I'd rather we do it together. No exceptions, no regrets, and that's a whole lot better than taking a chance and having to live without you."

"You remember?" He turned slowly, his eyes penetrating my soul, absorbing my words. The love in his gaze reached my heart, coursed through my blood, and swirled inside my mind.

"Of course I do." I nodded. "You asked me if I trusted you, and I can tell you in all honesty that I do now."

His eyes twinkled brighter than the stars dotting the night sky.

"You have a problem trusting my dedication to you, but you trust me in a life-and-death situation?" he asked in disbelief. His delicious lips twitched at the corners. I couldn't help but smile because it was the truth.

I wanted to reply when his brows shot up. I followed his line of vision and saw Brian signaling something before heading back to his car.

"Three minutes left," Jett said, his attention turning back to me. His hand lingered on my face as he brushed a strand of hair out of my eyes. "You're like no one I've met before," he whispered.

"I hope that's a good thing."

"It sure is." He smiled, revealing a pair of gorgeous dimples to die for. "I like that you trust me. I can work with that."

He cupped my face, his thumb stroking my skin as he leaned in to kiss me, his tongue meeting mine in a tender embrace. It barely lasted a few seconds, and yet it was the best kiss of my life.

"I truly believe you're the greatest thing that's ever happened to me," Jett said softly, "and there's nothing I'd ever change about you. You know that, right?"

He kissed me again. It was only when he leaned back to pull on his gloves and turn the key that I realized our kiss might have been our last.

24

IT WASN'T THE roar of Jett's car, nor the fired shot signaling the start of the race what sent my intestines into icy knots. It was the moment a black car pulled up next to us that I knew the time had come.

The passenger window rolled down, and Doug's gaze met mine. He was in his early twenties, with blond curly hair that fell into his blue eyes. His features were roughened, and his posture was confident. But what made me wary was the self-assured smile on his lips. It wasn't so much a smile as a smirk. Jett nodded and let out a low chuckle. In that instant I knew. Two men engaged in a battle of egos equaled a hell of a ride. And I was trapped inside this nightmare with no way out. Jett sped up and changed gears, the muscles in his arms straining. He didn't seem bothered by the way Doug's car kept coming too close—or that Doug bumped into our car when he overtook us shortly before we reached the first cross-point.

Someone made a hand signal. Doug turned to the left and Jett followed. I expected Jett to swear, but instead he hit the pedals harder and we sped off. No signs of his nervousness. My fingers buried in the armrest when the tires hit a bump in the road and I shot forward against the seatbelt. I wanted to scream, but the sound remained trapped in my throat. Jett needed my support. He needed my trust, because doubt and fear would take us nowhere.

But fear choked me, made me gasp for air and wish I'd never have to set foot in a car again.

I hated the way the car kept jerking after each bump and the engine roared like it might be about to draw its last breath. Every muscle in my body hurt, and my mind was spiraling into a giant hole of panic. Each second felt like an eternity. At the second cross-point, Jett overtook Doug. Adrenaline pulsed through me as I realized we still had a chance to win. Jett knew what he was doing, and his focus gave me courage. We were so close. So near I could already see the headlights of countless cars marking the finish line. Soon my ordeal would be over.

I recognized Brian's blue Ferrari in the distance. He was leaning casually against his car, the lights illuminating his features. We were almost there, barely a hundred feet. Fifty feet. But Jett didn't slow down. He was going way too fast.

If he didn't stop in time, we'd crash into Brian's car.

"Slow down," I shouted. He didn't acknowledge my command. Was he so high on adrenaline that he didn't realize what was about to happen?

"Jett!" I screamed, bracing myself. "You're going to kill him."

"It's okay." He didn't seem affected in any way. My heart dropped. In horror I watched Brian jump out of the way. Just in time, Jett swerved the wheel and drove past his car and the finish line.

"Serves him right for dragging you into this," he mumbled, and hit the accelerator again.

I shook my head at his stunt and let out a sigh of relief that nothing bad had happened. And we were the first to reach the finish line, meaning we had won. I turned to Jett. His fingers remained clenched around the steering wheel.

"Where are you going?" I asked, frowning.

"Back to the city." His calm tone, which I suspected was supposed to comfort me, only managed to alert me.

Why would he drive all the way back to the city when we were supposed to pick up his award or whatever?

I narrowed my eyes. "I thought you were going to stop. You said so yourself."

"Yes." He dragged out the word, not looking at me. "Once it's over. The race isn't finished yet." He took a left onto the main road. In the distance stretched out the illuminated highway and the New York skyline.

"What do you mean?"

"The rules are: whoever arrives first, wins."

"*What?*"

He wanted to drive all the way back through the city? Through the traffic to the warehouses? How the hell would he win without getting a speeding ticket? Or worse yet, becoming famous on national TV? In my mind, I could already see a helicopter circling over us, relaying the news that a driver had run amok, and people being warned to stay off the streets. We'd be all over national TV. So much for keeping a low profile.

"But—" I shook my head, realizing the finish line was the warehouse and we were taking a detour. What he was about to do was crazy. I checked the rearview mirror. Doug followed closely behind.

"You thought it'd be that easy?" Jett asked, answering my unspoken question.

"You call that easy?" I muttered. "I'd say crazy, insane even." I clasped my hand over my mouth. The truth crippled me. Apparently, Jett had every intention of continuing this madness through the busy streets of New York City. "Oh, God."

"I warned you," he said. We overtook one car and then another. After a few minutes Jett hit the brakes. We slowed down to below the speed limit. I shot Jett a confused look.

Doug drove past. Jett didn't seem to notice. When we halted in the middle of the road, I knew something was wrong. As much as I wanted to believe Jett had stopped because of me, I couldn't shake off the feeling he'd never give up.

"What are you doing?" I asked. Doug disappeared in the distance. Judging by the way he wound his way through traffic, he'd either crash or win. Cars stacked up behind us, but Jett ignored them—and me.

"Jett?" My fingers barely touched his arm. "What's wrong?"

"Did you notice Doug stayed on our tail but didn't take the lead—until now? He thinks he can catch up in the end, which is possible, given that it's one of the tricks I taught him. I'm devising a different strategy." He peered at me briefly before turning his attention on the rearview mirror.

I feared the answer, but felt compelled to ask. "Which is?"

"A shortcut he doesn't know," Jett said calmly.

Ah.

Somehow I didn't like it because, knowing Jett, shortcuts were never "shortcuts" as in "the easy way."

I didn't just suspect.

I knew.

Doug had almost disappeared from my vision, but if I craned my neck I could still see him stuck at a red light.

Jammed in with other cars, he couldn't possibly follow Jett.

"It's not so much a shortcut as a plan," Jett continued. That sounded even worse. "We're taking the same route, only the opposite way."

I had no idea what he was talking about, but had no time to ask because Jett went into full reverse. The car spun around, earning us more honks, but he didn't seem particularly fazed by the swearing drivers as he navigated down a narrow strip of lawn, swerving straight into oncoming traffic.

"Are you fucking crazy?" I shouted.

Ignoring me, he floored the accelerator, and the car jerked forward. We were driving so fast I wanted to cry. Instead I made do with burying my nails into the soft leather of my seat. My breath came in labored heaves each time cars drove out of our way to let us pass, or we dodged them.

"Please stop," I whispered in the hope Jett might listen to me for a change.

"We can't. This is the only way."

"But Doug's stuck," I argued. "Can you at least—"

Slow down.

Jett shot me a strange look, and I clamped my mouth shut to stop myself from whining. At an intersection Jett took a sharp left into a quiet one-way road. Straight ahead was the main road.

We were in the city.

So many people, so many cars. Jett didn't seem concerned as he continued to race through the streets. I caught the flashing blue lights of a police car before I heard the siren.

"Shit!" Jett floored the gas pedal, turning the wheel expertly as he crossed a red light. The police car followed behind.

"We need to stop, Jett." My voice came so low I wasn't sure he heard me.

"We can't. Trust me, we'll get out of this."

Oh, God.

His shortcut involved driving like a madman. If I didn't know any better, I could've sworn the brakes weren't working.

"Relax," Jett whispered, his voice was strained but by no means nervous. I always knew Jett was a risk-taker. Now I realized the guy was crazy beyond my wildest dreams, because he apparently thought anyone could relax with him behind the wheel.

Relax?

I felt physically sick. In fact, I prayed I'd just pass out and wake up when the nightmare was over. My heart pounded hard against the layer of frost spreading over me. I buried my face in my hands and started to chant in my mind.

Stay calm. Be quiet. Breathe in. Breathe out. Think of sunshine, of calming waters, the sound of seagulls. Think of violins, of heaven.

No. Bad idea. I didn't want to think of heaven.

Think of walking on the beach. Healthy. With Jett and a baby. Happy. Alive.

"Oh, God," I muttered. "Oh, God."

My fear intensified and transformed into a growing chill that could turn into ice and shatter me into pieces. The car chase in Italy had been bad. It had been horrendous. But Jett racing through New York City's streets with a police car trailing us was a living nightmare.

"Baby, just close your eyes," Jett said.

Close my eyes and pretend it wasn't happening? That had been the plan all along.

"I'm trying," I muttered.

"Just continue to keep them closed," he replied, encouragingly.

"Oh, God," I muttered. "Oh, God."

Please, please, please, I prayed. *Help us win. Help us arrive safely. Help us make it out alive. Help that nobody gets hurt.*

Could I have that many different wishes at the same time?

"They lost us," Jett said at last. Confused, I opened my eyes. He had slowed down and we were cruising a half-empty parking garage.

The sirens echoed in the distance.

Jett drove out of the building, past several blocks, and turned onto a highway for a few minutes. I recognized buildings in the distance before Jett exited the highway and drove along the fence. To my utter disbelief, we had made it unscathed.

I frowned.

"Is that—"

The warehouse, I wanted to ask until I saw Jett turning the wheel, spinning the car. He floored the gas and drove past the gates. The finish line had to be on the other side. In the distance I could see car headlights. Jett hit the brakes, and the tires screeched. My head jerked forward, and a pang of pain shot up my spine.

I smirked. My eyes fell on the crowd of people. They looked surprised, as though they didn't expect us to come from the back. And then the cheers began and more people gathered. Jett ignored them as he drove into the open garage. Doug's car wasn't there. Jett switched off the engine and turned to face me. His dark hair stuck to his temples, and sweat rivulets were running down his neck.

My legs were trembling so hard I pressed my soles into the floor to stop them from shaking. My whole body felt numb.

"We've won," Jett said, calmly. Was that a hint of pride? "You okay?" I shook my head, because I wasn't okay. "Don't worry, we have a fake license plate." The corners of his lips curved upward. So I had been right. He *was* proud. Maybe even elated.

"A speeding ticket isn't what I've been worried about," I muttered.

Fury burned inside me—at Jett's reckless driving, at his whole alpha "I do everything to win" attitude, and at a million other things. How could he smile when barely seconds ago he'd scared the hell out of God knows how many people, including me?

"I fucking hate—" I struggled for words, the shock rendering me unable to form a coherent sentence.

"How much you love me?" His dimples appeared, and for a moment I felt torn between hitting him and kissing him.

I stared at him, and then I started to laugh.

"Yeah. I do, and how crazy is that?" I knew it was hysteria and the adrenaline pumping inside my veins. That, or gratitude that we were still alive.

I didn't know what came over me, but seeing him hot and sweaty, with that amused glint in his devilish green eyes, I wanted him. I wanted him badly. Madly. Furiously. And I didn't care if it happened here, right on the spot, and if his ego grew sky high. I climbed over to his side and moved on top of him. My fingers buried in his hair as my lips descended upon his mouth with the kind of hunger that demanded immediate gratification.

"I knew there was a wicked side to you, Miss Stewart," Jett whispered against my mouth, and pulled back.

"You forgot crazy. I was crazy to come with you. I was crazy to think I could make it out with my sanity intact," I said. "I'll never do anything like this again."

"Never?" His eyebrows shot up in mock surprise. "What happened to 'no exceptions, no regrets?' I really liked that one. It sort of gave me leverage to try new things with you."

I shook my head. "I'll do anything for you, but no car races. No more stunts."

"I like a challenge. You know that." He grinned. "According to our arrangement and my rules, I still have several hours left."

I groaned.

Not that horrendous bet again!

"You've won. Get over it," I mumbled.

"Just one more stunt, baby." His eyes twinkled. I shook my head. "How about you let me change your mind?"

"Nice try, but I'll pass." I'd had enough of an adrenaline rush to last me a lifetime.

"I've heard second times around can be pretty good, too," Jett said. "Let's sneak out of the party and spend time together. It's long overdue, anyway."

The way he said it, he made it sound like a date. We hadn't gone on a date in forever. Actually, since breaking into Kim Dessen's house. But it sure felt like an eternity. "What party?" I asked.

"Call it a welcome party," Jett whispered. "Time to meet my gang." I had no idea what he was talking about, but the prospect of spending more time with him sounded tempting.

"Let me take a shower first," I said. "And no more stunts, Mayfield. I really mean it."

"No stunts, I promise." He grinned.

I rolled my eyes. Hadn't I heard that one before?

"At least for a while," Jett added.

My smile matched his as he pulled me to him for another kiss.

25

THE UPPER FLOORS of the warehouses were converted into bedrooms. Brian had arranged that Jett and I would take a shower and change in a room upstairs, which was pretty much the opposite of how I envisioned it: tiny but tastefully decorated in cream and brown with an adjacent bathroom and a shower cubicle. A four-poster bed lined the east side. A soft cream couch was set up in the middle in front of a TV set mounted on the wall. Everything looked neat and tidy. Whoever had decorated it obviously had taste.

"This used to be my room," Jett said.

"Really?" That really changed everything. I spun around slowly, trying to take in the details I might've missed. I walked over to the bed and lay down. The mattress was soft and the covers smelled fresh, as though they'd been changed recently. There were no pictures on the walls, but for some reason, I could feel a younger Jett's presence, his spirit and attitude. He had been tormented, yet he had also been happy.

"I like it here," I said, softly. "I'm happy we get to stay for a while."

Someone—I assumed Sylvie—had brought over clothes and as soon as I closed the bathroom door behind me, I stripped off and stepped into the shower, eager to let the hot water relax my tense muscles and calm my frayed nerves.

I had barely shampooed and rinsed my hair when the bathroom door opened and I saw Jett's silhouette clearly outlined through the curtain. He took his clothes off and peered behind the curtain, his impossibly green gaze a mixture between hesitation and desire.

"Brooke." His deep voice saying my name sent a jolt of fire between my legs. "I want to do something dirty to you. Something you'll never forget."

My pulse picked up in speed, and a rush of excitement washed over me.

"What do you have in mind?" I whispered.

He pushed the shower curtain aside and joined me in the cubicle, naked in all his glory. My mouth went dry at the beauty of his sculpted body with bulging muscles beneath taut skin.

Sex incarnate.

As though reading my dirty thoughts, Jett smiled, and our mouths met in a heated kiss. His tongue slipped inside me, prodding, demanding that I open up and give him what was his to take. At the same time, his hand settled between my legs. I moaned when he started to circle my clit. He didn't just make me wet; he made me ache for his fingers inside me, to touch him and test if he was real.

My fingertips grazed his swelling shaft.

"You're turning me on, baby." His whisper turned into a guttural rasp when my fingers began to work up and down his hardening shaft, mirroring his movements as his fingers circled faster around my clit, until I felt I couldn't bear it anymore.

"I want you inside me," I moaned against his mouth.

"Not yet."

He lifted my left leg, and I let go of his bulging erection to hold onto his shoulders for support. Ever so slowly he began to thrust one finger inside me, then two, igniting a blaze.

Oh, God.

Water kept pouring down on us, and I was sure that wasn't the only thing running down my leg. My body began to rock back and forth against him, seeking the pleasure only he could unleash. He pushed two fingers in and out, fast and furious. I moaned and leaned into his hand, ready for complete abandon. Just when I thought he'd take me over the edge, Jett slowed down—unbearably hot, unbearably painful—and then pulled out. His fingers continued to circle my clit without giving me the release I desperately needed.

"More," I said. "I want you to fuck me now."

It wasn't an option; it was a demand.

"As you wish." His eyes bored into me as he pressed me against the tiled wall and forced my left leg up higher. I could feel the slick head of his erection at my entrance, circling and nudging, doing anything but filling me. Impatiently, I stirred against him, my eyes begging him to take me.

"Is this what you're looking for?" He pushed the head inside me, stretching the soft flesh, while kissing my earlobe. My heart almost stopped from the sudden sweltering sensation gathering deep in my abdomen. I was so close. Just a few more inches.

"More," I whispered.

His erection plunged another inch into me, teasing me by moving gently, building the momentum until I felt like cursing him for torturing me.

"Fuck, Jett!" I swore. "You're killing me."

He laughed that deep laugh of his that always made me tingle all over. "As you wish."

I gasped as he shoved his entire length into me—fast

and determined. One full thrust. My flesh tightened around his shaft. The pain of him hitting an aching spot inside me disappeared quickly, and more pleasure began to build inside my abdomen. Consuming me. Burning my insides like hot lava.

He quivered, alive with fire, waiting…waiting for what?

My mind was too clouded to ask a question, too high from his scent and the taste of his mouth, too starved from his touch.

I needed him. He had to be moving. He had to before I exploded. Or else…

I ground my hips against him in need of more. My thigh muscles began to hurt from the effort, but I didn't mind. I needed release, and if he wouldn't give it to me, then I was ready to take it.

"I could stay inside you forever," Jett whispered—almost dreamy, almost regretful. He circled his hips without thrusting. "Remember the feeling of me inside you. We're together. Not you, nor me, but us."

The rawness of his hot words sent another ripple through my core, pushing me closer to the brink of an orgasm. It felt good. He was so good. I wanted to tell him. As if sensing my desire for him, he smiled. Our eyes locked with such intensity I felt lost in them, unable to tell where I ended and he began.

"You know I can't decline when you're like this." His

lips crushed mine. "So wet. Baby, I could do this forever."

Finally, his entire length began to move. I could feel every hard inch of him getting bigger, filling and stretching me. Pushing my boundaries.

Moaning into my open mouth, he began to thrust, first slow and then hard and harder. Faster and faster, sending my world into a whirlwind of lust and exhilaration. I closed my eyes to savor the sensation as the room began to spin around us. All I could feel was the hardness of his body spearing me.

"Jett." My breath quickened, and I plummeted into a sea of ecstasy. From the periphery of my mind I heard his final moan and felt his hot moisture spilling deep inside. My body melted into him, trusting him for support, as his waves of pleasure washed over me, taking us both to new shores.

I didn't know how long we stood in that shower, our bodies merged, the water cooling our feverish skin. Eventually, when the water began to turn cold as ice, we stepped out of the shower, dripping all over the floor. My legs were shaking from the effort, but my heartbeat had slowed down to a normal speed.

"Thank you," I whispered, so low I didn't think Jett would hear me.

"For what?" He wrapped me in a towel and kissed the tip of my nose.

For being amazing.

I shrugged and smiled, keeping my thoughts to myself.

26

BY THE TIME we finally arrived, the party was in full swing. The entire first floor was abuzz with people, Doug included, and more were flooding in by the minute. An indie band was playing in the corner. The air was thick with cigarette smoke. The tables were littered with alcohol bottles, half-empty glasses, and snacks, reminding me of my college days. Everyone seemed to be enjoying themselves. It was going to be a long night, I could see that.

Jett led me through the crowd, his possessive hand resting on the small of my back. I nodded even though I couldn't hear a word he said and continued to scan the room for Sylvie—without much success. We made it over to Brian. A girl sat on his lap. I recognized her as the one who had urged me to hurry up and change into the racing suit. The moment she saw us approaching, she stood and left.

I frowned.

Not only did she not like me, she had no problems showing it.

"Good job." Brian patted Jett on the shoulder and then turned to address me. "People owe me a shitload of money. I knew Jett would win."

So it was all about money?

Jett cocked his eyebrow. "Did you also bet on winning the drinking game tonight?"

"Are you challenging me?" Brian laughed out loud. "'Cause I'm a champ all the way. I have a high tolerance level. No fucking way you'd beat me."

"Who said I'm in?" Jett said. "No drinks for me tonight, but I know someone who'd knock you off your feet."

"In case you've forgotten, I'm Irish," Brian said. "I've won against everyone."

"Except for your sister." Jett nodded at the red-haired woman standing behind Brian. "She's in town, visiting."

Brian turned, his smile gone. "Crap."

"My money's well invested." Jett shot me a reassuring smile, and I knew he wasn't being serious. "She's going to strip you of your title big time."

"Hello to you, too, big guy." The woman smiled at Jett and turned to me. Her hazel eyes reflected her curiosity, but there was something else in them—warmth, which led me to believe Jett and she had been friends, and nothing but friends. "News spreads fast. When I heard you were back, I had to come and see for myself."

"Brooke," I said, reaching out. She grabbed my hand and gave it a good shake. For a moment, we just looked at each other, assessing. She was in her mid thirties, with a full-bodied voluptuous figure, pale skin, freckles, and an infectious smile. I decided to like her instantly.

"I'm Cassidy," she said. "I've already heard so much about you. The bastards who're after you will pay." It took me a moment to realize she was talking about Alessandro's club. "Brian knows how to find them. He's like a bloodhound." She roared with laughter.

"I hope so," I said. "Jett and I could do with a little peace." Cassidy's gaze brushed my abdomen, and she nodded knowingly. I wondered how she'd found out, but instead of asking I just smiled.

We chatted until Brian hit the stage, drawing everyone's attention to us by declaring Jett as the winner of the race, as if the world didn't know already, and then he went on to recount Jett's little stunt, including our car almost crashing into Brian's Ferrari. The room filled with laughter, Brian's included. Brian finally left the stage, and people flooded over to congratulate Jett, Doug among them. I stepped aside to give Jett his moment. Either the race had changed everything, or maybe everyone had been waiting for Brian's approval, but the ice was broken.

For the first time I saw Jett relaxed and easy-going in a public gathering. As if the person before me wasn't the Jett Mayfield I knew—the rich, reticent millionaire whose only purpose was to ensure the success of his company. Kenny had been right. The gang was Jett's family. Jett had more in common with them than he might ever realize because they had shaped him. They had helped him after his father kicked him out. For the umpteenth time, I wondered what had gone so horribly wrong that Jett returned to his father.

"Want to leave, baby?" Jett whispered in my ear. "You look so good in your tight jeans you're turning me on." As though to prove his point, his hand brushed my ass and his lips grazed the sensitive skin on my neck. A delicious jolt pulsed through me. If it weren't for the dozen people around us, I would've ripped open his shirt and pulled down his pants to enjoy his glorious body.

"We've just arrived and you want to leave already?" I asked, amused. "What happened to partying through the night?"

"Is that a trick question?" His hoarse tone sent another shiver through my body. Slowly he began to nibble on my earlobe. "When I want something, I don't wait."

"You take it. Got it." I swallowed and turned around, facing his deep green eyes the color of sin. "What are you suggesting?"

"I have a good idea, Miss Stewart." Heat traveled somewhere south at the insinuation in his voice. "Let me show you something that will make your panties wet."

Again?

He grabbed my hand and motioned for me to follow him. We were almost out the door when Brian blocked our way.

"Did anyone show you your way around?" Brian asked, addressing me.

"No need," Jett said through gritted teeth. Did I detect a hint of irritation?

"But I insist."

I shrugged at Jett, who shot me a glare. I shrugged again. This was Brian's territory, and he was proud of what he had built. We were guests, so obviously we had to behave as such. Jett could take off his pants later.

"Sounds great," I said. "Lead the way."

Brian talked all the way through the tour, while Jett's mood seemed to plummet to an all-time low. Amused, I gaped at the hugeness of the place. The warehouses were interconnected by a subterranean maze of corridors, which I had already suspected. The upper floors had all been converted to rooms and apartments. From outside the walls looked like they might be about to crumble, but the interior design showed Brian had spared no expense. The furniture was minimalistic but modern and expensive, the technology high-tech. Abstract paintings in red and blue with golden swirls hung on the walls, each showing the same signature. I wondered if one of the guys was an artist.

"You all live here?" I asked, impressed.

"Some of us. Others prefer their own place," Brian said, and opened the next door, leading us into a huge living room with a fireplace and yet more paintings displayed on the walls. "You're welcome to stay here for as long as you want. The top floor is all yours."

"My old room will do just fine, Brian," Jett muttered.

"I thought your girl might prefer something more—" Brian drew a long breath, considering his words as he regarded me "—upscale."

"We appreciate it," I said. "But I'd love to stay in Jett's old room, if that's okay."

Jett's arm wrapped around my waist. If I didn't know better, I would have said he was pleased with my answer—and possessive.

"If you need anything, let me know." Brian hesitated and turned to Jett. "Can I have a minute with you?"

I wondered if talking with Jett in private was the reason why Brian had insisted on coming with us.

"Sure."

"Take as long as you need," I said to them. The door shut and I was alone, but I could hear their voices loud and clear.

"I've arranged for a meeting tomorrow to find out who the unidentified recipient is. How much money are we talking about?" Brian asked.

"Fifty mill," Jett replied.

"Fucking hell."

"The company's going bankrupt." Jett hesitated. "I'm a CEO. If I don't sort out this mess, I could be held liable. I could lose everything; my money, my home, my investors in the new company, my reputation. But first I need you to focus on finding out who's responsible for Brooke's kidnapping."

"We're working on decoding the disk," Brian said. "Give us a couple of days."

"I don't have days. I need it as soon as possible. My father wanted the book, so it must be valuable. As long as we don't know who we're dealing with, Brooke's not safe."

"So you're assuming your father's in on it? What if he had no choice?"

"Don't give me that crap, Brian. You know there's no other explanation. My best guess is he transferred the money to keep some for himself. However, the question is why? I need to know if there's anything we don't know. I need you to check out possible risks. The last thing I want is my father getting us into deeper shit than we're already in."

"We'll keep you updated."

"Good," Jett said.

For a minute they talked about Cassidy. I walked over to the bed as soon as I heard footsteps crossing the room. The door opened and Jett entered.

"How much did you hear?" he asked after he closed the door behind him.

I winced, unable to hide my guilty expression. "How did you know I was listening?"

"It wasn't hard to guess. I know you, Brooke. Besides I don't want to keep secrets from you." He tilted his head, scrutinizing me. "So, how much?"

"Almost everything, actually. But I already know that Mayfield Realities are trouble, so it's no big deal," I admitted. "Your brother mentioned that you were working on setting up a new company."

He looked up, surprised. "And what are your thoughts?"

"I'm thinking you're going to be great," I whispered. "Many people don't know when to cut their losses when it's over. They choose to stay in a dead-end situation until everything comes crashing down on them. You're doing the right thing, Jett."

"Sacrifices before losses. I'm happy you get me," he said. "I'm sorry I didn't tell you about the missing money sooner."

I shrugged. "It's okay. I would've loved to help you, though."

"I could use your expert opinion in everything I do, Miss Stewart. How much do you charge?"

"A lot." My grin matched is. "And I know exactly how you can repay me." I pointed at the couch behind us. "Brian was kind enough to give us a nice room. We could commence our negotiations right now."

I walked over to the couch. Jett followed me and sat down, pulling me onto his lap. His hands pushed aside my hair to caress the nape of my neck. I closed my eyes, relishing his touch.

"Too bad we're not staying for long," he said.

"Why not?"

"I still don't trust them. It's too dangerous for you. And second—" His breath tickled my skin a moment before his lips parted in a tender kiss. "I want to spend quality time with you."

I turned to regard him. "Brian helped you find me. He's trying to locate your father and find out what the club's all about. Don't you think you're overreacting a little bit with the whole trust issue thing?"

"It's not that simple," Jett said grimly.

Well, it sort of was to me.

There was something in his expression that made me clamp my mouth shut and listen. He was angry. But why? Wasn't he happy to be back in touch with his old friends?

"I don't understand, Jett. This used to be your family." I

removed myself from his lap and kneeled before him, my elbows resting against his knees, as I looked at him. "You guys share so many memories. I thought you'd want to spend time with them."

His face resembled a grim mask. Something I'd said was wrong, and it made my mind frantic to figure out my misstep. I touched his leg to get his attention. Jett didn't react.

"I'm sorry," I said, unsure what I was apologizing for. "Do you want to tell me what's going on?"

The silence between us seemed oppressing. Voices carried over from outside the door—the chatter, music, and laughter building a strong contrast to what was going on inside Jett's tormented soul. I could sense that if I probed too hard, I'd go too far, and I didn't want to push him. I watched Jett's fingers curl around the picture frame on the side table. On it were a group of men sitting around a bonfire. With his tanned body and gorgeous dimples, I recognized Jett instantly. I bit my lip as I tried to imagine what could have caused Jett's sudden change in mood.

"I killed my best friend," he said, as though reading my thoughts. His voice was so low I wasn't sure I'd heard him right. His finger pointed at a blond man sitting next to him, holding a beer in his hand and laughing.

"Was it an accident?" I asked, breathlessly. It had to be. Anything else wouldn't make sense.

"No." He shook his head slowly. "Not really." His voice was raw, and his eyes filled with moisture. His face reflected so much pain that it seeped from his every pore. The thought that Jett was a killer didn't quite fit the picture inside my mind. I couldn't imagine him doing anything terrible, and yet I knew it was possible. Somewhere in the back of my mind, I remembered the gunshots. Somehow I knew Jett had shot the men who had been about to rape me. If it happened once, there was at least some possibility Jett had hurt people before.

In the silence of the room, my glance moved from Jett to the picture in his hands. It seemed to have been taken an eternity ago. But I couldn't ask the question burning a hole in my brain. Instead I waited patiently until he was ready.

"Joe did stupid stuff," Jett began. His words came slowly, struggling. "He had owed everyone, me included, because he was a gambling addict. He was so deep in shit, he couldn't even tell me he had borrowed money from loan sharks." His voice faltered, and he took a deep breath.

I swallowed. I had never seen Jett this way, his usual self-composure breaking down. Not even when he talked about his father.

"One day he needed a driver to pick something up. I didn't think much of it, so I drove him to the place without asking questions. But picking up wasn't the only thing he did that day. He killed someone. Said it was an accident. He confessed to me about various loans and the odd jobs he had been doing to repay those people. I promised I'd have his back and help him if he stopped working for them. But Joe didn't want to listen."

His voice was so heavy I knew there was more to the story. I watched him take another breath and put the picture back on the side table. My body urged me to touch him, but the man standing in front of me was trapped by memories, and I was seemingly forgotten, a shadow that couldn't reach him.

"That day he was supposed to take back the money he stole. Instead he hid it somewhere inside the warehouse and told me he'd leave the city, hide until he had made enough money to repay his debt and the high interest."

I shrank back a little at the intensity in Jett's eyes. He didn't need to tell me what he felt—the pain was written all over his face, inside his soul, inside his mind. His hands were balled to fists. I didn't need words to figure out that things had gone horribly wrong.

"What happened?" I asked quietly.

He pressed his lips in a tight line, struggling, his eyes moving back to the picture, as if it held the answers he was looking for.

"The money was gone the next day. Joe accused me of stealing it, and we had a fight." He smiled bitterly. "I was so angry about his accusation that I went to Brian and told him the truth about the loans. The job. The money. I wanted to help Joe. But Brian—" Jett took a deep breath, his tone angry. "He wanted Joe out of the gang. Said he was a liability."

I looked up, confused. "Why?"

"Because we already had problems with other gangs. It's the way this world works. Brian said that Joe posed a risk to all of us because he'd get us involved with the big guys and the real shit, like drugs. Brian took me in when I had no place to stay. He was always there for me. I went to him, trusting his judgment. When Brian wanted to kick Joe out, I begged him to give Joe a second chance, because without a gang he would have had no protection from the sharks. Brian was reluctant but eventually agreed under the condition we taught Joe a lesson and—" Jett paused, taking his time "—I offered to do it. Even though I was angry with Joe, he was my best friend, and I wanted to have control over what would be done to him. I suggested a race with the plan to simulate a collision with Joe—just to scare him, break a few bones, lock him inside a hospital for a while, where we could help him. Brian agreed. But it went wrong." He trailed off.

The air charged with heaviness. I knew what was coming, and it broke my heart.

"I lost control over my car and killed him," Jett said slowly, his eyes hard and cold. "It was my fucking fault."

I swallowed down the lump in my throat as I stared at the picture and the man sitting next to Jett. Jett never lost control while driving. I had seen it with my own eyes.

"How is that even possible?" I asked.

"I didn't see the tree on his side of the road." He cast his gaze on the floor. In spite of the dimmed lights, I could see the moisture shimmering in his eyes.

"But he did," he whispered. "When I hit him, he spun the car, pushed mine aside, and crashed right into the tree. By doing so, he saved my life but sacrificed himself. I watched his car explode."

"I'm so sorry."

"Don't be. I don't deserve it."

I loved Jett. I loved him with all my heart. I didn't want guilt to consume him. I grabbed his hand and pulled him to me, forcing him to look me in the eyes.

"It was an accident, Jett."

"No, it wasn't." His voice was angry. "See, there's always a huge risk. I knew it when I made that suggestion. I knew that it could kill him—or me. Yet I made that mistake and it defined me. It changed everything."

I kissed his hands softly. Inside I was shaken by his confession—not so much about what had happened, but by what he thought of himself. "Jett, your mistakes do not define you. You're far more than the sum of a few bad decisions in life."

He laughed darkly. I could see he didn't believe me.

"If I hadn't raced that day, he'd still be alive. My mistake cost his life," Jett whispered. "And when I found out that Brian knew about Joe's problems all along, that it was he who took the money and returned it to the sharks to prevent the place from being raided, I left the gang. If he had told me, I'd never have suggested the race and Joe wouldn't be dead. So no, I can't trust Brian. Joe had been more than a friend to me. He was like a brother."

There was a long silence. The muscles in his jaws began to work, but his eyes were glued to my hands, touching me without actually touching my skin. The air felt prickly and dark between us. I didn't know where to start or how to help him, even though to me Jett wasn't guilty. But how could I convince the man I loved that it was an accident— that he didn't do it on purpose—when he was the only person who could convince himself?

"If Brian knew about Joe's problems all along, maybe the sharks threatened him and he returned the money to keep you all safe," I suggested. "Have you ever asked him?"

"No. I left." He shrugged, his face a hard mask of denial. "But you don't understand, Brooke. The race was my idea. It was my *fucking* idea, not Brian's."

"Do you really think Joe didn't know what he was getting himself into?" I whispered. "He knew the risks, and he wanted out. Even if he hadn't died that day, he'd have owed a lot of people a lot of money. Dangerous people who would've come after him for taking that money. It wouldn't have ended well."

It was a twisted kind of logic, but it was the brutal truth. And Jett knew it, whether he wanted to admit it or not.

"We don't know that," Jett said, choosing to stay in denial. "For all we know it could have ended differently, if only he'd gotten the chance to turn his life around."

Jett was right. He didn't know if Joe wouldn't have been okay—like I didn't know if my sister would have stopped seeing Danny if I hadn't let her leave the house that fateful night. But when I trusted Jett with my secret, he helped me cope with the guilt that had been torturing me for years. I felt connected to Jett because I thought he understood my pain. My confession was my key to feeling free and safe around him and within the confines of my mind. Now that I knew about his past, I longed to help him build that same connection to me.

I moistened my lips, considering my words carefully.

"Right after I told you about my sister, you said to me that no one can help a person if they don't want to be helped. Remember?" I paused. When he nodded, I continued. "I know this hurts, but your past isn't so different from mine, Jett. You couldn't have helped Joe because he had made up his mind. For what it's worth, you gave it your best shot, given the knowledge and life experience you had at that time. Deep in your heart you cared for Joe. You suggested a car race because, like Kenny said, it was what you knew and did best. Not because you wanted to hurt your friend, but because you wanted to help him. I'm sure Joe knew that. He would've forgiven you. The fact that he saved your life shows that he cared for you, too."

Jett looked up into my worried face. His expression softened, and the warmth in his eyes returned.

"Has what I told you today changed your mind about me in any way?" he asked at last. He sounded nervous. It took every ounce of my willpower not to shake some sense into him.

"You have no idea, do you?" I asked in disbelief.

He shook his head. When he remained silent, I realized that he had been serious. I got up from the floor to sit on his lap, my legs going around his waist so I could face him.

"Jett, I love you for who you are. And that includes your dark side as well. One wrong choice doesn't make you a failure. It doesn't mean you're doomed to fail again," I whispered. "And to be honest, I don't care what you did or didn't do. It's in the past. And you can't change it. But I know this. You're a good person. You're a good friend."

The corner of his lips twitched in a half-smile, and one of his gorgeous dimples appeared. I stared at the perfection of it. It was one of the many reasons I'd fallen in love with him. There was something genuine about Jett. He really cared about the people he welcomed into his heart.

"All my life I've never felt this close to anybody," he whispered. "If shit didn't happen, I'd never know how to treasure my blessings." His thumb trailed the contours of my lips slowly. "You're my blessing, Brooke. I don't want to keep dreaming or take risks because, for the first time, reality is better than anything I could ever envision."

I smiled. "Is that the reason you didn't want to race today? Because you thought tragedy could strike again?"

Jett nodded. "I couldn't afford another mistake. Losing Joe was hard, but losing you would have killed me. It was another reason why I didn't want to beat Doug in an open race. I knew he'd try to block us or move in for a PIT maneuver."

I frowned, and he continued to explain, "Fishtailing. Anyway, I would've done the same to him. He was never particularly good at keeping hold of the wheel." Jett sighed and rolled a strand of my hair around his finger, curling it and letting it loose, the way he always did when he was about to say something that bothered him. "You know, Brooke, when I met you I experienced happiness for the first time in my life. Brian thought I'd be too scared to race, but he got it all wrong. I didn't want to—not because I'm scared, but because I don't want to risk what I have with you. I want to see our baby grow up. You both mean the world to me."

There were so many feelings inside me that I feared there might not be enough space to fit them all in. I drew in a long breath and let it out slowly as realization kicked in. Jett and I were in his old room, and he had just declared how much I meant to him. My heart threatened to burst with emotion. Or maybe it was the result of his smile penetrating even the deepest layers of my soul, warming my body like no one could.

"I want you to be mine forever," Jett whispered. "To ensure it, I'll always make you happier than any other man could. I want to be the best thing that's ever happened to you."

"You already are." My fingers brushed over the stubble covering his strong chin. So hard and yet so soft—just like the man hiding behind the most beautiful face I had ever seen. His eyes locked on my mouth, and slowly his lips met mine. A moment later our tongues tangled in an erotic dance, and his hand squeezed beneath my shirt to explore all that would be his forever.

27

"JETT, WE KNOW where your father is." Kenny stood in the door of the community kitchen, his laptop tucked under his arm. I motioned for him to come in and he sat down at the kitchen table where Jett and I were having afternoon coffee and snacks. In the last few days my appetite had quadrupled, and as much as I wanted to blame it on the baby, I couldn't rule out Jett's sexual appetite as being the culprit.

"We hacked into his accounts," Kenny said, opening his laptop. "As luck would have it, we also found a couple of things that will interest you."

"Like?" Jett sounded as interested as a student after a long Friday afternoon class. Bored, he barely regarded the laptop's screen as he took a swig of his latte and cracked the shell of a peanut, handing it to me, then opened one for himself and popped it into his mouth. I suppressed the need to giggle. Ever since we had arrived here five days ago, he had made himself comfortable in an odd way I hadn't seen in him before. His shirt was open and his hair a sexy tangled mess—as if he couldn't stop boasting that his sex life was great, which was the truth. But did he *have* to be so obvious? We had been making love almost nonstop, his sexual thirst increasing by the day, just like my appetite.

"We checked his phone logs and found that he called Brooke's number when she was in Italy." Kenny looked at me. "You remember a call from abroad?"

I froze at his question as the memory came flooding back: the hot summer day when my phone rang while I was pretending to Sylvie I wasn't seeing Jett. I had been so engrossed with the estate that I forgot all about the mysterious caller.

"I do," I said slowly, my glance sweeping from Kenny to Jett. "Remember when I asked you if you had called me?" I raised my brows to jog his memory. "I wasn't sure, because the person hung up."

The confusion on Jett's face cleared as he remembered. "Are you sure it was my father?"

"Damn right I am." Kenny frowned at Jett popping another peanut into his mouth. "The day before he *died*—" Kenny made quotation marks "—he tried to reach her on her landline. Sounds like he was trying to talk to her in private, but that's not what I wanted to show you. Look." He pointed at the screen. "When I searched through his phone records, I discovered that besides Brooke, he had called two other people on that same day." Kenny turned his laptop around to show us.

Now my interest was piqued.

Leaning forward, I tried to decipher the numbers, but all I saw was a bunch of html code and yet more code. No names. I had no idea how Kenny could read any of it, but I guessed with him being a hacker he knew how to get details and see connections.

"Yeah? Well, he's a company owner. You'd expect he talked to more than two people," Jett said and gave his usual *what do I care about this shit?* shrug before his hand poked the bowl of peanuts in front of him. Kenny's brow furrowed as Jett took another peanut and cracked it open, the sound so loud it made me chuckle.

"Are you planning on eating the whole bowl, man?" Kenny asked Jett, his voice dripping with irritation. "I'm trying to have a serious conversation with you both."

"This better be good." Jett let out an exasperated sigh and pushed the bowl aside.

"It is. Trust me." Kenny pointed to the screen. "He phoned a hotel service and an attorney. The attorney happens to have the same name as the person your father transferred money to."

"Could be attorney fees," Jett said.

Kenny shook his head. "Not fees. The full fifty mill, dude, in small transactions. Your father transferred the money through the attorney's account into an unidentified recipient's account. Do you know who the recipient is?"

Jett and I exchanged interested glances. Finally Jett said, "No idea. You?"

"A charity called ETNAD." Kenny paused, waiting for our reaction.

"Never heard of it," Jett said.

"You better have."

"Why?"

"Let's see. First of all, it's a lot of money for one charity." Kenny leaned forward until his elbows rested on the kitchen bar. "And then there's the fact that the attorney your father called is the same guy handling the Lucazzone estate's affairs. He works for Alessandro Lucazzone and Brooke."

That was the moment I heard the needle drop. Or maybe it was a bomb. The silence in the room was so ominous a shudder ran down my spine.

"Clarkson?" All of a sudden I felt faint.

Even Jett looked up and asked, "Why would my father transfer money to him? It doesn't make sense."

"It didn't make sense to me, either, until I told Sylvie and something completely unrelated crossed her mind. If she's right, we might've found our connection between your father and why he wants the book." Kenny smiled pleased, enjoying every second of his show. "She mentioned Clarkson's slanted handwriting. Brooke, when Clarkson sent you letters he wrote your name and address on the envelope, right?" I nodded, unsure where he was heading. "Well, Sylvie thinks the handwriting's the same as the one in the book."

"Is she sure?" Jett asked. "For all we know, he could have an assistant. It could be her handwriting."

I grimaced. Clarkson most certainly had an assistant, but would he really drag her into any dirty affairs and risk exposure?

"No," Kenny said slowly. "Sylvie *believes* to remember. So it's a wild guess, I know, which is why I brought this in the hope you might recognize it."

He pulled the black book out of his bag and pushed it across the table toward me. I flicked to the first page. The handwriting was slanted and old-fashioned, but I didn't remember whether it was analogous with Clarkson's handwriting because I never paid attention to the small details. Who would have?

"What makes her think it's the same?" I asked.

"She recognized the letters 'B' and 'S.' The curved 'B' and 'S' in your name look pretty much like those." He pointed to the "S" in Statham and "B" in Bradley.

"How would she remember something like that?" It wasn't really a question; more like awe. Sylvie referred to herself as a scatterbrain, but her keen eye for detail never ceased to amaze me.

Kenny answered anyway, "She said not many people write like this anymore, which is why she remembered it so well. The possibility didn't cross her mind until I told her about the money transfer." He let out a long breath. "Do you have anything from Clarkson? An envelope, signature, anything at all?"

I lapsed into silence as I tried to remember. "The estate's financial reports were stolen along with the envelope, but before I met with Clarkson for the first time, he sent me a letter. I might still have it at the apartment. No promises, though."

It had to be there because I had never sorted through my stuff, what with Jett lying to me and my consequent heartbreak, the sudden departure to Italy and our getting back together. And upon our return, I had barely had time to grab some of my stuff before I moved in with him.

"Where's Sylvie anyway?" I passed the book to Jett absentmindedly. "I thought she was coming today."

"It's her employee induction day," Kenny said.

"She took the job with Delta & Warren?" I asked surprised. "I thought you guys were going on a road trip."

"We still are. Sylvie's trying to get two weeks off."

Kenny hesitated, grinning. "It's her first day and she's bargaining already."

"Sounds like her," I said, my attention returning to the book in Jett's hand. "I'm sorry, Kenny. I don't recognize the handwriting, but I'll head over to our apartment and get the envelope so we can compare it."

My head was spinning with facts. I massaged my throbbing temples. "Even if it were Clarkson's handwriting, it still wouldn't make sense why Alessandro's attorney would write down a few names and numbers, then hide the book in his client's basement."

As I spoke the words, I realized I had never taken into account the possibility that my lawyer might not be the kind person I thought he was.

"Unless Clarkson's also involved in the club and they all work together," Jett said, "and as such the book has importance for all of them."

"That's what I figured," Kenny replied matter-of-factly. "I'm sorry, mate," he added to Jett.

"My father led me to believe he and Lucazzone were enemies. If Clarkson works for both of them, then my father lied to me." Jett's entire demeanor had changed. His eyes were like layers of frost, devoid of compassion. "Yet another lie."

"What do you know about the charity that received the money?" I asked, changing the subject.

Kenny shrugged, signaling he didn't know more than we did. "It's private. Apparently it supports the fine arts. That's all I could find out."

ETNAD? The letters echoed in my head. ETNAD. Why did it sound so familiar when I was sure I hadn't heard of it before?

I grabbed a pen and wrote down the name to visualize it.

"Can you run it through a database or something and find out what the letters could possibly stand for?" Jett asked.

"I was trying to show you, but you were too busy munching," Kenny said mockingly, and opened a new window in his browser. "The most likely—and only answer—is Electronic or End Transactions Numerical Analysis Data."

They continued to chatter, their words no longer reaching me because my brain kept circling around the charity's name.

ETNAD

So far and yet so close.

I thought of Scrabble and possible combinations.

ETNAD. Five letters. The only five-letter word I could think of was anted, but the answer was on the tip of my tongue. I tapped the pencil against my lips as I fought hard to grasp it. When it didn't come to me, I began to combine four-letter words on a blank sheet of paper.

"Are you playing Scrabble?" Jett asked. Nodding, I shushed him and read through what I had so far: etna, ante, dean, date, neat, tend, dent. Each of them sounded familiar, trying to tell me something, and yet they weren't quite right. And then I read from right to left and my blood froze in my veins.

ETNAD was DANTE.

Dante.

The man who had wanted me. A cold chill made me shudder as I recalled the events before Liz was raped.

"Brooke?"

"What?" I glanced up into Kenny and Jett's worried faces. Had I spoken out loud?

"What's wrong?" Jett asked, his hand touching my arm gently but protectively. My glance fell on the pencil in my hand, broken in two. Jett's fingers burned my skin, or maybe I was frozen, not just my mind, but my entire body. "You okay?" Jett persisted.

"The charity your father's involved with," I began, my voice shaking, "if you read ETNAD from right to left, it spells Dante."

I didn't have to speak the obvious. Jett's face turned into a mask of fury, and his jaw set. His fists balled, and something sparkled in his eyes.

"Fuck! That sick bastard." He wiped a hand over his

face, but it did nothing to diminish his anger. "He lured you in."

Kenny looked from Jett to me, the confusion on his face lifting, meaning Jett must've told him everything. "Anyway, guess where he called from when the explosion happened?"

"I don't give a shit," Jett cut him off. "I have a bigger problem now. He's still involved with the club, and there's no doubt in my mind he's responsible for what happened to Brooke. I need to know why."

"Why don't you ask him, Jett?" Kenny asked quietly. "Your father's staying at the Richton Hotel, room number 113, under the name Paul Anderson. I'll go with you and we can—"

Ignoring him, Jett walked out and slammed the door shut.

"Tell him I'll be waiting for him outside," Kenny said and smiled apologetically. "Sorry. It's a fucking mess."

"It's okay. I didn't expect it any other way." I returned his weak smile and followed after Jett.

I found him in his former room and closed the door behind me. In the silence of the walls, it was just Jett and I, two tormented souls. From the doorway, I watched him retrieve a gun from a drawer and check that it was loaded.

"Please don't hurt him," I whispered. "We don't know for sure what's going on."

"How much more proof do you need, Brooke? He's a

fucking liar," Jett hissed. "He claimed he and Lucazzone hadn't been in contact for years. And then I find out he transferred money to a bogus charity that's connected to the club in some way." He shrugged into his leather jacket and squeezed the gun inside the holster at his back.

I moved closer until we were mere inches apart. "Please, Jett. Don't."

He scanned my eyes, his frown deepening as he cupped my face in his hands.

"Look, I know what I'm doing. Okay? My father's my problem, and I have to deal with him by myself. The least he'll do is answer my fucking questions."

"Let me come with you, then," I pleaded. I had a horrible feeling about the whole situation.

Jett shook his head vehemently. "You're staying here. After what he's done to you, I don't want him anywhere near you, Brooke."

I moistened my lips as I considered my words. There were so many loopholes that I just couldn't wrap my head around the entire picture.

"He could have killed me in the car, but he *didn't*." I held onto Jett's arms, forcing him to listen. "His driver was shot. He arranged for a fake identity and money. He didn't have to do any of that, which is why I don't believe it."

Judging from his expression, Jett didn't believe me. Even I found it hard to believe, but the arguments inside my head kept telling me Robert Mayfield was innocent. The thought that Jett's father not only hated me so much he wanted me out of his son's life, but also hated me so much he wanted to kill me, was too wicked to believe. He had to be innocent, because I couldn't imagine anyone being so horrific and cruel.

"He threatened your family and friends' lives. Isn't that good enough a reason for you?" Jett asked. "As long as I don't know what's going on, you're staying here, and Kenny's keeping watch on you."

He also threatened your life, but that I didn't add. Instead I looked up into Jett's beautiful eyes. My heart raced wildly at the thought of him going in alone.

"Your father has bodyguards. I want Kenny to come with you."

A few moments of silence passed between us.

"Okay." He sighed, giving in. "But you're staying here. I'll have Brian watch you."

The decisiveness in his tone irritated me. I didn't like it when Jett handled me as if I had no say in the matter.

"Don't treat me like I'm some fragile butterfly, Jett." I folded my arms over my chest and regarded him. "I'm going to make myself useful by returning to my apartment to find out whether Sylvie was right about the handwriting. I think I know where Clarkson's letter is. Brian can accompany me."

Anger crossed his features before he shook his head.

"No." His voice was forceful. "I'll be back before evening, and we'll go together. First I'm dealing with my father, and then we start digging into Clarkson."

"You're worrying about me when you're the one walking around with a gun," I murmured dryly.

"I've heard women like a guy who knows how to fight and defend himself." A hint of a smile appeared on his lips. He was trying to be funny by pretending he had everything under control, but the cagey expression in his eyes gave away his real thoughts.

I ignored his statement.

"Not when you intend to hurt someone." My fingers brushed his cheek gently. "Promise me you won't hurt him. He's your father, and you'll only end up hurting yourself."

"I can't make that promise. You know that," he said. "But I can promise you I won't do anything I'd live to regret."

He pushed my hand away and walked over to retrieve the phone on the sideboard, then handed it to me. "I want you to carry this with you. If something happens, call me. Okay?"

He kissed me on the cheek, and then grabbed his jacket. I watched him walk out the door and close it behind him.

"I'd rather you gave me a gun than a stupid cell phone," I muttered, and pushed the cell inside my handbag. It was true. I never would've imagined I might want to carry a gun. In fact, the thought of having a weapon in the house used to scare me. But now, after seeing what had happened to Liz and having been subjected to violence myself, I had never wanted anything more than to be able to defend myself.

28

JETT'S WHOLE "WEAK woman/strong man" attitude was ridiculous. I didn't want to feel useless while he did all the hard work. If Jett thought he could treat me like some fragile flower that had to be protected at all costs, he was wrong. I harbored no plan, no intention, no desire to be that way. The thought alone made me livid. I, weak? I could take care of myself. Besides, Jett wasn't the only one who needed answers. I, too, sought to get rid of the nagging questions inside my head. I wanted to find out if Sylvie was right about the handwriting and maybe shed new light on the whole Lucazzone secret.

Peering through the window, I watched him leave with Kenny, and then grabbed my handbag. The kitchen was empty. Jett's buddies, Brian included, had gathered in the open-space living room slash hall on the floor below Jett's room. Thank God for football games accompanied by the usual male shouting and yelling. I sneaked past them and had reached the first floor when I felt someone's hand on my shoulder.

"Where are you going?" Tiffany, Brian's girlfriend, asked. Regarding her oversized turquoise sweater and her short black hair with violet streaks, I begged my mind to come up with a good lie.

"Jett wants me to get a feel for his car. You know, acquaint ourselves." I groaned inwardly at my lame excuse.

"Cool." She shrugged. "But you can't drive it."

"Yeah, that's what he said." I rolled my eyes in mock irritation, ignoring her patronizing tone. "I'm just going to sit in it for a while. He's an amazing driver, and it looks so easy."

"It's not." Her lips curved into a fake smile and disappeared a second later. "The keys are in the locker room in a box on the wall. Have fun!" She walked away. We had been staying for a few days, and I still didn't know what her issues were. I climbed down the stairs, passed the security cameras, and let myself out.

The buildings looked more ominous than ever—maybe because it was a cloudy day promising a rainy night.

I crossed the backyard and reached the gate. The guard frowned but didn't comment as I walked through and called a taxi.

During the drive to Sylvie's apartment, I could no longer ignore the thoughts inside my head. There were too many loose ends, especially the part where Alessandro Lucazzone worked together with Robert Mayfield. If I didn't get answers, I'd never find peace. My fear would continue to consume me. I couldn't spend my life hiding. I missed work, shopping, and meeting for coffee with Sylvie; most importantly, I wanted a normal life with Jett so I could prepare for motherhood.

Eventually we reached the apartment, and I let myself in. Everything was quiet, but the air smelled of Sylvie's perfume and memories. So many happy memories.

Fighting the sudden onset of nostalgia, I removed my shoes and walked barefoot to my former room. Everything was tidy, the bed made. Just like I had left it when I moved in with Jett. I headed for my desk and began sorting through the mail pile Sylvie had kept for me. And there was a lot of it. It took me a while to find Clarkson's letter.

I scanned the old-fashioned writing. The "B" and "S" were curved—as though he was into calligraphy. There was little doubt the owner of the book was the same person who'd written down my name and address on the envelope.

I jumped in my skin when something clicked in the hall and footsteps thudded on the hardwood floor.

"Sylvie?" Pressing the letter against my chest, I peered out the door. "I didn't expect you home so early. Kenny said—" I broke off as I stared at the one face I never expected to see. In front of me, standing near Sylvie's large bookcase, was Nate, his hands buried in his pockets.

"What are you doing here? How did you get in?" I asked, unable to hide the shock in my voice. For some reason I thought there had to be a perfectly reasonable explanation.

"The door was open." He pointed behind him.

"Are you looking for Jett? He's not here, but I can call him."

"No need." He smiled. "I've been waiting for you."

It was the strange smile on his face that made my heart beat frantically in my chest.

"Why?" I whispered.

The apartment felt small, the air too thick to breathe.

"I knew you'd be coming." He took slow, measured steps forward, his blue eyes scanning me. I inched back.

"You haven't answered my question. Why are you here?" I was missing something; I just couldn't put my finger on it.

"Oh, Brooke." He laughed, the sound sending a shiver down my spine. "I *have* answered your question. Weren't you listening?" His tone was contemptuous. "I said I was waiting for *you*. You walked away from me last time, and I had no choice but to wait for you. After all, I paid a lot of money to have you. Your behavior didn't please me, but

I'm willing to look past your indiscretion."

What indiscretion?

My body froze, and my chest began to tighten with fear. Alarm bells rang in my head.

"You—" I choked on my breath. The thought was horrible. It couldn't be true. I couldn't even speak it out loud. He nodded encouragingly, and his eyes flickered with knowledge and pleasure. I stared at his evil smile, thinking how much he seemed to enjoy the moment he disclosed his identity.

When Danny claimed a man paid for me, I imagined him to be older. Never Jett's attractive brother. Clearly, he was a sociopath—charming and likeable on the outside, but twisted and sick to the core.

"You're Dante?" It wasn't so much a question as a statement. My voice was shaking and my throat was so tight I felt like I was being strangled.

"I am Dante." His eyes flashed with pride, as though the name had a special meaning. And it did, somewhere at the back of my mind; my paralyzing fear just wouldn't let me grasp it.

"You work for the club and the charity?" I asked in disbelief. On the rare occasions we had met, he had always been friendly, helpful even. He had claimed to be close to Jett. It had to be a misunderstanding.

"Not working." He shook his head slowly. "I'm *leading*

the club. I think there's a difference, Brooke. Clarkson convinced Lucazzone to leave everything to the charity, and the charity's mine."

My mouth went dry. The person I had been fleeing from had been among us all along.

"You seem surprised," Nate continued. "Didn't you think I'd be capable of such a grand scheme?" The expression in his eyes changed from pride to amusement, and back to pride. "My brother's so blind in love with you he even told me where you were staying."

"What do you want from me?" I asked again. I hoped it was the book, but in some way I knew he hadn't arranged to kidnap me because of it.

"You know the answer, Brooke. Deep down." He took another step forward and stopped, like he had all the time in the world. "The estate. You. The company. All the things I worked hard for. All the things I deserve. I'm here to take them all."

He pulled out a hunting knife.

He was going to kill me.

The realization kicked in hard. I had to stall until I found a way out. "I don't understand." I took another step, and my back hit the wall. The living room was to my right. This was my last chance to run. Turning, I dashed past him in the hope I could lock myself inside the living room and open the window to call for help. I hadn't even reached the door when he slammed me to the floor and, turning me around, his hand tightened around my throat.

"We're not finished." His grip was so tight I thought I might pass out. My palms flew upward to push him away as my eyes filled with moisture from the lack of oxygen. His face inched closer until I could feel his breath on my lips.

"Right from the beginning, you were nothing but a millstone in my big plans, Brooke. You die. And I get everything. Simple as that," Nate said. "I bet you didn't see that coming."

His hands released my throat. I pulled myself up on my knees, gasping for air, ignoring the pangs of pain shooting through my ribcage. So the car chase in Italy hadn't been about the book; our pursuers wanted to kill me. Nate flung me on my back and held the knife against my throat. Tears began to trickle down my cheeks, not out of fear but out of shock.

"Now, don't cry, little one. All those years, Alessandro had the choice to pass the estate on to me," Nate began. "But he kept looking for an heir, leaving me no choice than to trick him and everybody else. So I bought his late wife's favorite charity organization and made sure that Clarkson squeezed in a clause that if anything happened to you before you signed the inheritance papers, everything would fall to ETNAD. Then, after he signed the will, Lucazzone died." Watching me, he tilted his head. "That was a few weeks ago, right before I convinced Jett to meet with you to discuss a potential partnership."

I shook my head. It wasn't possible. While I knew the will was drawn up prior to my meeting with Jett, Alessandro hadn't died. Thus, the timeframe was wrong.

"I don't believe you," I said. "I met with Alessandro a few weeks ago. He's in a coma but alive."

"Clarkson works for me, Brooke," Nate said matter-of-factly, as if that was the answer to all my questions. "The old man you met was an actor I hired. Or why else do you think the nurse never left you two to talk in private? He was a bit senile, and we had to make sure he didn't make a mistake, revealing too much." Nate laughed and played with the knife pressed against my throat, obviously excited by his own madness.

"You and Jett were played from the beginning. Or did you think it was fate?" he asked. "I set up the meeting between the two of you. I even chose the bar. As his new assistant you were supposed to travel to Italy, meet with the old man, and never make it back alive. What I didn't expect was Jett to fall for you and figure out there was something wrong with the estate, but you've done me a favor, Brooke. It makes sense that my brother would shoot you in a jealous fit and then kill himself, unable to live with the guilt."

"He'd never do that," I whispered.

"You're right. But with my help, he will." Nate's blue

eyes shimmered. I realized he was crazy. Literally crazy. A psycho. "Jealousy can be such a strong motive. And everyone who knows Jett knows he's a passionate man. It's a good plan, isn't it? And when Jett dies, I get his shares of the company as well."

My heart pounded fast, and desperation washed over me as I looked into Nate's hard, cold eyes—the eyes of a killer.

"Please," I whispered. "You're talking about your brother. Don't you care about your family?"

"I'm sorry things have to end this way," Nate said. "But business is business, and everyone has to fight for himself."

"Let her go, Nate." A familiar voice carried over from the door. Nate eased enough on the knife, and I followed his line of vision to Jett's father pointing a gun at us.

"So it was you all along? How could you betray me, Nate?"

"Dad?"

"Move away from her and drop the knife." Robert waved his gun. "I'll tell you one more time, Nate. Let her go."

Nate took a step back, his knife dropping to the floor. I crawled toward the living room door, putting some distance between us. Nate seemed frozen, probably processing the news that his father was still alive. A few seconds passed. Robert spoke first.

"I raised you as my son," Robert said, inching closer.

"And this is how you repay me? After all I've done for you?"

I stared at him, confused. Wasn't Nate his biological son? And what about Jett?

"Who was the guy I saw at the morgue?" Nate asked accusingly. His voice was tinted with a hint of anger.

"Some dead guy who was already dead when we got the body from the morgue," Robert replied.

Nate remained silent as he stared back at his father. His eyes moved from his father to the knife on the floor. Eventually he asked, "Why did you fake your own death?"

"When I told you about the club years ago, I did so to protect you from its influence. But you joined it behind my back and blackmailed me all those years." Robert shook his head. "I thought I could trust you, but all you did was stab me in the back."

"I had no choice, Dad," Nate said slowly. "I was blackmailed, too."

Robert laughed bitterly. "Bullshit. You went around our backs and manipulated everyone. When I sent Clarkson the money, I already suspected you were the actual recipient. But I wasn't sure. All I knew was that it had to be a relatively new member, someone who knew my every step by watching me. When Clarence Holton told me you were the new club leader and interested in Brooke's estate, I couldn't believe it. I had to see for myself that the son I raised like my own could do this to me." He paused. "So I led everyone to believe I was dead while I tried to keep Brooke safe and get the book. It was the only way to find out my blackmailer's identity."

"Why the book?" I asked.

Robert Mayfield's eyes narrowed on me. "The numbers are combinations to P.O. boxes containing videos taken during various—" he hesitated "—club meetings. I figured the blackmailer would feature in one of them." His attention turned back to Nate. "I'm sure if I looked hard enough, I'd find proof that you've been blackmailing members for years. Not that I need it now. Your standing here is proof enough that you betrayed the trust I placed in you when I told you about the club. I've been watching the apartment for days because I knew if Brooke stopped by, you would too." He shook his head, his face a mix of anger and grief. "I'm deeply ashamed of you, Nate. Of what you've done to the club. Of what it's become."

"I'm sorry, Dad." Nate's manner changed. His face looked guilty, and his voice filled with sadness as he stepped forward, hands outstretched. "If I had known I was a disappointment to you, I would've changed a long time ago."

He was such a good actor—the sudden realization scared me more than anything. In slow motion, I watched Nate pull out a gun.

"No!" I shouted, but it was too late. A muffled shot echoed from the walls. Robert dropped to the floor, and blood began to pour out of his chest.

"Why don't you admit you're jealous, Dad? That you could never accomplish what I've achieved?" Nate picked up his father's gun, his eyes fixed on the old man, as he pushed it inside the belt holster at his back. I kneeled next to Robert and pressed my hands against his chest to stop the blood flow.

"What did you do?" I shouted to Nate. The blood began to spread so fast it stained everything. My hands. Our clothes. The floor.

"It's been long overdue," Nate said. "And it's all your fault, Brooke. If you hadn't run away, my plan would've played out neatly."

"We need to help him, Nate," I pleaded. "Please call an ambulance, or he'll bleed to death."

"I don't care about him. He's not even my father."

I gaped at him in shock. "How can you say that?"

"It's the truth." He shrugged and checked the gun. "Years ago I opened his safe because I needed money and he wouldn't give it to me. That's when I found my birth certificate. He took me from my real parents. Nobody asked me if I wanted to be raised by him."

"I took you in from an orphanage, Nate," Robert whispered. "Your parents abandoned you." His face was distorted in pain.

"You're lying." Nate raised the gun again. "You're fucking lying." He walked back to his father, his brows drawn in anger. Now I understood why Jett saw his father the way he did. As volatile. Competitive. Even heartless, and sometimes cruel. Robert was about to die, but he preferred telling the brutal truth rather than make amends.

"You were an orphan, Nate. Your mother abandoned you in the gutter when you were barely three days old."

Even though it was a poor excuse for his actions, for some reason I understood the pain Nate must've gone through all those years after finding out he belonged nowhere. The past he had was based on a lie.

"You wouldn't have paid a dime if it were the truth," Nate growled. "The fact I could blackmail you all those years so easily shows me you're guilty of taking me away from my real parents."

"Nate!" His father choked on his breath, his face distorting. "I built the company. I didn't want to deal with any scandal or bad publicity. Everything I did was so you and Jett could have a carefree future. Showering you with millions to make you believe you were my own son and that you had a father was a small price to pay. It doesn't change the fact that you were abandoned."

"I fucking hate you," Nate whispered. He held the gun to Robert's head. "And I don't care about anything you say.

I'll just fucking kill you both."

He meant business.

My gaze swept over the room, taking in anything I could use as a weapon. Anything to keep the psycho from killing us. I just needed a distraction.

The thudding and voices outside the door made me flinch, and Nate turned his head. I used the opportunity. Grabbing the vase on the side table, I smashed it into the back of Nate's head. He swayed, and the gun dropped to the floor. I lunged for it and pointed it at him. My hands were shaking badly because I knew Nate had another gun tucked in the holster at his back.

"Don't even think about pulling it out," I hissed. "Or I'll shoot."

Nate chuckled, unfazed, and took a step forward. "Look at the way you're holding that gun. You can't even shoot."

I lifted the gun higher.

"I swear I'll do it."

He dove for me. I shot—and missed.

Shit.

The door bolted open, and from the periphery of my vision I saw Jett and a few guys storming in. Nate turned around, his arms spread out, a horrified expression on his face.

"Thank God you're here, Jett," Nate shouted, his gaze brushing nervously over the gun in Brian's hands. "She shot our father. She's involved in his shit and now she's trying to kill me."

I gaped, my speech failing me.

Un-believe-able.

The guy wasn't just a good actor; he was a born liar.

Jett pulled out his gun and pointed it at Nate. "I don't believe my girlfriend would ever do that."

In slow motion I watched Nate retrieve his gun out of the holster. Jett aimed. An instant later a muffled gunshot resonated from the walls and Nate slumped to the floor, blood pouring out of his leg, his face a mask of agonizing pain.

I had no idea that Jett could shoot that well. Brian and another guy lifted Nate up and dragged him out the door. But my mind was already elsewhere.

Jett's hands were all over me, inspecting me for wounds. "Are you hurt?"

"No, but he is." I pointed to his father, who lay in a puddle of blood. The smell was overpowering, and I couldn't stop shaking. "Nate shot him while your father tried to protect me. We need to help him."

"Shit," Jett muttered, kneeling beside Robert as he pulled out his cell phone and called Sam.

By the time a private ambulance arrived, I was a nervous mess.

I buried my face in Jett's chest. "I hope he'll make it."

He didn't reply. The silence was oppressing as we drove to Sam's hospital.

"How did you find me?" I whispered. We had been sitting in the waiting room for two hours until Sam could confirm that Jett's father had passed the critical phase following surgery. Avoiding the subject was easier than looking at the hard facts. It was easier than admitting that Jonathan Mayfield had been playing Jett all along, and Robert Mayfield might die because of his adopted son's greed.

"Your cell." Jett smiled softly. "Besides, you're stubborn, so I figured you wouldn't listen. It wasn't a hard guess."

"But what made you come looking for me? You said you wouldn't be back before evening."

"Kenny found out Clarence Holton had also transferred fifty million to Clarkson, so my next guess was that someone must've blackmailed them, and it wasn't my father." His eyes met mine, and for a moment they took my breath away. "But then Brian called to tell me his girlfriend saw you leaving, and I drove over."

"I'm glad you did," I whispered, refusing to think of what might have happened otherwise.

His shoulders slumped. "I never would have expected this from my brother."

"That's what your father said, too." I leaned my head

against his shoulder then recapped the events from the beginning. "What are you going to do with Nate?" I asked once I had finished.

"I'm going to find the videos and hand them over to the authorities, and let them decide. He deserves all that's coming."

I sat up to regard him. "What about your father?" He couldn't possibly reveal his father's involvement in the club without risking Mayfield Realties' collapse. I wouldn't let so many people lose their jobs.

"I don't know, Brooke," Jett said, defeated, "but I'm sure we'll figure something out."

29

THE NEWS ABOUT ETNAD and the elite club was splashed all over the newspapers on a Monday, a little more than a week after Jett's father was shot. Someone had tipped off the authorities and now investigations kept popping up all over the States and even Europe. New names were revealed every day, including Jett's brother.

I was standing in Jett's kitchen—our kitchen—brewing a large pot of coffee to see me through the busy night ahead. It was early evening, shortly after dusk, and the sun had just disappeared behind the thick curtain of rain clouds that had been hovering above New York City for the last few days. We had arrived back from the office and dinner in a nearby restaurant, and Jett was still in the shower so I was alone with my coffee and thoughts as I sat down on the couch, cross-legged, and spread the newspaper around me.

I had gone through the articles countless times, but for some reason I kept coming back, unable to grasp the fact that my nightmare had finally come to an end. That Nate had been involved for many years still shocked me. Jett refused to talk about him, as if his brother wasn't worth mentioning.

Robert Mayfield was mentioned in the business section—the man, who had allegedly been involved in a freak explosion, only to come back from the dead. The hole in his chest had remained a well-kept secret. We had visited him in the hospital the day before. Even though the doctors kept him in an induced coma for days, I had wanted to see him. Knowing he'd tried to protect Jett and me—granted in a strange way, but still—the meeting had felt different. And while I knew we'd probably never meet for Thanksgiving or Christmas dinner, I planned on getting to know the real Robert Mayfield as soon as his health recovered, for both Jett's and the baby's sake.

With Kenny's help the missing money would be returned into the corporate bank accounts, and Jett could finally focus on launching his own company—that's where all the coffee and my undying support came in. I didn't just love him; I was proud of him and his achievements, and I was going to see his dream come true, no matter what. Even if that involved working at the office during the day and helping him with the launch of his business at night.

"Do you want to call it a day, babe?" Jett said, appearing around the corner.

"There's still so much to do." I pushed a cup of steaming coffee into his hands, marveling at the perfection of his broad chest and his electric eyes that reflected the light in a million facets of green.

"Maybe I want to focus on something else for a while." He placed the cup on the table and pulled me against his hard body, his mouth burying in my hair at the nape of my neck. To smell, to kiss, to bite—I had no idea, but work was waiting, and I could sense he was about to idle.

Ever so slowly Jett began to unbutton my dress. I pushed is hands away before he could rip off my bra.

"Sorry, Mayfield, but if you want to call it a day, I'll have to insist you use the remaining twenty something hours of your win now, because I'm not giving you any more for free." I pointed at the front of my dress. "Unless of course—" I smiled "—you surrender your win and let me be in charge once and for all."

"There is no way in hell I'm surrendering, Miss Stewart." He fished a set of keys out of his pocket and dangled it in front of my face. "Brian has changed the license plate for our little trip."

Oh, God.

"We're not racing anywhere," I whispered, petrified at the thought of Jett behind a steering wheel.

Jett's eyes twinkled. "Which is why I thought *you* might want to drive her."

I overlooked the part where he kept calling his car a *she* in favor of the fact he was letting me drive his beloved. I had never driven anything so expensive and shiny. I was almost drooling at the thought.

Grinning, I grabbed the keys before he changed his mind. "Now you're talking. How could I possibly resist going for a ride in your baby."

"I hope it's not going to be my only ride tonight." He winked in case I missed the sexual undertones.

Heat scorched my cheeks. Did he *have* to be so blunt?

"That depends." I inclined my head in mock confusion. "Where are we going?"

"Back to the Hamptons," Jett said, amused. "I forgot my bag."

***

It was a little past eight p.m. when we arrived at Kim Dessen's place. With the moonlight casting an eerie glow, magnifying its large windows and the narrow path lined with rosebushes leading straight to the private beach, the building looked more beautiful than I remembered it. Jett unlocked the door and turned off the alarm, but didn't switch on the lights.

We climbed down the stairs past several doors and entered a dark room. Jett pressed a switch and the entire pool was lit up in soft blue and green colors, the underwater light bouncing off the dark walls like it was the only source of light. I gasped at the magnificence and the size of the place. On the west side were lounges and a bar. The pool had a huge elongate side, and a smaller circular one. Opposite from it was a large plasma television set fitted on the wall.

"Wow." I spun in a slow circle. "This place is heavenly."

And tranquil. Much more amazing than any public indoor swimming pool or spa I had ever seen. I watched the color-changing water, immersed in the sparkling underwater lights.

"I love it. Completely love it," I said, unable to hold back my enthusiasm.

"Care for a swim in the pool? Or should we try out the theater?" In the darkness, my gaze searched for Jett and found him standing at the stairs of the pool. He had kicked off his shoes and his feet were in the water, his eyes beckoning me to inch closer.

"You're giving me a choice?" I asked, faking surprise.

"More like a question what you want to do first, because we'll be doing both." He grinned, revealing the two most gorgeous dimples in the world. "We have a long night ahead, during which I intend to push your boundaries and see what makes you tick. Or squeal. I'm going to discover all your secret spots."

"My secret spots aren't so secret any more," I said.

"I'm sure you've kept one or two hidden." He flashed me a grin that made my heart sink in my chest. "I know a thing or two you don't yet know about yourself."

Slowly he began to remove his clothes. His jeans. His shirt. His underwear. The pool lights bathed his skin in a soft glow; the shadows did nothing to hide his perfection.

I found myself smiling when he strolled into the water naked. I could've stayed transfixed to the spot, watching him for hours.

"Come in, Brooke," Jett said, slowly.

"Shouldn't we be taking a shower first?"

"You're right." He stepped out of the water and came toward me. I thought he'd show me the way to the bathroom but instead he lifted me in his arms and walked with me back into the swimming pool.

Hovering in his arms above the surface of the water, I squealed and fought his iron grip when a cold wet sensation seeped through the material of my dress and reached my butt. It was cold. Scratch that. It was so freezing I thought I might see ice cubes floating around me. An instant later, Jett's arms were gone, and I plunged into the water, the coldness spreading around my limbs.

"Seriously? I hate it when people do that," I said the

moment I broke the surface of the water and wiped my eyes, probably smearing my make-up all over my face. My dress was soaking wet—floating like a halo because the thin fabric was so light it didn't stay underwater. Jett laughed. No. Make that he laughed hysterically.

"Stop laughing like a hyena." I splashed him.

"I'm sorry." He grinned sheepishly.

"No, you're not."

I tried to swim to the edge when he grabbed my waist and pulled me against his naked body. "You're cute when you're angry, Brooke."

"I'm not," I said, unable to stop my teeth from chattering. "It's frickin' cold."

"You'll be warmer once you get out of this dress." He didn't wait for my reply. Within seconds his expert hands had undone the zipper and pulled the dress down my shivering body, then tossed it on the edge of the pool.

"Better?" he asked. There was a spark of mischief in his eyes. And he was still grinning. I frowned when he disappeared beneath the surface. Was he going to retrieve my high-heels?

"No, it's still cold." I doubted he heard me. Looking down, I saw him diving. His naked body shimmered underwater, heading straight for me. Like a fish. Or was he supposed to be a shark?

Oh, God.

He wouldn't dare, would he?

He did.

He grabbed my left foot and pulled me underwater until my face was at the same level as his. My eyes were open as he drew me to him and kissed me, his lips pressing against mine. For a moment, I almost forgot we were underwater. It was the feeling of freedom. It was perfect, so perfect that words failed me.

He let go of me and together we broke the surface.

"I've always wanted to do something like this," Jett said, laughing. His hair looked like a sexy mess.

"You've got balls, Jett. Pulling me under like that." I had loved it, but I wasn't ready to admit it because I was still shivering.

"It's not that cold."

He was right. It wasn't *that* cold.

It was damn icy—so cold I couldn't even feel my limbs.

"You know it's freezing," I said, "and kissing was your solution to keep us warm?"

He shrugged. "You always manage to heat me up. Do you want to try again?"

"No." I shook my head and stopped him before he dived. "Don't even think about it. I don't want to get hypothermia."

"You won't," he said. "Just keep moving."

I tilted my head. "Easy for you to say. You're a man.

You don't feel the cold like I do."

"You're right, babe. That's because seeing you naked always raises the temperature a few degrees." The corners of his lips twitched.

I frowned, suddenly seeing the connection. "Is that why you asked me to get out of my dress?"

"I'm not sure. I thought it'd help." He held up his hand in an innocent gesture. "I'm just saying it would turn every man on. It sure turns me on seeing your nipples harden."

"Listen, Tarzan." I poked a finger in his chest, unable to remain pissed off. "No more funny stunts." The water barely reached my chin. I rubbed my arms to infuse some warmth into them. It didn't help.

"It's going to get warmer, I promise," Jett said. "Give it a few minutes until the pool heats up." He wrapped his arms around me and pulled me against his chest.

Warm water began to pulsate from all directions. The knots in my muscles began to ease and I grew more relaxed with every minute. The underwater lights changed from blue to a fluorescent green—dark and shimmering beautiful like the color of emerald. Just a few shades lighter than Jett's eyes.

"Have you ever done this before?" I asked.

Jett shot me a sideway glance. "What?"

"Breaking and entering."

"I'm not exactly breaking in."

"You're right. You had a key, on both this and the previous occasion." I put on the most serious expression I could muster. "Unlocking and entering, then?"

"The only thing I need to unlock is you." He laughed out loud. "Honestly, it's the first time, but you've got to admit Kim has a nice house." He swam in a circle and then pulled me close again. I wrapped my legs around his waist, knowing well he couldn't resist. "We should do it more often," Jett whispered. "Visit properties, make sure they're well maintained. Unlock all the places we have to see."

He wasn't talking about houses.

Jett grabbed my ass and I looked up into his eyes. They were glinting, full of mischief. Full of hope and promises.

With my legs wrapped around him, he carried me. I didn't put up a fight. Even if I tried, I wouldn't have been strong enough to push him and swim away.

"Where are we going?" I asked.

"The middle is heated," he said.

Every pool is heated, I wanted to point out.

"You know I can't resist seeing you wet." He gave me a sly look, and I remembered we were intruders.

"I can't believe you jumped in naked. What if someone caught us?"

He laughed at my mortified expression. "So what? It's worth the trouble. It's worth everything when you're with me. Not taking the risk is far riskier."

We stopped at the side of the pool, right below the sculpted statue of a Greek goddess towering over us. The water was warmer here.

"Ready?" Jett winked and pressed his palm against what looked like an inconspicuous white tile. Instantly, hot water began to shoot from small openings, shifting around my thighs and lower back in a fast spiral. I had been in a Jacuzzi before, but this was different because the bubbles didn't reach the surface. My arms went around Jett's neck, and his eyes met mine with such intensity it took my breath away.

The lights in the pool began to change, turning darker and darker until the surface was almost black and the lights underwater twinkled like stars in the night sky. I felt as though we were floating in a galaxy amidst stars. A minute passed, then another, and the lights changed to green again.

It was out of the ordinary. Nothing I had seen before.

It was so hauntingly beautiful I wished I could take a picture and hang it on the wall in my office. In the serenity around us, I brushed my fingertips along his jawline, praying I could freeze time and hold onto this moment forever.

"It's amazing," I said. "I want to capture the moment of us and treasure it forever."

"No need. Our future holds plenty more of such moments." He traced the contours of my lips, sending a tingle down my neck, right into my heart. "You're not just any girl for me. You're the only one that matters, and I have no intention to ever let you go because every moment with you is a little more than amazing."

"You're lying." I laughed even though I felt a little bit like crying because his words matched the way I felt about him.

His magnificent green eyes bored into me, and it took my breath away. "Why would I be? I've no plans to give you anything less than you deserve, and you deserve the world," he whispered. "I wish I had met you sooner."

I didn't reply. I couldn't because my heart was doing cartwheels, and my mind was spinning.

"Even knowing I might have pushed you away? Or fallen pregnant?" I asked at last.

"Especially because of that. I love a challenge, and you provide plenty of that," he whispered. "We both know you pushed me away because you love being chased. You got pregnant because you wanted my baby."

I slapped his arm.

"You couldn't keep it in your pants and *that's* the reason." I returned his smile. In spite of the tranquility inside me, life tugged at me, growing, a reminder our future would bring many challenges. "I'm so afraid I'll get huge and ugly like a walrus."

"What?" He laughed. "You could never look ugly."

"How do you know?" I whispered. "In a few weeks I'll

be all bloated and the size of a balloon."

"I just know," he replied. "Every time you tell me your hair's a mess and how much you hate it, I find you the most beautiful. I can't wait to see you grow, knowing that our baby is part you and part me, our best qualities merged into one being, and there's nothing ugly about that." He smiled gently. "I cannot promise that carrying this child will be easy, but I can promise I'll carry you when you need me. I'll support you all the way."

I leaned my head against his shoulder, and he wrapped his arm around me, drawing me close. In the silence of the room and in the stillness of the water, Jett's presence was overpowering. He was everywhere, inside my mind, in every cell of my body, settled deep within me. He was like water, pouring into me, filling me to almost overflowing, drawing me under. Soon I'd be drowning in my feelings for him. Soon our passion would become a current, drawing me into the depths to keep me with him forever, and claiming me as *his*.

His eyes glistened in the soft glow of the lights, and in the tranquility of this place his love for me was unmistakable, and his passion was definite. He didn't have to ask me what I felt for him or what I wanted. He *knew*. I knew. The whole world did.

I could see my own feelings and lust reflected in his eyes and feel them in the way he touched me. Strange that we had voices to talk, and yet our hearts spoke louder. Asking and yet not requesting. Pleading and yet not forcing. Making us aware there was one single truth in that single moment: we were in love.

Holding onto each other. Crazy about each other. Lost in our jungle of passion and fulfillment, we were insatiable. We were two of one mind.

His eyes probed mine with a gentleness that took my breath away. Even if I wanted to talk, I couldn't. I was afraid to break the moment because it was *ours*. In the solitude of the walls around us, it didn't matter where we came from or what journey we had been on. It didn't matter how much pain we carried or whether the world was coming to an end. All that mattered was there was still an *us*—after everything that happened. The future was uncertain, but his love was not.

Jett leaned in and kissed me gently, the tip of his tongue arousing me. His lips were soft, not demanding, as if he had all the time in the world. His hands touched my back, my hips, sending jolts of lust through my body. On the outside I was shaking—not from the cold but from want. On the inside I was trembling, pulsating, asking—with need. He pressed me against the wall hard, and I wrapped my legs around his waist. My hands ran through his hair and gathered at the nape of his neck as his growing erection brushed my entry.

Jett's expression triggered a surge of arousal inside me. My core pulsated, asking for him. My whole being burned and flickered, boiling with a growing desire only he could still. He pushed me up high against the wall, and his body pressed into me, his hands cupping my ass.

I let my hand glide between our bodies to guide him, even though he didn't need guidance.

Jett never did.

I moaned, and his hard erection entered me, filling every last corner. I shifted my hips to let him slide just a little deeper, even though he was too big to bear, his unnatural warmth searing me.

And then he began to move, the warm water rolling gently around us, just like the thick shaft inside me. My insides clenched as the thrusts became harder and deeper, stretching me. With every thrust he hit my core, sending a pleasant shot of pain through me that made me call out his name. Pressed between him and the warm wall, I rocked against him until I could feel the release, and when I came, his body became my sanctuary.

30

MY DRESS WAS dripping wet, the thin fabric completely transparent. I had only two options: walk around the house in a wet—and see-through—dress, or stay naked. I figured there wasn't really a difference.

"Great." I glanced around me in the hope I might spy something suitable to protect my modesty. "You could have warned me before pushing me into the pool."

"I told you I needed you wet." His tone was casual, but I didn't miss the amused flicker in his eyes. "Wet is good, baby. I like the way it feels."

Holy mother of double meanings!

My cheeks caught fire at his insinuation and, like on cue, moisture gathered between my legs. He always got me wet, whether I wanted it or not. And, unfortunately, he knew it.

I watched him slip into his jeans, which he left

unbuttoned, revealing rows of hard muscles and bronze skin. I pointed to his shirt he picked up from the floor. "Good for you. At least one of us is dry." I caught him glancing at the watch. "What's your next plan?"

"We're going outside."

I narrowed my eyes. "Where?"

He tilted his head. "To the beach."

"No break?"

"Nope." His gaze was relentless. "I'm not wasting one minute."

The dress then. I bent down to pick it up and caught Jett glancing at my naked ass. No surprise to find him grinning.

"I hope you're not going to wear that." He pointed to the dress in my hand. "I love the way you are right now."

"Naked?"

The corner of his lips twitched. "Yep, au natural. With no flavors, no additives, no make-up. Stripped of all the layers." He smiled his most saccharine smile. "Just raw pureness."

"Please don't ask me to run around naked, Jett."

"I wasn't going to ask." His eyes twinkled—probably at the thought of having me at his mercy. "I was going to plead."

"No way." I slipped into the wet dress. It was useless. It was so transparent that I could see the outline of my nipples. And judging from Jett's grin, that had been the plan all along. I crossed my arms over my chest and put on my most serious expression. Grinning would only encourage that inflated ego of his. Actually grinning would encourage him to do naughty things, and I'd probably end up playing along just for the sake of it.

Or maybe because you want him as much as he wants you.

"You can wear this, baby." He pushed his dry shirt into my hands. I pressed it against my chest, realizing it was shorter than my dress and would probably barely cover my butt.

"Seriously?"

He was standing before me half naked, with nothing but his jeans and muscles on display. He caught my appreciative gaze and in response flexed his chest muscles, the movement making his tattoo come alive. But that wasn't what made me swallow hard. He was hard and defined. Like a bronze statue. His body was so sexy I wanted to trail my tongue all over it.

"Are you shy? Or are you just pretending?" He removed my arms from my chest and held them up. Inside the pool water had covered my body. Now it was just the thin layer of my dress, and under his gaze I felt exposed.

"There's nothing to hide, baby. You're sexy and you're beautiful. I love every inch of your body." His gaze swept over me in a way that made me blush. He placed my hands on his hard stomach. "I like you touching me. And that's not the only thing I want you doing to me."

His eyes met mine, and I couldn't stop my mouth going dry at the thought of having him inside me again.

"I'm beginning to think you're insatiable, Jett," I muttered. "Either that, or you're a sex addict."

"Maybe I am." He grinned. "Or maybe I'm just saying that I can't get enough of you."

He drew my mouth to his and kissed me softly.

"I was thinking we should skip the beach walk and just watch a movie. You realize we've never done that?" A wicked grin appeared on his lips. "In the darkness, just you and me."

"Now that sounds tempting." I liked the idea of darkness and Jett, and the way he said it made it sound like he shared my naughty thoughts.

He held open the door. "You first."

I walked in, turning to see if he was following me, and found his eyes glued to my ass again.

"Nice view." He nodded appreciatively. I shook my head and kept on walking. A side look into one of the large mirrors reminded me I looked horrible. My hair was a complete mess. And my make-up had vanished. By the time we reached the long foyer, I had made a mental list of all the things that needed taking care of.

Change into something more suitable.

Blow-dry my hair.

Apply make-up.

I even pondered how long it'd take me to dry my dress with a blow dryer. And I had to insist on cleaning the house before leaving. No way would we leave clues of our breaking and entering behind. The last thing we needed was our DNA prints or fluids scattered all over the place.

"Can you give me twenty minutes?" I asked on the way to the living room.

"Ten minutes." He kissed my cheek and opened the door. "We only have twenty-two hours left and I'm not deducting your minutes from my meager hours." He grinned and then slapped my ass playfully. "Don't keep me waiting too long, woman."

The southern accent again.

I giggled and headed for the stairs, then remembered this wasn't our home. We weren't even guests. I stopped in the middle of the stairs. Jett hadn't moved from his spot.

"What about the house?" I pointed to the wet footprints on the marble floor. "We need to clean up."

"Don't worry your pretty head about it," Jett said. "Cleaners are coming in for an open day next week. They'll take care of everything. Besides, Kim knows." He winked. "She even gave us her blessing."

EPILOGUE

IT WAS OUR first vacation together. Jett and I had arrived at the lush Hawaiian resort three days ago and had barely left the room for anything other than to eat and give the poor cleaning lady some space.

"Care for a visit to the beach?" Jett asked. In the moonlight flooding through the restaurant's window, his face was nothing but beauty and pure sexiness.

I shrugged and interlaced my fingers with his. "Sounds good. It's not like I can sleep."

"I'll help you change that," Jett whispered, and led me out of the restaurant and down the path of trees, shrubs, and bushes to the beach.

It was true. Ever since I was held hostage and woke up in the hospital, I couldn't sleep because fear kept me awake, which was why Jett had insisted on taking this vacation. I was supposed to rest, to live and forget. I leaned against his arm, enjoying the delicious sensation the sound of his voice sent through me.

The sky was pitch black, dotted with thousands of stars. I had seen it before, but this time it seemed more beautiful than ever. As if my bad experiences made me appreciate the view more. Or maybe because whenever Jett was around, the whole world seemed different. Serene and colorful. Full of magic and mystery. Pure perfection—just like the man I loved.

He spread his jacket on the soft sand and sat down, the water just inches from our feet. Slowly, he wrapped his arm around my shoulders. Engrossed in our thoughts and each other's presence, we watched the waves of the ocean crashing against the shore.

I smiled at him and rubbed my cheek against the roughness of his stubble, wishing I could collect the magic of the moment in a bottle and keep it forever.

"It's so beautiful here," I whispered, and looked up at the sky. He didn't reply. At some point I realized Jett was looking at me—as if I was the only star in his night sky. I turned to regard him, and Jett kept looking at me, his eyes meeting mine with gentleness.

For once his silence didn't worry me, because no words were strong or expressive enough to capture the beauty of the moment. No words could express the magnitude of my feelings for him, or how much I wanted us to have a future. No words could express how much I didn't want to let him go—not yet, not now, and surely never. It was sad, really, because if we were in a dream I'd wish we'd never wake up from it.

But it was reality, and while I wanted to forget the past, there were ugly reminders that lingered at the back of my mind. Danny. The estate I never wanted, but had inherited nonetheless. The lawyer, Clarkson, who'd disappeared. In this reality, with the way things were progressing, I knew life would go on, and the little moments I spent with Jett would not stay forever.

Like bubbles, this moment would rise to great heights until someday, I just knew, it would burst—little droplets we'd struggle to hold onto, falling, until the fragments disappeared, leaving behind nothing but a fleeting memory. A dream. I swallowed hard, reminding myself never to take any moment with the love of my life for granted. Because it'd pass too fast. In a heartbeat. Lost forever.

"What are you thinking?" Jett asked. "You just had the strangest expression on your face."

I pondered for a few seconds whether to tell him or not, when I remembered Sylvie's advice on relationships and honesty. In the serenity of the night, with the soothing sounds of the ocean enveloping us, I knew I could trust him the way I had trusted him when I told him about my past. By confiding in him, we had become one mind—connected in some way, like the water to the moon. Like the tides.

"I want to keep all my happy memories with you, because they're the only thing that remain of the past, but I don't know how." I rested my head against his shoulder. "I see the stars in the sky, and they make me think of life. Of the many plans dwelling inside my mind, but how few memories I have. No matter how hard I try, I can't choose which memories I want to keep or which I can forget. So I've been wondering what's the purpose of creating memories if I can't keep them all?"

Jett took a deep breath and let it out slowly. "You don't have to try so hard to remember them, Brooke," he whispered. "The moments that mean the most to you stay etched in your mind. They might be few, but those are the only ones that matter."

I turned to him, taking in his beautiful eyes. "How do you know?"

He shrugged. "Do you know why I had the tattoos done?"

His question threw me off balance.

"No," I admitted.

He lifted his shirt. Under the moonlight, his skin shimmered golden, the black tribal tattoos hauntingly beautiful. "I had them done to help me remember all the things I don't want to forget." He pointed to the upper one on his shoulder. "This one helps me remember how hard my father was and all the lessons he taught me. It also reminds me that true power comes not from submission or gain, but from controlling my inner demons. Because our true enemies live within ourselves and feed from the lessons we failed to learn from our pasts." He arranged his shirt back in place. "Ever since I got my tattoos, my bad memories have become good memories. Even valuable."

"Maybe I should get my own tattoo," I said.

He laughed and tilted his head to the side. "I'm not sure I want your skin covered in ink. I love it the way it is just now." As though to prove his point, his fingertip brushed my collarbone, sending a shiver down my spine.

"Are you telling me what I can't do with my skin?" I raised my eyebrows, which made him laugh harder.

"If we're talking about a small one." He pointed to my ankle. "A tiny one that's not noticeable, then feel free to come along. I'm getting a new one soon."

"You never told me you wanted a new one."

"Yeah, well, I didn't know until I met you."

He lowered me onto my back and settled on top of me, his dark green eyes lingering on me. Beneath me I could feel the sand on my skin. It was cold but not unpleasant. "You know the feeling you get when you think you hear music, and it makes you stop in your tracks, completely absorbed? Well, that's how I felt when I kissed you for the very first time. I knew right then that I could love you. The night in the bar? That was the best thing that ever happened to me, and that's what I want my next tattoo to remind me of. I want your face on my skin. Something to look at when you're not around."

"No way," I said, laughing. "You're not doing that. What if we fight and you come to regret it?"

He shook his head slowly. "Never." He was so serious that my laughter died in my throat. "I've never been this much in love. And never before did I feel the desire to have someone as much as I want you in my life. So, you're stuck with me, Miss Stewart. Whether you want it or not."

"I hope I'll be stuck with you for a long time," I whispered. "Because moments pass way too fast."

"Not if I hold onto them," Jett said, adding softly, "Not if they're real."

He smiled, and for the first time I felt hopeful.

"I hope our child gets your long eyelashes," he said, his breath warm brushing my lips as his hands caressed my face. "In fact, if we have a girl, we're naming her Treasure."

Whoa, he had chosen our kid's name already? Without me?

"Hell, no." I snorted.

"Why not?" His hand trailed up my thigh, gathering in

the waistband of my jeans. "I said it once and I'll say it again. You're my treasure, Brooke, so the name's perfect for her."

"That's debatable." I tried to push his hand away, but it was a feeble attempt. "Besides, what makes you think it's a girl?"

"It has to be." His lips curled up at one corner. "But in the off chance I'm wrong, I'll let you pick out a boy's name." His mouth found mine, and under the stars, no kiss could've been more perfect—a moment I hoped would never end.

Life's uncontrollable, unpredictable, and a hell of a mess. Without fear, loss, and the wrong choices we made, we wouldn't be who we were. And while some of our decisions had broken us, the pain glued us together. Without the passion, we wouldn't have surrendered and conquered what we never thought could be ours. Without Jett's love, I wouldn't have learned the true value of our relationship.

When Jett saved me, he saved not only my life, but also my hopes and our future. He allowed me to believe that our love would never fade away. He left a memory I didn't want to forget, and now I was ready to treasure his love forever.

The End

WHAT'S NEXT FROM J.C. REED

Ever since Surrender Your Love was released, I've been asked to continue Jett & Brooke's story. While Treasure Your Love concludes the Surrender Your Love trilogy, like many readers I've found it incredibly hard to part with my characters, and so I've decided to give Brooke and Jett a special edition volume starting in early 2014:

NO

EXCEPTIONS

Experience how the past never stays the past.

No Exceptions is not part of the Surrender Your Love trilogy. It's more of an added short novel collection for readers who want to find out what happens after Jett and Brooke's happily-ever-after, and to Sylvie and Kenny, Danny and Liz.

A THANK YOU LETTER

There are so many things I want to say at the end of a book, and particularly at the end of such an emotional journey. First of all, the story of Brooke and Jett teaches that love, if it's the real deal, can't be broken. It's worth the pain and any bad experiences that may come with it. And while Treasure Your Love is fictional, I wrote it to show that life is a wild ride, and there are no guarantees.

Because reviews are hard to come by, and because readers rarely write them, I want to thank everyone who's taken the time to leave one, no matter how short.

My utmost gratitude goes to my friends and bloggers (many of whom I've had the pleasure to call friends), and to all who have supported me and helped spread the word on Facebook, Twitter, and on blogs. You've been nothing short of amazing.

I want to thank my editors for their hard work. I had an amazing time working with you.

But, most of all, I want to thank my readers. You have amazed me with your kind messages, and while I can't hug you all, I can at least write this note to tell you how thankful I am for your support. Thank you for reading and enjoying this trilogy.

THANK YOU from the bottom of my heart.

Jessica C. Reed

***

Connect with me online:

http://www.jcreedauthor.blogspot.com

http://www.facebook.com/pages/JC-Reed/295864860535849

http://www.twitter.com/jcreedauthor

Made in the USA
Lexington, KY
09 July 2015